BARBARA TRAPIDO

BROTHER OF THE
MORE FAMOUS JACK

PENGUIN BOOKS

PENGUIN BOOKS

Published by the Penguin Group
Penguin Books Ltd, 80 Strand, London WC2R 0RL, England
Penguin Putnam Inc., 375 Hudson Street, New York, New York 10014, USA
Penguin Books Australia Ltd, 250 Camberwell Road, Camberwell, Victoria 3124, Australia
Penguin Books Canada Ltd, 10 Alcorn Avenue, Toronto, Ontario, Canada M4V 3B2
Penguin Books India (P) Ltd, 11 Community Centre, Panchsheel Park, New Delhi – 110 017, India
Penguin Books (NZ) Ltd, Cnr Rosedale and Airborne Roads, Albany, Auckland, New Zealand
Penguin Books (South Africa) (Pty) Ltd, 24 Sturdee Avenue, Rosebank 2196, South Africa

Penguin Books Ltd, Registered Offices: 80 Strand, London WC2R 0RL, England

www.penguin.com

First published by Victor Gollancz 1982
Published in Penguin Books 1998
12

Copyright © Barbara Trapido, 1982
All rights reserved

Printed in England by Clays Ltd, St Ives plc

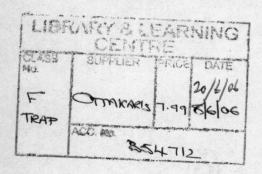

ABOUT THE AUTHOR

Barbara Trapido was born and educated in South Africa and came to London in 1963. She now lives in Oxford.

Her first novel, *Brother of the More Famous Jack*, one of the most highly acclaimed first novels of the eighties, was awarded a special prize for fiction at the Whitbread Awards in 1982; her second novel, *Noah's Ark*, published in 1985, was 'even better' (*Financial Times*); while her third, *Temples of Delight*, to which *Juggling*, published in 1994, is a sequel, was shortlisted for the 1990 *Sunday Express* Book of the Year Award. It was followed in 1998 by *The Travelling Hornplayer*, which was shortlisted for the 1998 Whitbread Novel Award.

For
Stan, Elaine and Susan

1

Since I have no other, I use as preface Jacob's preface which I read, sneakily, fifteen years ago, when it lay on the Goldmans' breakfast table, amid the cornflakes:

'I cannot in good conscience give the statutory thanks to my wife,' it says, 'for helpful comments on the manuscript, patient reading of drafts or corrections to proofs, because Jane did none of these things. She seldom reads and when she does it is never a thing of mine. Going by the lavish thanks to wives which I find in the prefaces to other men's books, I deem myself uniquely injudicious in having married a woman who refuses to double as a high-grade editorial assistant. Since custom requires me to thank her for something, I thank her instead for the agreeable fact of her continuing presence which in twenty years I have never presumed to expect.'

It was a marriage characterized among other things by the fact that Jacob was alternately infuriated and enchanted by Jane's resolutely playing the country wife. There is no doubt that it influenced the paths that I chose to tread.

I met Jacob Goldman when he interviewed me for a university place in London, during my final year in the genteel north London day school to which my mother had sent me. My mother, the widow of a modestly comfortable local green-grocer, had done so at some sacrifice to herself in the hope that I would acquire the right accent and be fit to mix in the right circles. As parents are destined to be disappointed, I believe she was disappointed that her decision ensured instead that I acquired a collection of creditable 'A' levels and became one of Jacob's pupils. Jacob—an impressive and powerful left-wing philosopher up from the East End—talked to us with a marvellous and winning fluency about the transcendental dialectic, in a huge cockney voice full of glottal stops, like a plumber's mate. He was the Professor of Philosophy in that labyrinthine Victorian edifice and quickly became my father figure and cultural hero. I had read Lord David Cecil's references to his 'rooms' at Oxford, but Jacob interviewed me in nothing one could dignify with such a word. He interviewed me in what appeared to be an aerated cupboard.

'I'll be frank with you,' he said. 'I had you up here because your Head's report on you is so unfavourable, it leads me to suspect that you may be somewhat brighter than the Head. You may of course be no more than an opinionated trouble-maker. Which do you think you are?' He fixed me under his black horsehair eyebrows with what I took to be smouldering animosity. It was, of course, well before the day I saw him ask into his kitchen a collection of rain-soaked Jehovah's Witnesses and offer them cups of tea, for he was the kindest of people. He had hair to match his eyebrows sprouting, intimidatingly, like sofa stuffing from the neck of his open shirt. I must have shrugged in an unprepossessing manner. How could I put across to him how it was with me? How much I was driven timorously by a desire to please and yet found myself stubbornly unable to do so by obedience to any values but my own? Since my values were not shared by those around me, I couldn't possibly win. The lack of recognition, I think, made me show off in an attempt to force it from those in authority over me.

'Sometimes I show off,' I said.

'Me too,' Jacob said.

I was, in a minor way, a trouble-maker at school, always polite, guilty of little more than reading James Joyce under the desk in religious education classes, truanting from all sporting occasions and disregarding the finer points of the school uniform: balking, in short, at those aspects of school which seemed to me peripheral to the educational process. Education, as I had always hoped for it, is what I got from Jacob. Jacob clearly identified to a degree with trouble-makers, having, I discovered much later, come before a kindly Tory magistrate once in the course of a troubled youth. The magistrate's Toryism had taught Jacob, I think—with Toryism and other forms of villainy—to hate the sin and not the sinner. A thing he was very good at.

'Tell me what you like to read,' he said. He smoked his disgusting proletarian cigarettes which he lit from a large box of household matches and gave me the floor. Somewhat to my retrospective embarrassment, I remember telling him, among other things, that I thought Wordsworth had 'possibilities,' that I thought Jesus Christ had been a Utopian Socialist and that I didn't like the sex in D.H.Lawrence. It is a tendency I have, now kept in check, to compensate for my natural timidity with odd flashes of bravado.

'The wife doesn't care for it either,' he said, which surprised me not a little. 'She considers it not so much sex as indecent exposure. But is there not—forgive me, since this isn't my cabbage patch—is there not an element of zealous pioneering about it? Is it not a little ungrateful to climb on the shoulders of the past and sneer?'

'I don't know,' I said. 'But I don't much like having to be grateful for things.' Jacob took this with an encouraging suppressed smile.

'To be sure I've never been hit with the Chinese jade,' he said. 'I've had the Heinz tinned oxtail thrown at my head and miss, but it doesn't have anything like the same symbolic power.' I went on then to make heavy weather of the only philosophy book I had ever read—a small Home University Library publication of Bertrand Russell's which I had bought in the Camden Town market, I suspect to annoy my mother, who believed that I was becoming a blue-stocking and frightening away nice young men. It was I who was frightened of men, of course, but it worked two ways. As Robert Frost says, 'There's nothing I'm afraid of like scared people.' I told Jacob then that *Emma* was my favourite novel. He allowed himself to remark at my expense that there was, at least, no sex in it. Sex, had I but known it, was one of Jacob's favourite subjects. I blushed and said hotly to cover myself, 'Of course there's sex in *Emma*. Mrs

9

Weston has a baby. It grows out of its caps, remember? You don't get babies without sex do you?' Jacob produced a wonderful Rabelaisian laugh and volunteered some coffee which we acquired down the corridor from a dispensing machine.

'Listen Flower,' he said when I took my leave, 'people who come here do so on the back of the British Taxpayer. I expect my people to work. If they don't I do my best to have them thrown out.'

During the summer vacation I received notification—Jacob's ultimate compliment to me—that the department would have me on three Es.

2

Not long afterwards I met a man called John Millet in Dillon's bookshop.

'Just the jam and the poetry?' he said into my ear. I didn't know who he was. He approached me in the stacks as I browsed. He spoke BBC English and wore a slightly preening twisted smile. In my string bag, over my shoulder, I had a jar of cherry jam and a paperback John Donne. I blushed deeply, embarrassed by the cliché of his good looks, because John Millet looked like a man in an Austin Reed shirt advertisment. He was clad in stylish pale linen and had a squashy packet of Gallic fags jutting from his breast pocket.

'Careful I don't make you blush again,' he said, relishing my embarrassment. 'It doesn't match the clothes you're wearing.' I was dressed on that day in an outsize purple football jersey which I had worn to my interview with Jacob. I wore it, as was then the fashion, well over half way up my thighs. Pulled over one eye I had a small crocheted string hat which I had made myself. I have a great love affair with clothes. They are consumingly important to me and I often pull off a successfully Voguey look. Once when I was crossing Tottenham Court Road a team of Japanese photographers began to click their shutters. I was more than chuffed that they should have risked the traffic for my image. I like crafty clothes especially. I like shepherd smocks and intricate knitting. I can knit prodigious landscapes into my jerseys. I can do corded piping in seams and beaded embroidery. I like to make quilted cuffs and bodices.

John Millet that summer was wearing his middle age with a casual grace. That afternoon he drove me along the Embankment to the Tate Gallery in his white Alfa Romeo, which he had recently driven across the Alps. He was an architect just returned from four years in Rome. Lined and brown, he stood among the smooth pebble-white Henry Moores. In the basement café with its charming murals he fed me doughnuts and talked about the Portland Vase. Enclosed by the rustic idyll of the walls, watching the smoke rise from his Gauloise, I thought, romantically, of a goat-boy playing the flute. Three days later he told a hairdresser in Sloane Square how to cut my hair.

'Like this. Like this,' he said.

I watched my hair drop in pale clods to the floor. The effect, I had to admit, was astonishing. With my almost non-existent breasts and my narrow hips, I looked alluringly herma-phrodite. I came out holding my head high, reaching for the gallant curtle-axe I felt upon my thigh.

'That's better,' he said, running his thumb down the newly exposed groove in the nape of my neck. He was considerately restrained always in his touchings. We dined in an Italian restaurant where before my eyes he devoured a daunting plate of snails with a squeeze of lemon, while I wrestled with my pasta. My understanding of foreign foods at that time was limited to the conviction that paprika in the stew made it Hungarian and tinned cocktail fruits made it Caribbean.

'Like this,' he said, demonstrating with fork and spoon, Roman-wise. When I achieved, with this technique, something the size of a cricket ball wound onto the end of my fork he was charmed by it as a symptom of my innocent youth.

'It's not good enough, you know,' he said, eyes smiling. 'Florentines manage it using only the fork. I'm spending a couple of days with some friends in the country,' he said. 'Will you join me?' Olive oil on my chin was enough to make me feel daringly bacchanalian.

'Yes,' I said. 'Yes, yes.' From the deserted offices of his archi-tectural partnership in Hampstead he telephoned his friends.

'Jane,' he said wooingly. 'My sweet and lovely Jane, may I bring a friend?' I sat perched on the desk beside him, hearing every word. His friend had her mouth full of marbles and replied after a pause with caution.

'You know I don't like people, John,' she said. 'Would I like your friend, do you think?'

'Definitely,' John said. 'I guarantee it.'

'And tell me, John, if I may make so bold,' she said, 'are you and your "friend" together or apart?' John smiled at me reassuringly as I glowed with the excitement of no retreat.

'Together,' he said.

My mother coincided only once with John Millet. The day before we left for Sussex. He caused her a burst of subsequent indignation.

'He's queer,' she said, priding herself on her instinct for nosing out sexual deviance. 'The world is full of nice young men. Why do you go out with an old queer?'

3

The house, as it presents itself from the road, is like a house one might see on a jigsaw puzzle box, seasonally infested with tall hollyhocks. The kind one put together on a tea tray while recovering from the measles. We are in the Sussex countryside, not far from Glyndebourne. We are in Virginia Woolf country. Mrs Goldman is in her vegetable garden, but leaves it and comes over when she sees us. She puts down a gardener's sieve containing potatoes and a lettuce and takes John's hands warmly in her own.

'Darling John,' she says. 'How truly lovely to see you. You're as handsome as ever, but I have to tell you you are going grey.' Her voice is a stylish combination of upper-class vowels and tongue-tied sibilants.

'You're pregnant,' John says reproachfully, still holding her hands. 'You were pregnant when I left.' She smiles at him.

'But not quite as pregnant as this, was I?' she says. Jane Goldman has that indiscreet full-term bulge women get when the foetal head engages. She stands hugely in strong farmer's wellington's into which she has tucked some very old corduroy trousers. She has these tied together under a man's shirt with pyjama cords because the zip won't come together over the bulge. Bits of hair are falling out of her dark brown plait. She has a face like a madonna. She wears a contained, ironic smile which makes dimples in her cheeks and is blessed with the bluest of eyes. A neglected Burne-Jones, she is, in wellingtons.

'New babies have such lovely legs,' she says in her own defence. 'That's an awfully nice pullover thing you're wearing, John. What elegance you always bring to our establishment.' John Millet has clad his torso in an impeccable sky blue velour

14

article with sleeves that blouse into ribbed wristbands.

'This is Katherine,' he says. Jane Goldman peers at me with her myopic blue eyes in the bright sunlight.

'Hello there,' she says, taking my hand and bestowing her smile upon me.

'Why have you grown your hair?' John says possessively. 'This heavy Teutonic hairstyle. I don't like it.' Jane laughs.

'It's not a hairstyle. It's neglect,' she says. 'Go and admire my daughter. Rosie is over there. Isn't she nice?' She gestures to where her leggy, dark nine-year-old and friend are making a tent with a garden bench and a collection of dusty Persian rugs.

'Your children are dragging your heirlooms in the mud,' John says. Jane surveys her worldly goods with marvellous indifference.

'Any such heirlooms you see are what my mother sneaks out of the shed,' she says. 'How are you, John? Did you have a lovely time?' John doesn't talk about himself. He prefers forms and artefacts.

'You never came to see me in Rome,' he says. She smiles at him tolerantly.

'Have you stopped to think of the cost of getting the Goldmans to Rome?' she says. 'Anyway, Jake likes day trips to Worthing. He doesn't like holidays abroad.'

'Worthing smells of seaweed,' John says. 'Your husband is mad. You could have left him at home.'

'You should be so lucky,' she says. 'And aren't all the best people mad?'

'Your garden is better than ever,' he says, taking in the lovely wildness of self-seeding flowers.

'I give it no attention,' she says. 'I spend all my time among the cabbages these days. I've been having words with Jake about it this morning as a matter of fact. He says I give it too much of my time.' She laughs briefly. 'What he means is that he needs a proper wife who will type his manuscripts and listen to him carping over the Sunday papers.' John smiles.

'How is Jake?' he says.

'He couldn't be better,' she says, making the admission sound like a conspiracy. 'I would say things were going rather well for him. He won't admit it to you of course. He's such a

posturing old bastard. He likes to suffer in public. He is spending the weekend grumbling over his proofs. He's taking his
new book to London tomorrow.' John clearly finds reassurance
in the fact that his friends are unchanged. He needs them to be
unchanged.

'Let's go in,' she says. 'He'll be very glad to see you.'

'And your children?' John says as we walk slowly toward the
house.

'The children are lovely,' she says. 'Roger and Jont are giants
with deep voices and big feet. Roger is about somewhere.
Jonathan is fishing as always but he'll appear at lunchtime.
They're much the same really. Roger is gorgeous and Jonathan
is trouble. Equally gorgeous, but trouble. Rosie is a dear little
creature, but idle and spoilt. I believe she has the art of making
herself pleasing to men,' she says. 'Jacob at any rate is charmed
by her. She does nothing but swim and turn cartwheels. The
babies are delightful. They're no more bother than a pair of
kittens. Neither of them can count to ten. Do you remember
Roger at four, John? How he discovered Infinity while standing
at the window counting MGs? It struck him suddenly that
numbers could go on forever. Do you remember how Jacob
made us go out and spend the milk money on sticky buns to
celebrate? Weren't we daft?'

'I've always felt indebted to Roger,' John says, gallant and
gently humorous. 'He told me when he was three that the
sperm whale enjoyed occasional snacks of small shark and I
have never forgotten.'

'He read all those remarkable dinosaur books,' Jane says.
Roger Goldman has recently won an *Observer* competition, it
appears, with a bogus essay in natural history arguing that the
earth is flat. John makes a reference to this which pleases his
mother. He has seen it in the *Observer*, which was of course
available to him in Rome. John Millet pronounces his name
like the grain, not like the painter. It typifies his air of well-bred
understatement. He has clearly been expressing his love for
Jane Goldman in courtly tributes these twenty years.

4

In the sitting room, in the company of two dark and curly tots and surrounded by a great volume of Sunday newsprint, is my philosophy professor: a coincidence which leaves me feeling more than compromisingly marginal to a middle-aged reunion of old friends. He wears his shirt unbuttoned and reveals to me, thereby, that the hair grows like a blanket to his navel. I assume this to be a minor deformity which he bears with fortitude. He booms a welcome to John and gets up, buttoning his shirt.

'You're grey,' he says, inspecting him jovially. 'You look like an eminence. Jesus, John, you look like the Chairman of the National Coal Board.' He embraces John effusively, like a football star. John speaks quietly, but with no less pleasure in the meeting.

'I've heard it rumoured that you're on the BBC these days,' he says in self-defence. 'How are you, Jake? You look terrific.'

'Tottering on,' Jacob says. 'Tottering on.'

'I have brought a sweet young woman for you,' John says. To say that he offers me to Jacob in any real sense would of course be misleading. In his manner he likes to imply more than is there. Jacob is in any case too resolutely monogamous, too involved with Jane to contemplate others and too upright in matters of fraternizing. He says it perhaps to compromise us both or to create a myth for himself which makes more legitimate his flirtation with Jacob's wife.

'This is Katherine,' Jane Goldman says. My presence seems to cause him no discomfort.

'Well, well,' he says enigmatically. 'Katherine, is it? And these are my lovely children. Sam and Annie.' His little twins

17

have made a mountain by gathering every cushion in the house and in it they are merrily trampling about. One of the cushions has burst its seam and is spewing out foam chunks onto the carpet which is in any case full of coffee stains and dust. 'Aren't they big?' he says. 'Too late to put them down for Eton.'

'One of them appears to be a girl,' John says. 'Hey, Jake, your wife is pregnant. What's the matter with you people?'

'We like fucking,' Jacob says. The word drops like a rock onto my uninitiated sensibilities, but does nothing to shake his wife's composure, or John's.

'Don't be evasive,' John says. 'I want to know what's the matter with you. Four children I accept is perhaps not an intolerable number—and I can appreciate that nobody could have predicted twins. But six? Why do you have six children?' Jacob won't be drawn, sensing, perhaps, a degree of unwitting prurience in John's insistence.

'I like to get her knickers down,' he says. 'I like her, for Christssake. She's my lawful wife.'

'But you're not Catholics yet, are you?' John says.

'You want her to swallow hormone pills and get cancer?' Jacob says extravagantly. 'Or would you prefer her to stuff copper hooks up her cervix?' (I had no idea until this moment that I possessed such a thing as a cervix and the knowledge caused me, prophetically, to contemplate my pelvic region, for the first time, as a potential disaster area.) 'A hundred years ago women ruined their health swallowing lead pills,' he says, 'and poking at themselves with crochet hooks. Now they ruin their health swallowing hormone pills and pushing copper hooks into the neck of the uterus. You may call it progress if you like.' I have never before heard private parts made public. I find it quite astonishing.

'As I understand it, childbirth is also dangerous,' John Millet says.

'That's as maybe,' Jacob says. 'But childbirth is natural. It's a nicer thing than pills and hooks.'

'You sound like Malcolm Muggeridge,' John says. He offers Jane one of his cigarettes, which she accepts. He lights it for her and watches her inhale appreciatively. She looks all the time remarkably serene and as if containing some benign, ironic joke.

'If you want the truth, John,' she says, 'you won't get it from Jake. I'm pregnant because it seemed a delightful idea to him and me after we'd blown all the twins' birthday money last winter on an extravagant drunken lunch. I'm afraid it impaired our judgement. We made eyes at each other over grilled lobsters and resolved to jettison our humble rubber goods. I agree with Jake about the pills and the other things. You may not, but then you haven't been on the slab in the Family Planning Clinic. Anyway, the point is that any day now we'll suffer for it. My darling Jake will hold bowls for me half the night, while I vomit in labour and botch the breathing exercises, which I always do. Then he'll spend the next three years suffering his insomniac's agony after being woken at night. And he'll put up with us having our bed peed on and his manuscripts scribbled over. Jonathan woke him up nearly every night for four years. He and Roger are violently allergic to each other. Rosie caused him to slip a disc last summer. He had to spend all his income tax rebate on what Sammy here calls his fizzy old therapist. Oh, if only they weren't always so lovely, John, it wouldn't be half so tempting.' John smiles at her.

'You are both insane,' he says. 'I've brought you some very special wine, by the way, from a vineyard near Amalfi. I've got it in my car.' He has seated himself by this time in a small, beautiful lyre-backed chair. The seat is loose and the legs are splaying outwards at the joints. Anyone in my mother's circle would have done it up years ago in tasteful Dralon.

'It wants some glue here,' John says moderately, inspecting the joints. 'I'll do it for you if you like.'

'Please do,' Jane says. 'Before my mother comes to see us next week. She has a special thing for that chair. Lady Gregory gave it to her mother. She thinks that Yeats might have sat in it.' Jane Goldman's family is patrician Anglo-Irish. She has married her Mile End Jew in defiance of them.

'Yeats, William Butler,' Jacob says. 'Brother of the more famous Jack, of course.' He turns to me, to where I have seated myself, alongside the children, in the heap of cushions. 'Jane went to a local auction sale once, Katherine,' he says. 'Chap spells his name for the auctioneer. 'Yeats,' he says. 'Gates?' says the auctioneer. 'No, no,' says Jane's chap, 'Yeats, *like the poet.*' Does that amuse you?' he says. It obviously does because I giggle appreciatively.

Jacob's small daughter has decided suddenly to flatter John with her intimacy.

'Jane's baby is going to get born through a very stretchy hole,' she says. 'And only girls have them. If you are a boy or a girl you stay a boy or a girl, you know.' There is more sex education about than I have encountered in all of my life.

'Absolutely,' John says, full of sober conviction.

'And when the baby is inside, it can suck her nipples from the inside, can't it?' she says.

'I think you may be wrong there,' he says without displaying a hint of mirth. 'I think there's another system for inside.'

'Something to drink,' Jacob says decisively. 'Come with me, Katherine. I'll find my son for you.' He is seeking to protect me from the fantasy, which John Millet allows me, that I am one of the grown-ups. In the back hallway before the kitchen door is a large laundry basket, such as is used to accommodate Falstaff, which contains a great tumble of wellington boots. All the visible ones say R.J.GOLDMAN in marking ink, presumably because his oldest son Roger wears them all first. It underlines for me Roger's glorious ascendancy. At the kitchen table Roger Goldman is poring over the *Observer* theatre reviews, stretching long denim-clad legs before him. He has, on his comely dark head, a remarkable floppy black beret which gives him the look of having come but late from Wittenburg. He is scratching idly at his dandruff where his hair protrudes at the back of the cap.

'I'll give you that hat, shall I?' Jacob says agreeably.

'Thanks,' Roger says, still reading and scratching. Jacob pulls the cap over his eyes.

'Stop reading for a moment, will you?' he says. 'It's only the routine Sunday pap for the *lumpenintelligentsia.*'

'Fuck off, Jake,' Roger says, tensing with antipathy. He looks up, however, and sees me. He has the same stunning blue eyes as his mother and a similar fine face.

20

'This person is Katherine,' Jacob says. 'She's a pupil of mine. Look after her for me.' He pulls out a chair for me. A Windsor kitchen chair with wobbling spindles in the back. 'Jesus,' he says, 'there's more bloody hopeless chairs in this house than makes sense. Has Goldilocks paid us a visit? Stick this one in the shed, Roggs. Use it for bails and stumps.' As Roger begins to get up, Jacob changes his mind. 'Forget it,' he says. 'How many bails and stumps can one family reasonably use?' He pulls out another for me. 'Have this one, Katherine,' he says. 'We'll save the other one for unwelcome guests. Give her a drink, Roger.' He plants before Roger a half empty bottle of white wine from the fridge and two glasses. Then he carts off the hard stuff to the sitting room.

Roger, for all he is endowed with distinguishing beauty and the benefits of his parents' bold, radical iconoclasm, is as shy and awkward with me as any other sixth-former. We punctuate awkward silences with snatches of factual information and seek refuge in the newspaper. Roger has the advantage here, but I have never found reading upside down all that difficult. Roger is going to Kenya for a year on VSO before going to Oxford the following summer to study mathematics. I venture so far as to tell him I like his hat.

'It's a German student's hat,' he says. 'It belonged to Jake's father.' Jacob's family has fallen and risen again in defiance of Hitler. Inwardly, a little sycophantically, I admire the impressive ethnic muddle of his origins.

'Try it,' he says. He puts it briefly on my head, while I blush and think of dandruff.

'You look very nice in it,' he says shyly and, averting his eyes, he takes it back. Outside somebody has begun to groan noisily over the pulling off of wellington boots.

'Roggs?' says the voice. 'That poovy Millet has brought a woman with him. Have you seen her?' Roger tenses in an agony of embarrassment.

'Don't shout,' he says, a little piously.

'Listen, Shitface,' says the voice, 'this doll is worth a bloody sight more than the Queen's Christmas message.' He comes in, having slung the boots roughly into the basket. He has large bare feet and has evidently been going sockless in wellies. His eyes widen with shock when he sees me, but he is not half so embarrassed as Roger and starts to laugh.

'Okay, what's your 'phone number, then?' he says facetiously.

'Don't be cheeky, Jont,' Roger says hurriedly. 'She's one of Jake's pupils.'

Jonathan sits down. 'Does that mean you actually pay to listen to him?' he says to me. 'Roggs and I would pay to shut him up, wouldn't we, Rogsie? A sponsored silence, like they have in the Brownies.'

Jonathan Goldman, who is sixteen, is taller than his brother and coarser looking. He has unbecoming frizzy hair and, underneath his boisterous humour, a slightly menacing adolescent belligerence. He looks, when I come to analyse it, not unlike Jacob—or as my mother would put it, who has none of my liberal squeamishness—he looks 'like a Jew.'

'That Millet makes the parents twitter,' he says cheerfully. 'Do you think he gives Jane the flutters?'

'They always twitter,' Roger says in disgust, fixing his eyes somewhere beyond the kitchen clock. 'All of them. This time next week, I'll be on another continent.'

The kitchen is large and dauntingly grotty. There is excess rubbish piling up in a Heinz bean carton beside the overflowing rubbish bin. Where the legs of the table meet the floor there are encrustations of toddler food. The tops of some home grown vegetables are wilting on the work-board alongside seeping used tea-bags and half-eaten bowls of that morning's cornflakes. It is also perfectly apparent to me that the Goldmans write their telephone messages all over the wall. Alongside the kitchen telephone the wall looks like a defaced urban street hoarding. Rosie has scratched up a conspicuous message in black marker pen for her father. 'Jake must fone criss,' it says. Underneath it, Jacob has written, 'If criss fones me again tell him to phuck off.'

5

I leave the kitchen and find Jane Goldman alone in her vegetable garden, stringing onions. She asks me to join her at it when I approach, which I do. She says apologetically that it looks a little William Morrisy, but that it makes sense if you don't want them to rot. To me, straight from the outer reaches of the Northern Line, it looks positively Robinson Crusoe and I tell her so.

'But I'm good at knots and weaving,' I say, recommending myself. Mrs Goldman gives me a friendly smile.

'Jake is a very urban person too,' she says. 'If you mention the Northern Line to him he goes quite starry-eyed. He likes to see Coke tins in gutters. He likes to be five minutes' walk from the Hampstead Everyman. He finds this hopelessly countrified.'

'It's very nice here,' I say. 'Your house. It's very nice.'

'And very dirty,' she says. 'Do you mind the dirt, Katherine?' I am surprised by the question. It requires a quick decision from me and with a sudden instinct to emulate her, I commit myself against the grain to the ideology of dirt.

'It's nice dirt,' I say. She looks up at me, trying to make me out.

'It saves us from people, this house does,' she says. 'I'm very fond of it. Tell me where you met John.'

'In Dillon's Bookshop,' I say.

'How wonderfully highbrow,' she says. 'I met him in Woolworths when I was about your age. It's very flattering, I think, to be noticed by him. He says he likes the quattrocento profile.' But Jacob, who has picked his way along a row of her inverted jam jars, is there behind her.

'Quattrocento lahdeedah,' he says. 'He likes women with no

tits.' To be sure, neither of us is particularly well endowed in that respect.

'Give me the nuts and bolts of the sleeping arrangements,' he says. 'Where are these chaps going to lay their heads?'

'In the guest room,' she says. 'Roger has done it already. I asked him to.'

'This young person is one of my up-and-coming first years,' he says. They look at each other with meaning.

'Really?' Jane says. 'Now there's a thing.' I feel myself on the rack with awkwardness.

'I'm very sorry about this,' I say. 'I didn't know I was coming here or I wouldn't have come.'

'Now see what you do, Janie,' he says accusingly. 'You make the sweet creature feel unwelcome. It only wants a little tact and delicacy.' Jane Goldman gives me a delightful conspiratorial smile which makes me feel a lot better.

'I see,' she says with quiet sarcasm. 'Well, fire away then, my tactful friend. I hope you're not planning to take a great stand.'

'The point is this,' he says. 'We all know and love John as a dear friend, not so?'

'Naturally,' she says.

'And we all know, of course, that some of our best friends go in for sodomy, buggery, child-abuse, you name it.'

'Have a heart, Jacob, there's no call for poetic licence,' Jane says.

'The point is quite simply this,' he says. 'I will not have this old faggot come here to my house in order to indulge a sideline in female children. Not with my pupils. Not with Katherine here. Is that clear to everyone present?'

I believe it is no exaggeration to say that I took a few steps forward that day. I had cried into my pillow the night my mother called John Millet queer, but I perceived a world of difference between that and Jacob's calling his house guest an old faggot. For one thing he said it so loudly that it filled the air without shame. It had none of the same prim moral censure. But I was a little taken with the idea of sexual induction. It was for John Millet that I had ironed my beautiful Liberty lawn nightdress and for him that I wore my palest consumptive stockings and high-heeled shoes. Jacob, with his unhesitating

24

way of bulldozing through to the heart of any matter, not only confirmed that my mother was right, but eroded my privacy, leaving me feeling like an Arab bride whose wedding sheets are being hung out for the villagers to inspect for blood stains.

'Perhaps Katherine would oblige you and accept Roger's bedroom?' Jane says. 'And Roggs can move in with Jonathan. Would you, Katherine? It's a lethal muddle of electronic wiring, I'm afraid.'

'Of course,' I say, making nothing of the momentous event, being by training polite and accommodating.

'You haven't fallen for this character?' Jacob says to me. 'Nothing more, I hope, than a little indulgent *sehnsucht*? No?'

'No,' I say, with my fingers crossed, wondering what *sehnsucht* could be. Jacob uses German words quite a lot. He had his origins in pre-war Germany and therefore has no difficulty with getting his Londoner's tongue round words like *Wirtschaftgeschichte* and *Weltanschauung*.

'That's my girl,' Jacob says. 'Tell him to use his own house, lovey, and don't you venture into the bedroom without taking a spanner with you.' To this day I don't really know what he meant by it, but it made me laugh a little which was a gratifying release. He turns back to Jane. 'And are we going to eat at all today, Janie, or have you forgotten us, as usual, here among your shallots? My sweetie, it's nearly half-past two.' He gains strength from the myth of his wife's incompetence.

'I never forget you,' she says mildly. 'But he's coming, husband, our maligned friend. Be sure to use your tact and delicacy on him, won't you?' John is strolling up to us, slapping his thigh lightly with the Sunday glossy.

'I thought you were incarcerated with your proofs,' he says to Jacob. He makes up to Jane, leching, as he does, without apparent intent.

'You smell very French,' he says. They laugh together, very close and affectionate.

'Balls, John,' she says, 'it's onions.'

'I'm revising the sleeping arrangements,' Jacob says, tenaciously. 'We're giving you the guest room, as befits your station as our more senior guest, and bunging Katherine in with the children. Okay?'

25

'What, what?' John says vaguely, looking at all of us in turn. 'What's this?'

'Katherine here is one of my students,' Jacob says.

'I know,' John Millet says. The swine, I think, wretchedly. He knew all the time. Did he set it up to have an audience? Did he in his urbane wisdom merely not give it a thought? Did he hope to make Jane Goldman jealous by requiring her to share a niche in his pantheon of superior women?

'I have no wish to be charged with corrupting the youth of Athens,' Jacob says coldly. 'Let's not ruin our Sunday over it, eh? Let's just leave it at that.' But John can be fairly persistent, and all of them having been absent from each other, they are now feeling their way back into a tolerance of each other's idiosyncrasies.

'Is your husband being serious, Jane?' John says. 'Has he become a member of the Church of England Committee for Moral Reform?' Jacob is incensed at this supercilious use of Jane as intermediary. He appears suddenly very large.

'I *am* the Church of England Committee for Moral bloody Reform,' he says ominously. 'And much more besides, as you'll find out if you try me.' Jane takes John's arm.

'Please don't rise to him, John,' she says. 'It's not worth it for any of us. We both know how frightfully rhetorical and hysterical Jake will get. If you make an issue of this, Jake and I could well end up screaming at each other, because that's the way it works, isn't it? It's an awful bore for the children and Katherine will feel wretched. Now, if you will just kindly fetch us that very special booze you have in your car, we can drink it with our lunch. I've worked like blazes on this lunch, I don't mind telling you, though Jake hasn't noticed. The babes have made you blackberry tarts and whipped up great quantities of cream. Please, John. You must know that with enemies like Jake you don't need friends.' This proves with John to be an effective piece of diplomacy, but Jacob is, alas, not pleased with it.

'Jesus Christ, Janie,' he says angrily. 'I'll thank you not to bloody well talk about me like that. "Humour the old bastard because he's a harmless lunatic." All that. I pay the bloody mortgage here and I'll lay down the bloody rules if it bloody well suits me. I say who sleeps in what bed here and don't you

26

forget it.' Jane Goldman is impressive in the face of male paranoia.

'I won't stay and listen to this, Jake,' she says quietly. 'And neither will Katherine.' We go ahead into the house, where I watch her frying courgettes.

'I'm bound to say you weathered all that with admirable composure,' she says. 'My congratulations to you. Are you as composed as you look?' To my embarrassment I find that I am crying. Jane embraces me remorsefully.

'Sweet child,' she says. 'How awful this must be for you. What sods we are.'

'I think I'd like to go home,' I say. She embraces me. I find it strangely comforting, the contact with a highly pregnant woman. I am the only child of my parents.

'I find that very understandable,' she says. 'But I should be very sorry to see you go.' I cry fairly copiously into her shoulder, wiping mascara onto the yoke of her shirt.

'What an old bastard he is to bring you here,' she says, 'and raise all this hue and cry. You don't half get all sorts when it comes to men. As for my Jacob, you want to pay him no attention. He behaves like Heathcliff to everyone, you know.' She gets me a wad of kitchen towel. 'He's very kind, if the truth be known. You wouldn't happen to be his young woman who likes Mrs Weston and her baby's caps, would you?'

'I think I must be,' I say, sniffing inelegantly.

'Well now,' she says cheerfully, 'my old man is *most* impressed with you. He thinks you're terrifically bright and he thinks, between us and the gate post, that you've got the best legs since Marlene Dietrich. What a delightful coincidence to have you here. I can't let John Millet drive you away. I insist that you stay. Can I say, in Jake's defence, that he wouldn't ordinarily snoop into your sleeping habits? It is a bit compromising isn't it, for him, though God knows why he has to make a five-act play about it in the vegetable garden—stalking about and bloodying everything, but that's the way it is. I should think it's quite enough to make you consider going to university in Leeds or Bristol. If you're feeling better I might tell you about the time I met John, shall I?' I say yes. I like autobiography and I like her.

'He asked me to come and see him at his place in Belsize

Park. I was spending the summer with my aunt in Cadogan Square at the time. When I got there I found him on the chaise-longue with a beautiful young man. They were kissing each other passionately on the mouth. I wasn't anything like as sophisticated as you. I was very straight-laced, Katherine. I was a dear little flat-chested, upper-class Christian, buttoned up in cashmere. The product of a Scottish nanny and a girls' boarding school. Jacob found me white-faced in the hall. He was John's upstairs neighbour, you see. The two of them got on like a house on fire. He took me upstairs and succeeded in persuading me that there were worse things afoot in 1945 than a little aberrant sex. He was very kind to me and also very amusing. He took my head apart while I scrambled for the bits and determinedly stuffed them back. I spent the night with him,' she says, 'to my very great surprise. I was such a little prude, you see. John spent the night downstairs with his boyfriend. We met for breakfast. There was a shared kitchen. I in Jacob's pyjamas, John and the boy friend in matching Norwegian fisherman's jumpers, as you might see on a knitting pattern. The V-neck and the button through. John's mother had knitted them—one for John and one for the boyfriend. Splendid woman, John's mother. Jacob naked from the waist up, sprouting hair from every follicle.'

I find her wonderfully gossipy and conspiring. We are drawn together into an intimacy not only by the melodrama in the onion patch, not only by a happy accidental affinity of mind, but because I believe that I answer a need. As women do, she has sacrificed distant female friendships on the altar of a contented marriage. She has been assimilated into her husband's tribe of male academics, male bohemians, male politicos and predominantly male children. She makes rapid commitments with the logical clarity of hallucination. She tells me at once that she jacked in Oxford after knowing Jacob for three days and went to live with him instead.

'He was much more fun. And all that sex, Katherine, was so unexpectedly jolly,' she says, in her headmistressy voice. 'One had been led to believe that it would be such a hurdle.' As she catalogues her early life for me, it assumes all the properties of an eighteenth-century burlesque. There is the runaway daughter, the intractable father, the foreign-born lover, the instant romantic commitment, and, of course, the routine poverty. Her father, a highly conservative Oxford theologian, now retired, cut her off like the blight along with his sister in Cadogan Square.

'My brother declared himself determined to avenge my lost honour,' she says. 'But he never came, poor Henry. I think he got wind of the fact that Jake was a pretty big chap. Jake looked very ferocious in those days. He was bearded, you see, like whatshisname. The old biddy in Highgate Cemetery.' She got pregnant immediately to pre-empt any attempt her family might make to tear her away.

'And you lived happily ever after?' I say.

'We fought like cat and dog as it happens,' she says. 'I'm quite sure I'd have picked up my little baby and run back home if it hadn't been made so clear to me that I wouldn't be welcome. Culture shock is no small thing, you know. Once I ran into Henry as I was pushing Roger in his pram on Hampstead Heath. He walked straight past me. I remember thinking, funny, I used to toast marshmallows with that person. I went home to cry over Jake, but he had his whole damned *Kapital* reading group all over the furniture. I was obliged to cry over John instead. I was often obliged to cry over John. Jacob was always too busy flogging leaflets or mounting the tub on street corners in those days.'

When Jacob and John come in, having made their peace, she and Jacob mime brief reassuring kisses to each other.

'What have you been hatching?' Jacob says, noticing the glow in her cheeks. He puts his hands over her breasts. He has no restraints about laying hands on her in public.

'I have been filling in Katherine on my past,' she says without apology.

'Not a thing to inspire imitation,' he says. 'Why do women always talk intimacies about themselves? To listen to women talking is like sitting in on an encounter group. I cannot wander among the library shelves without being a party to whispered confidences. They will spread their personal lives like jam all over the stacks.'

'I must tell you something amusing, John,' Jane says, 'if you promise you won't start with Jake. My father is on the Church of England Committee for Moral Reform.'

6

It is temporarily impossible for me to enter the Goldmans' dining room because Jonathan has been gunned down by Sam with a plastic machine gun and has thrown himself in a convulsive dying agony across the doorway. I consider stepping over him but it occurs to me that the little bastard might well use the opportunity to look up my skirt. Rackatackatackatack.

'Get up, Jont,' his mother says briskly, in her hot potato voice. 'Katherine wants to come in.'

Jane has made us some aromatic, garlicky iced soup for lunch, served with hot garlic bread and followed by pork loin simmered in milk. There is also an abundance of her home-grown vegetables.

'What is it I can taste?' John Millet asks her solicitously.

'Coriander,' she says. 'You roll it up with coriander and seal it in butter. Then you pour boiling milk over it which forms a crust and reduces to this pleasant grainy stuff around the meat.' John and she do some rather in-group cookery talk, being the only ones that know about it. John is a kind of gastronomic Lionel Trilling and likes to pursue every morsel down his throat with analysis and appraisal. 'It's dead kosher,' she says, to amuse him.

'It could be neither more sinful nor more delicious,' Jacob says graciously. 'You may produce lunch two hours late, but you make it worth the eating, Janie.' Each in their own way, they honour the same mistress, 'Thank you,' she says. Jacob, with a forkful of pig meat seethed in milk celebrates perhaps not so much a release from ethnic taboos, as from the distant nightmare of his own truncated childhood, the marvel of his latter-day bourgeois *gemütlichkeit* in which I suspect he can never quite believe.

John Millet, as he hands me the salad, passes messages of bottomless innuendo in his smiles. I hold nothing against him. On the contrary, I have become rather elated. I consider myself, after talking with Jane, to be rather stylishly at the point where it all is. Where I always wanted to be. In the company of urbane, emancipated people. Some of my best friends are Jews and homosexuals. Besides, the idea of the sex act is so bizarre in any case, so appalling, so terrifying, that the element of the participant's gender hardly signifies. I am not shocked by his versatility.

'Do you still play that fiddle, Roger?' he says.

'He's the best violinist in the National Youth Orchestra by a mile,' Jane says. She has a tendency to answer questions for him as if he needed her as a buffer between himself and a hostile world, her lovely first-born child. But Roger chooses to answer for himself. He chooses to take a stand, holding his head high, his Adam's apple twitching slightly in his throat, armed strong in undergraduate righteousness.

'I don't play a fiddle,' he says. 'I play the violin.'

'Don't you be so damned churlish, you miserable nitpicking boy,' Jacob says rather violently. He and Roger exchange a moment's hatred. Roger wears his principles, a little provocatively, high on his shoulder like a schoolboy's dufflebag.

'I am merely pointing out that to call a violin a fiddle is a form of name-dropping,' he says coldly. 'It's a familiarity you earn the right to use—that's if you like name-dropping.'

It may appear melodramatic for me to interject here that in the face of that impressive vulnerable zeal, that high-minded verbal coup, I fell in love with Roger Goldman. I remember the moment as vividly as I remember the turn of his head. I cannot send up the emotion as I do so much of my youthful self, for though I have made many compromises with it it has never completely left me.

'Save your Oxford style till you get to Christ Church, sonny,' Jacob says, with terrible put-down. 'And in the meantime remember that to pick nits at my table, with my guests, is a form of bad manners.' Jonathan, promptly and hair-raisingly,

31

throws a large chunk of garlic bread at Jacob's head. It misses him and hits the wall behind.

'Fiddle schmiddle,' Jonathan says. 'What's all this "my table" crap, Aged Parent? Ma bought this table from the shop that closed down. What makes it yours? You really like to make a big patriarchal spiel over grub, don't you, you big Jewish yobbo.'

Nobody requires him to remember either his manners or the starving. Jacob merely instructs Sam in the subversive art of throwing the bread back. They appear to get on extremely well, do Jacob and Jonathan. Jacob is sufficiently opinionated to appreciate in Jonathan so much of himself.

'Make us some coffee, Flower,' he says benignly.

'Make it your bloody self, you schmuck,' Jonathan says.

'Sweet Jont,' Jacob says, 'be kind to us.' Rosie takes a whole plum out of her mouth to air a profundity before putting it back in again.

'Jonty is showing off,' she says. Jonathan laughs good-humouredly.

'Okay, Jake,' he says. 'I'll make it, but only if I can make instant, mind? I'm not going to stand over that cocked-up filter. It takes forever.' Jacob licenses what to me is an alarming amount of blasphemy, insubordination and defiance. He seems to set it up. It's as though he were all the time taking his children through an assault course in defiance. Jane by contrast is surprisingly school-marmish and she clearly believes in child labour. She could surely rise to a dish-washer, but she prefers to use her children. She believes that a row of children chopping vegetables is a better thing than a machine.

'Make the coffee, Jonathan,' she says icily. 'We'll have the real thing and brought to us in the sitting room.' Jonathan goes with the alacrity of Mustardseed. 'Stack the dishes, Rosie,' she says, 'so that Roger can wash them.' She is more demanding with Roger than with any of the others. Before the day is out I see her accost him where he engages in chewing grass on the front lawn and say to him, 'Go and have a bash at the G Minor, Roggs.'

'The G Minor is hard,' Roger says.

'Of course it's hard,' she says, working on him with her

powerful elitism, 'but not altogether beyond the likes of you, my darling.' I find this more than rigorous, coming as I do from a world where Purcell is a washing powder.

John Millet, over the coffee, talks lyrically about Rome. About the bell tower near his flat in Trastevere, about the fading gradations of mud-brown paint on the house fronts, about huge stuffed tomatoes in the piazza restaurants and the macho roar of Fiats. The images incorporate themselves into the composite romantic blur of my impressionable aspiration. Thereafter, while Jacob consumes what remains of the afternoon working on his proofs, John Millet reads the Sundays in a deck-chair with his shirt off. I read Dr Seuss books to Sam and Annie, and Rosie borrows my earrings to try on upstairs. Jane plays the *Suite Italienne* with Roger, and Jonathan on his bicycles sets out to take his fishing tackle to the stream. With the heat of the day he has taken off his jeans and is wearing fraying shorts and nasty, algae-ridden tennis shoes. He gets to the gate but then wheels round, hunched over his racing bike which he controls with one hand since he has his fishing rod in the other. He stops in front of me.

'Want to come fishing?' he says. He has a bold stare and big legs. He is the kind of schoolboy one avoided sitting next to on the bus home from school. 'You could use Jane's bicycle,' he says.

'She might need it,' I say.

'She can't use it at the moment,' he says. To be sure, Jane would have some difficulty squeezing herself in behind the handlebars in her condition. 'If you're scared, we can walk,' he says, 'I don't mind.' Silently, I curse Jonathan for plucking out the truth and handing it to me with such offensive frankness. I last rode a bicycle at the age of nine. I fell off and broke my arm the day after my father died. Jonathan and Roger, by contrast, are the kind of people who use bicycles with the accomplishment of Vietnamese peasants, capable of carrying children on crossbars and luggage carriers—and simultaneously bringing home great loads of shopping in back-packs. The kind of people who inspire a belief in the future for intermediate technology.

'I'd need to find you some shoes you could sludge around in,' Jonathan says, eyeing my strappy T-bars. I find it difficult to look back and realize that the single most important factor among my reasons for turning down Jonathan's offer was the prospect of having to put on hand-on wellington boots from the laundry basket.

'I think I'll just stay and listen to the music,' I say. 'I think catching fish is cruel, actually.' Jonathan throws me a look of impatient contempt. 'Spare a tear for the bait,' he says, as he takes his leave.

7

At six o'clock in the afternoon Jane brings us tea and toast on the grass. Jacob emerges from his work room for this pleasant ritual and Jonathan is back from his fishing. Rosie's friend, who disappeared at the lunch-hour, has reappeared to continue improvements to the play tent. Roger, who is flushed from the effort of playing his violin, makes a tangram with a slice of toast as he stretches on the grass.

'Give it to Rosie,' Jane says. 'See if she can put it together.'

'Give it to Katherine, Roggs,' Jacob says. Roger hands me the plate, lying on his belly in the grass, stretching out an arm. He watches me as I do it. It takes me some time, but I do it. John Millet applauds me. Roger averts his eyes self-consciously as I look back at him. On the bum pocket of his Levis he has a brightly coloured embroidered butterfly.

'We oughtn't to be letting John know that us Goldmans eat pre-sliced, steam-baked bread,' Jane says gaily. 'John is a believer in superior food.'

'So are you, Jane,' John says. 'You cover it under a veil of inverted snobbery.'

'True enough,' Jane says contentedly. 'Each of us to his own necessary snobbery. We ought to make some music, all of us, before the day is out.'

'You have been doing nothing else all day,' Jacob says, 'but making music and cultivating your garden.'

'Producing food,' Jane says. 'Bringing you lunch and tea. What should I be doing, Jake? Taking a course in psychology at the Brighton Polytechnic? Earning extra money to buy you elegant sweaters like John's?' Jacob turns to fix her with a mixture of caustic resignation and love.

'I heard all that this morning,' he says. 'I don't need a replay. All I've got to say is if there's any more music brewing in this house, John and I are off to the pub. The rest of you can get your rocks off Nymphs and bloody Shepherds. A highly suitable pursuit, on reflection, for women and children of a Sunday evening.' He is sitting on the grass at her feet with his head between her knees. She is in an upright wicker chair behind him. Having put down her tea cup, she is running her hands through his hair.

'As if we don't all know you can't sing in tune,' Jonathan says, rising to him obligingly. Jane smiles. 'Quite so, Jont,' she says. 'There's never much to be gained from having Jake sing, other than the odd International Brigade song, got out of tune. Sweet husband, why not take John to the pub for an hour? Then he can make us amends and do us some lovely supper on your return.'

'With the greatest of pleasure,' John says.

They go, Jacob and John, in a spirit of attractive but excluding male cameraderie, snatching up cigarettes and keys.

'We'll take my car,' John says. 'There's just the two of us.'

'Call that thing a car?' Jacob says. 'I call it an ego trip.'

We sing 'O Worship the King' in four parts unaccompanied. It would be like being back in the school choir, were I not so dazzled by the sonorous depth of Roger's voice. Jane, who stands beside me, begs me to overlook her sibilant S. Then Roger and Jonathan sing for us. Two beautiful, mournful songs full of black despair and crystal tears. *Christall Teares*. The songs cause me ever after to speak the name of John Dowland with reverence.

'Here,' Jane says. 'These.'

'I can't sing tenor,' Roger says, declining the first with too much nicety for the spirit of the occasion.

'Oh for Christssake, Rogsie,' Jonathan says, coaxingly. 'Jane sings sounding as though she needs a new bloody washer in her larynx.'

'Thanks, Jont,' Jane says.

'I can't sing tenor, that's all,' Roger says. 'You sing it.'

'Okay, okay, I'll sing it,' Jonathan says. 'Give us the bloody thing.' He raises his hands like a stage pedagogue. 'Quiet,

quiet,' he says preciously. 'Absolute quiet please. Stick your chewing gum behind your ear, Rosie.'

> Go christall teares
> Like to the morning showers
> And sweetly weepe
> Into thy Ladyes brest.

The second is a duet. Jonathan, to my very great surprise, flukes his voice up into a piercing alto for this item. I have never heard a post pubertal male sing like a girl before and it confronts me at first like the shock of meeting a man in drag at a street corner. *Down and Arise* goes the refrain. *Down and arise I never shall.* With their respective appearances they contradict the song in its picturesque melancholia. Roger with his jaunty butterfly appliqué'd to his bum pocket. Jonathan with his hairy rugger legs and sockless feet. Both of them so manifestly on top of the heap and very like to stay there. Jane plays the piano for them. She turns to Roger when they get to the end.

'Very nice, chaps,' she says. 'Get the babies out of the bath will you, Roggs,' she says, delegating incorrigibly. As he complies, Jonathan fits his flute together, making trial blows over the mouthpiece. Rosie blows a wobbly minuet and shakes spittle out of her descant recorder. The little Goldman twins come in then, standing damp at the gills in their cotton-knit pyjamas, and listen to Jonathan, who plays them 'Tom, Tom, the Piper's Son.' They try to join in but forget the words, which makes Jane smile.

'Darling babies,' she says, allotting them a moment's casual attention. They appear on the whole to be the successful product of benign neglect. Jane is nothing if not eclectic and has her family make chamber music of the 'Yellow Submarine' on the flute, violin, piano and descant recorder. They end prematurely in laughter.

'You're too good for the rest of us, Rogsie,' she says. 'How do you bear with us?' From Roger's expression, it is clear that he does so only with difficulty.

8

Fish fingers and beans from a tin is what Jacob crams into his three youngest children upon his return. It is his weekly gesture toward domestic involvement. He processes both food and children very fast, giving orders like a genial scout master. I observe him at it, because I am in the kitchen participating in John Millet's prodigious soup making. He makes a soup with Jane Goldman's excess tomatoes, donning her butcher's apron and pushing up his sky blue wrist bands to reveal the bronzed sinews of his lovely wrists. He requires, for his creation, the addition of ground rice, egg yolks, a great deal of grinding in a stone mortar and some careful sieving. Jonathan and I are delegated to dip strips of bread first into a pool of melted butter and then into Parmesan cheese which Jane draws out of her larder in a large caterer's pack. These are then toasted in the oven and are to be eaten with the soup. Roger is at the table, once again in the cap, reading a Swahili phrasebook.

'Jont,' he says, 'listen to this. "Boy, I asked you to bring *all* my bags. You have brought me only three." ' There is more levity in his dealing with Jonathan than with anyone else. Jonathan laughs.

'Jesus,' he says.

'Who writes this drivel, Rogsie?' Jacob says. He takes the book from his son and examines the fly leaf. 'German missionaries,' he says in disgust. 'What can you expect?'

'The sieve is most important,' John Millet says to me. I have done with the bits of bread and have taken on the sieve. 'Don't put it back on the heat, child, or we'll have scrambled eggs.'

'Twiddled egg soup,' Jonathan says, playing the fool. Jane is sitting at the table with Roger, looking tired and pregnant. We eat at the kitchen table when the children have finished, and all agree that the soup is quite delicious.

'These infants must go to bed,' Jacob says. 'And you too, Mrs Goldman. You look like a corpse. You bang at that *klavier* all day when you should be in bed with your feet up.' He initiates the process of getting the children to bed by enacting an evening burlesque, making jokes and uttering threats which creates a crescendo of boisterous indignation. He is a great prima donna over precisely which bedtime stories he will and will not read. He vetoes everything the little ones propose.

'Ameliaranne Stiggins!' Annie screeches excitedly.

'Ameliaranne Stiggins?' Jacob says, affecting stern, incredulous disgust. 'Backwards is the only way I will consent to read Ameliaranne Stiggins. Now John here—he's your man. He'll do you Ameliaranne Stiggins translated into Italian.' John smiles. 'Give us "Mrs Stiggins sat bump upon her favourite chair" in Italian, John.' John doesn't rise to it.

'Children are your fix, Jake,' he says, 'not mine. I've left my cigarettes in the car.' He leaves to get them. Jane selects Jonathan to wash the dishes.

'Come on, troops,' Jacob says. 'Go on ahead of me. Ten seconds is all I need to finish my coffee. We'll have the *Just So Stories* or the E. Nesbit.' Surprisingly, Jacob is a traditionalist, it seems, when it comes to child literature. He swats his twins on the rump with Roger's Swahili phrasebook. 'Move,' he says. 'The lash falls heaviest on the last man to brush his teeth.' The tiny ones go giggling up the stairs. Rosie lingers in the doorway.

'I'm not a man,' she says, 'so I don't have to go.'

'Go, my love,' Jacob says. 'School tomorrow and your mother is grinding her teeth.' Rosie manifestly gets on Jane's nerves.

'I want to show you my handstand,' Rosie says.

'Why are you such a bloody nuisance?' Jacob says affably. She sits down in the doorway.

'I'm too tired to walk,' she says. 'Carry me.' Jane is beginning to get visibly tense around the mouth. Jacob gets up and slings her across his shoulder like a sack.

'Come on, Flower,' he says. 'And *go to bed*, woman. You're pregnant.' Roger, who suffers no slight degree of revulsion for Jacob's extrovert goings on, has quietly slipped away.

39

Jonathan, scuffling conspicuously in the sink, appears to take it on in kind.

'God, you're like a bloody storm-trooper, Jake,' he says. He does the accent. 'Prizes for ze first man to vash himself in his own soap,' he says. A remark which adequately exceeds the bounds of good taste. How much it does so, I realize only when I discover from Jane, as our acquaintance evolves, that Jacob's father disappeared in Nazi Germany—a fact which causes me to deduce at the same time that Roger doesn't balk at wearing a dead man's hat. A martyr's hat. He runs, as it were, not only the ordinary risk of leaving it on the bus, but the more profound risk of catching death by contagion.

'I've done your dishes, Ma,' Jonathan says, while John Millet is out of the room. 'Everything except for the sieve. I'm not picking that effing muck out of the sieve for your poncy geriatric friends.'

'They're not my dishes, Jont,' she says. 'Did you catch anything today?'

'I've given up fishing,' Jonathan says. 'It's cruel. Ask her.' He nods rudely in my direction. Jane smiles.

'Go on,' she says, 'I don't believe it. In a suffering world, Katherine?'

'Because some things are worse doesn't make it less cruel,' I say. Perhaps it is a foolish debate to carry on with the wife of a man who has worn a yellow star in his time.

'Think of the milk in your coffee,' she says. 'It was snatched from a suckling calf.'

'Don't talk to her,' Jonathan says to me as he moves to leave us. 'She murders greenfly.' He almost collides with Roger who re-enters the room. Jane looks at him, watching his face with surging maternal tenderness. Jane Goldman is manifestly a great admirer of male flesh in general, but has a special thing for Roger. He is undeniably lovely. She strokes his cheek as he sits down on the table beside her.

'Mother,' he says peevishly, 'if Jake is taking the car to London tomorrow, how am I getting to my music lesson?' She sighs impatiently, wanting to love him but not to solve his problems for him.

'You'll resolve it, Roger,' she says indifferently. 'People

played the violin before they drove motor cars.'

'It's twenty miles,' Roger says. 'Why can't he take the train? He always does.' Jane smiles at him knowingly.

'Villainous man, your father,' she says, 'to use his own car when it suits him. He needs to get about a bit tomorrow, that's the point. But, even so, if you tried asking him civilly he might leave it for you. He hasn't got three heads. Why do you never speak civilly to him?'

'I hate him,' Roger says. 'He snipes at me.'

'I'll tell you something, my sweetie,' she says, with her hand again on his cheek. 'If you talked to me the way you talk to him, I wouldn't snipe at you. I would black your eye. Now take Katherine to watch the television. I'm tired of you.' Roger sulks, feeling betrayed by her.

'Is my car any good to you, Roger?' John Millet says, generously. 'I'm going into Brighton tomorrow to look at a site, but I should be back by one o'clock.' Even Roger, infant wrestler with the Infinite, is not immune to the charms of a white Alfa Romeo. He stops sulking and looks up.

'I take it that the left-hand steering won't trouble you?' John says.

'No,' Roger says. 'I have to go at four, if that's all right. Thank you very much. But are you sure you don't mind?'

'Not at all,' John says. 'such a small favour after all. Come with me to Brighton, if you like, and give it a try. I thought I might take in the chapel on the way back. The one with the Duncan Grant and Vanessa Bell paintings. You know?' He fixes his elegant mind for a moment on walls adorned with fruit and flowers, as we sit under the Goldmans' Japanese paper lampshade, covered in fly spots and dust. The paper is beginning to come away from the wire frame and is spiralling gently downwards towards the table which it overhangs.

'How very kind you are,' Jane says appreciatively. 'Take Katherine too.'

'Now I'm going to take a spirit-lamp into your shed and mend some of your chairs,' he says. He kisses her cheek. 'Before one of your children breaks a leg,' he says.

Over our heads, Jacob is bawling voluminously, amid great hilarity, that he will lock in the broom cupboard anyone found out of bed after a count of five.

9

Roger takes me to the television. The Goldmans, being cultivated people, own a small and rubbishy television set which
they banish to the children's playroom. The playroom is a
devastation of Lego bricks and jigsaw bits. Faded children's
drawings hang with curling edges from a pin-board alongside
Rosie's swimming certificates which announce that she has
satisfied the County Education Officer that she can swim a
hundred yards, five hundred yards, one mile, and that she can
also save lives. The playroom chairs are those uncut moquette
iniquities patterned in red and grey blobs which one expects to
find abandoned by disused railway sidings. I dare say that
whatever the Goldmans' furniture says about them, it also says
that they are articulate enough to contradict what it might
attempt to say.

Jonathan has got to the playroom before us. Shamelessly he
is reading his way through the *Girls' Crystal Annual* for 1964.
Roger turns on the television. This being Sunday night the line
is relentless low-brow moral uplift. It offers us interviews with
people whose Christian faith has made possible for them the
conquest of adversity. Roger sucks uneasily at his teeth
throughout a resolutely positive account of paralysis from the
shoulders down.

'Jesus, Rogsie,' Jonathan says. 'Switch off this bloody drivel.
You really go for all this gangrene and snot disease, don't you?
No wonder you dream that your teeth fall out.' Roger laughs,
colouring a little, nervous and lovely. He fiddles with the knobs
to discover alternatives. They are the Royal Ballet in *Les
Sylphides* and Ava Gardner in an ancient safari drama.

'We'll have this,' Jonathan says. 'Let's for God's sake not have

Culture.' Ava Gardner's beauty, decked out in khaki, crosses the decades to us, even on the Goldmans' small screen.

'I'll bet you this is Kenya,' Jonathan says, with his eyes on Ava Gardner's boobs in drill cloth. 'They're all dressed up like boy scouts. Your clothes are going to be all wrong, Rogsie. You'll have to ferret about in the Oxfam shop for a bush ranger's hat.' Roger laughs again, tossing his lank dark hair from his eyes.

'I'm going to miss you, Jont,' he says. 'You're the only person I'm going to miss. You're the only person I know who is worth talking to, come to that.'

'Balls,' Jonathan says. 'And another thing. Mother is going to have me playing the flute double time once you and your bloody fiddle are out of the way. Or is it your violin? Why did you produce all that crap at lunch time, incidentally?' Roger shrugs.

'I felt like it,' he says. 'Both Jake and that Millet get on my nerves.'

10

John Millet is alone in the kitchen next morning when I come down, having exposed his face both to his electric razor and to the morning dewfall. He has taken a country walk before breakfast with his sky blue velour pulled on over his naked skin. The Goldman car is crunching on the gravel outside, because Jane has come back from delivering children to nursery school and to junior school. Jonathan has gone off earlier on his bicycle.

'Did you sleep well?' John says to me, meaning to amuse himself slightly at my expense as Jane comes in. He gives me a wild flower. A flower for the virgin.

'Woodsage,' he says.

'Woodspurge,' Jane says, correcting him. 'Is Jake still asleep? I left him asleep in our bed with Annie. Did you hear us prowling last night? Annie was sick three times. I think she has swollen glands.'

Jacob, when he comes in, grumbles ostentatiously that he has not slept at all and gropes for the coffee pot. This is a manifest lie since his wife has told us she left him asleep.

'I shared my bed with two women,' he says. 'One of them pregnant and the other vomiting.' It is a relief, I find, with the passing of time, to watch Jacob operating without the company of John Millet, who, for all that he is sexually ambidextrous, represents a threat to Jacob in his devotion to Jacob's wife and in his waspish high breeding. I am, to an extent, a pawn in Jacob's consequent displays of virility.

'How goes it with the conceptual framework this morning, sweetheart?' he says to me, as he slaps his proofs down on the table. What is one supposed to reply to such a question?

'Fine, thanks,' I say.

'Her conceptual framework is fine,' he says. 'Where's the bloody *Guardian*? Have those bloody lazy children not delivered it?'

'Oh come on, Jake,' John says coaxingly. 'You couldn't be through with yesterday's news yet.'

'Yesterday's news is what I'm after,' he says. 'It's what I get every day in the *Guardian*.' I find him on the whole a creative and inspired grumbler. Give him the CBI, the Queen Mum or the bourgeois press and with any one of them he will grumble new hypotheses into being. I like him enormously. More than anyone I know.

'Have some breakfast, Jake,' Jane says. 'Roger has got the *Guardian*. He's got it upstairs. Leave him alone.' Toast and coffee for Heathcliff, and marmalade.

'Why is it none of my socks match, Jane?' he says. 'Why is it other men's socks match? Do they have nicer wives?'

'Perhaps they wash their own socks,' Jane says. 'You ought to go now, Jake.'

'Now remember that child, Janie, will you?' Jacob says, as he begins to make a move. 'There is a *sick child* in the house. Can I rely on you to remember that?' Roger comes in with the *Guardian* and with his transistor radio. He is listening to a string symphony. 'Roger, Annie is ill,' Jacob says. 'She needs attention. Will you ensure that your mother gives her some? Will you get her to call the doctor if it's necessary?'

'Is that Purcell, Rogsie?' Jane says.

'William Boyce,' he says.

'Of course,' she says. She has occasionally a togetherness with him which reminds me wistfully of a time when my mother and I cried together during *The Sound of Music* when Julie Andrews went back to the nunnery. I look at the first page of Jacob's proofs, being a natural reader of other people's papers.

'I cannot in good conscience give the statutory thanks to my wife,' it says, etcetera. 'Without her, no books would be to me worth writing.'

'Your proofs,' Jane says, as he kisses her goodbye. 'Don't forget your proofs.'

'Good God,' he says, slapping his forehead. 'My proofs.'

11

Roger Goldman walks through the sea-front kitsch like a man in John Bunyan. The pedlars of human thighs modelled in candy, of corny hats with smutty messages, of Brighton rock, do but themselves confound. Such is his strength while I lust after hot dogs. All around us, families on holiday are pursuing relentlessly their forms of child-rearing. Educated parents lecturing babes in push-chairs, improvingly, at the appearance of every wave and seagull. Humbler parents indulging in that peculiarly Anglo-Saxon form of parental sadism which involves threatened smacks and offers of sweets. Toddlers all itching to get out of buggies as the sea invites. 'Shut up, Stephen, you've had your crisps.'

Roger is wearing his butterfly jeans and a voluminous collar-less shirt belted at the waist. He has the martyr's hat tucked into his belt. We walk well beyond the inhabited stretch of beach and come to rest eventually on some rather oily pebbles. Roger lobs aspirant stones into the sea with a strong bowler's overarm which makes me catch my breath.

'Are you glad you've left school?' I say.

'Of course,' he says. 'Aren't you?' I try to put across to him how heady I was with joy the day I left school. Perhaps I am a bit of a fool. I tell him how my best friend, my dearest and best giggling companion, and I stuffed our hankies in our mouths during the last absurd rendering of 'Lord Dismiss Us' at the final assembly; how we carted home a great quantity of accumulated litter from our desks in a plaid blanket which we carried between us down the hill. How we stuffed our school hats into a letter box and ate chips in the street, desecrating our uniforms.

Bless us all our days of leisure,
Help us selfish lures to flee,
Sanctify our every pleasure,
Pure and spotless may it be.

'I bicycled straight home with Jonathan,' he says. 'There wasn't anybody at my school I cared to celebrate with. My music teacher gave me a glass of terrible sherry.'

To meet up with John we walk up through the Brighton Lanes where I am too shy to stop and look in shoe shops lest Roger think me trivial. John, who is waiting for us, treats us to steak and chips like kids on a boarding-school outing. All my outings with him have this air of semi-lecherous avuncular treat. It could be, given his versatility, that he is savouring the prospect of either one of us. As he goes off to visit the men's loo the waiter brings me, as ordered, an apple pie with cream.

'Nothing more for you, laddie?' he says coaxingly to Roger.

'I'm not "laddie,"' Roger says haughtily. 'I'm Roger Goldman.' I start to giggle.

'Laddie!' Roger says to me in disgust when the waiter has gone. 'It sounds like dog food.' United suddenly by our delicious youth and the folksy word the waiter has chosen to emphasize it, we both get very high on uncontrolled laughter.

'Oh dear,' John Millet says patronizingly as he comes back.

The chapel is beautiful, hidden as it is among primeval green, being, as it is, more artfully lush within. John takes some photographs with a flashlight. It is as though the harvest festival were taking place on the walls. When I look down the nave, I see that Roger has mounted the pulpit. A thing I would never presume to do.

Roger drives us home with John Millet beside him in the passenger seat. We get back to find Annie is completely recovered and pottering in the kitchen with Jane. Jonathan, who is in his awful school uniform, is railing against the new English master who has put him down for detention, he says, for being cheeky.

'You *are* cheeky, Jont,' Jane says without concern. 'I consider it part of your charm, but you cannot expect others to do so.'

'The bloody fool asks me to paraphrase "heaven's cherubin, horsed upon the sightless couriers of the air," ' he says, thumping about. 'What's the fucking good of paraphrasing it? It sounds better the way it is.'

'What did you say to him, Jont?' Jane says.

'But don't you agree, Jane, it makes nonsense of it to paraphrase it?' Jonathan says.

'What did you say to him, Jont?' Jane says insistently.

'I said if he didn't understand it he shouldn't be doing it with us.'

'And?' she says archly.

'He said if I was so clever would I like to take the class. So I took the class. A bloody sight better at it I was, too, but he made me stop after about ten minutes because it showed him up. He'd better not try and be funny with me again,' Jonathan says. This is bigger and better trouble-making than I ever dreamed of. Silently, resentfully, I hand him the crown.

'You watch it, Jonathan, that's all,' Jane says. 'Neither Jake nor I will be on our knees before the Head, pleading on your behalf when he decides to throw you out.' She turns to Roger. 'The young ladies 'phoned for you, Roger. The ones with the tennis court. They want you to play tennis with them tomorrow.' Roger shrugs.

'They play tennis in white togs,' he says nastily, 'like walk-ons for *Cinderella on Ice*.' I quail before this snobbish indictment and thank God that I always hid in the library during games. If I had played tennis I would almost certainly have done so in white togs.

'Go on, Rogsie,' Jonathan says, as Jane makes us tea. 'I'd go for the one with the legs.' Roger says nothing. He goes out to fetch his violin. 'I have to go now,' he says to John, who gives him the car keys.

12

That evening, in the garden, Jane forgives me for picking a half-grown cucumber which I mistake for a courgette. Potatoes come out of the ground white, I discover. The brown skin forms afterwards. Jacob joins us on his return, in the company of Annie and Sam whom he has met at the gate. He has the *Listener* in his hand and a parcel of cheese wrapped in vine leaves for his wife.

'For you, my love,' he says. 'Not for anybody to share with you.'

'Not even you?' she says. She is touched. 'Oh, Jake.'

Wrapped in the *Listener* he has a Dillon's bag which he hands to me. In it is a copy of *The Ragged Trousered Philanthropists.*

'Take a holiday from The Great Tradition,' he says. I thank him, profusely, being honoured by the gift.

'A Young Person's Guide to the New Jerusalem, eh, Jake?' Jane says. 'I'm rather glad I got the cheese. I'm too old to be converted.'

'I'm coming out simultaneously in paperback,' he says to her. She rejoices and kisses him.

'Oh, wow,' she says. 'Oh, Jake, wow.'

'Come out with me tonight,' he says. 'Leave the children, leave the guests and come out with me. Hold hands with me at the pictures.'

'I have to tell you, Jake, that I've been having fairly regular labour contractions this afternoon,' she says.

'Christ,' he says. 'That's it then for the next six months. Or can one hire a wet nurse? Who needs an au pair? Why is the world full of au pairs? A wet nurse is what we need.'

'I'm sorry, Jake,' she says, 'I'd better not go anywhere tonight.'

'Sweetheart,' he says, accepting the inevitable. He turns to Annie and Sam. 'Jane will have a baby for you tomorrow. Rosie will be more than pleased to see you two lose your place as the family babies.' Jane laughs a little.

'She will, won't she?' she says. 'Poor Rosie.'

Jane makes the children's supper that evening, leaning against the table periodically, to breathe deeply as her uterine muscles contract. She has 'phoned the midwife and the doctor from the kitchen telephone. I find it all more exciting than I can say and am astonished at how cool she is.

'I thought people gripped a bed and screamed,' I say.

'That happens later,' she says. 'Later on is when I go to pieces. I've never been one of these insufferable people who does it all right.' Jacob and John are watching the television news in the playroom. Jonathan is doing some homework at the kitchen table. He had spread a newspaper over the spillage and has his Latin on top of it. I engage Rosie and the twins in a game of Snap on the kitchen floor, but Rosie's perception is, of course, too quick for the others. Nor is she old enough yet to indulge their urge to win.

'Snap!' she shouts relentlessly. 'Snap! Snap!' The babies storm her to grab back their cards. Jane despatches the twins sharply to the playroom to join Jacob before she goes into another of her spasms.

'Jont,' she says, 'I'm going to be sick.' Deftly, Jonathan grabs a large antique jug from the shelf beside him and inverts, onto the table, a small pile of paper clips, trading stamps and string before handing it to her.

'Heave into this, Ma,' he says, which she does.

'Get Jake,' she says, when she can raise her head. 'Tell him I'm going to bed. Tell him there's puke on the table.'

'Snap!' Rosie shouts. 'I've won.'

Roger comes home with his violin in its case.

'Hello,' he says. He turns a chair round and sits on it astride the back. He puts his violin on top of Jonathan's Latin. Rosie is doing a handstand against the kitchen door.

'Jane is having her baby,' she says, glad to be first with the news. Jonathan comes in.

'Mother is giving birth,' he says. He picks up the jug of vomit and goes to the door with it. 'Cheers,' he says, disgustingly. We hear him flush it away in the downstairs loo. Roger says nothing but the event puts him on edge.

'Let's go for a walk,' he says. We coincide with the midwife on the path to the front door. I eye her bag for signs of crochet hooks and lead pills.

'Which one are you?' she says heartily to Roger. 'Did I deliver you?' In spite of their differences, the Goldman children have the look of having come off the same conveyor belt.

'I am Myself,' Roger says witheringly. He has a powerful line in animosity. He pulls the Hamlet hat further over his eyes to hide from her. We walk across a field to the right of the house towards a stream. Beyond the stream, which we cross, is a rather morbid little chicken battery belonging to the neighbouring farm, and, alongside that, a blackberry wilderness where we pick and eat.

'Jane says you can get blackberries without thorns,' he says as he examines a scratch on his wrist. 'She's going to grow them.'

'Have you always lived here?' I say. He shakes his head.

'Since I was five,' he says. He hands me some blackberries which he has picked from beyond my reach. 'We used to live in Belsize Park. Where do you live?'

'Hendon,' I say. 'I take my cat to the vet in Belsize Park.'

'We used to live on Haverstock Hill,' he says. I grow silently desperate, thinking that Roger will be gone in four days and all we do is have these dead-end conversations. Suddenly Roger says, 'Once Jont and I were picking blackberries in Oxford. In my grandmother's garden. We tried an experiment to prove the existence of God, because the grandparents had been converting us. We were about four and seven, I think. We kept muttering abuse to the Holy Ghost to see if the wrath of God would come down. The neighbours heard and told on us. I've never been so embarrassed in my life. My grandfather tried to make us pray for forgiveness. I wouldn't do it. I couldn't.'

'Isn't praying embarrassing?' I say. 'Isn't it excruciating?'

51

'At least C of Es do it with a book so that there's an end,' Roger says. 'Quakers go on forever when the spirit moves them. Our headmaster was a Quaker.' He gives me another handful of berries.

'Pentecostals do it to a Wurlitzer,' I say. 'Get moved, I mean. I heard them on the radio.' I walk six feet in the air for noticing that I have made Roger laugh. As we walk back to the house, as I try not to break a leg in my silly shoes, I think admiringly that I have taken berries from the hand of one who does not balk at performing experiments on the Almighty.

13

At eleven o'clock, Jacob comes into the kitchen with the doctor, who takes his leave. I am there with John and Jonathan; Roger has gone to bed.

'Well,' Jacob says stoically, 'I've known worse.' He puts the kettle on to make Jane and the midwife some tea. 'She's got it all out. The babe is female and a very decent size.'

'How is she?' John says.

'Fine,' he says. 'Somewhat grey and washed out, of course. The human frame is not particularly well designed for the purpose. It's easier for cats and horses. The infant is nibbling happily. Come in and see her.'

Jane is sitting up in a very pretty old brass bed, propped on candy-striped pillows. Her face is lined and slightly puffy. The midwife is sitting on the bed with her, talking coaxingly, rather idiotically, to the baby.

'Come on, don't be a lazy girl,' she says, 'take the whole nipple, darling, or your mother will get sore. We can't have that, can we?' She pushes the dark surround of Jane's nipple expertly into the baby's mouth. The room smells faintly of menstrual blood. On a tea trolley at the end of the bed is an enamel basin containing an organ, in appearance not unlike an ox heart, as one might see in the butcher's shop, but trailing bluish umbilical cord. She sees Jonathan look at it.

'It's my placenta, Jont,' she says, reaching out to him. 'Nature is very messy sometimes. Would you like to hold her?'

'Okay,' Jonathan says. He takes the baby with its head in the palm of his hand, swaddled, as it is, in cellular blanket like an infant Christ. Quattrocento. 'Hello, little rat,' he says.

'She's beautiful,' says the midwife reproachfully.

'Just a good size to go in your saddle bag, isn't she, Jont?' Jane says. 'Would you like to take her to school tomorrow? Bumpety over the cobbles?'

'It is tomorrow,' John says. 'Katherine and I are off now, Jane.' He gives her a kiss. 'Don't exhaust yourself, will you? We'll meet again soon. Come up to London.'

'Come again, Katherine,' Jane says to me. 'Write me your 'phone number on the wall in the kitchen.' She kisses me. 'Jacob, make her do it,' she says. 'Where's Roggs?'

'He fell asleep,' Jonathan says, 'playing himself at chess.'

John drives us with grim and silent purpose to the nearest hotel and signs us in. I have no power to object. I feel, as I enter the foyer, that I have an electronic beeper on the third finger of my left hand announcing the absence of the wedding ring. I am morbidly fascinated by his preening beauty, which borders upon the physically repulsive in its narcissism. Although he takes the precaution of undressing in the dark I am aware of grotesquely enlarged male parts in silhouette, as you get in Aristophanes, tied on for ribald effect. As my mind connects, suddenly, with what the biology teacher told us about erectile tissue in the reproduction of the rabbit, I realize, with relief, that this is routine. There is no difficulty of access and no pain. Just a comforting and unremarkable filling of a gap. Easier than one's first tampon. John, presumably, experiences the additional pleasure of confounding Jacob's prohibition. In the morning, he drives into London and drops me off at the Hampstead underground station before going on to his office.

'I'll be in touch,' he says.

14

My mother had missed me. That was obvious. And I had not given her a thought.

'Did you have a nice time?' she said.

'Yes,' I said.

'What did you do?' she said. I had been deflowered in a hotel room and had taken blackberries from the hand of a beautiful young man who played the violin and routed the Holy Ghost. I had seen a human placenta and a new-born baby. I had learned about crochet hooks and copper clamps in the cervix and egg yolks in the soup. I had found an older woman to emulate and admire in place of my mother.

'I watched Ava Gardner on the telly,' I said.

'Is that all?' she said.

'I went to the seaside in Brighton,' I said.

'I missed you,' she said. My mother gave me a cup of coffee which I drank on the sofa, staring across at the painting over her fireplace. A painting of a child with Murillo eyes weeping a contrived glass tear. To my mother this sweat-shop Wool-worths oil painting said Childhood. I had never been able to compete with its posey guile. I asked myself reproachfully why one glass tear should be more acceptable than another, as I thought of the Goldmans singing Dowland. My mother would go to the ends of the earth if I lay dying, and once did.

'It was my professor's house,' I said, loosening up excitedly. 'The one who interviewed me. His wife had a baby last night. She had it in the bedroom. It got born in their bed.' Between the lines of what I said my mother read the message. The message was rejection, and it made her hostile.

'What next?' she said tightly. 'When you get to having a baby

55

you'll realize the place to have it is in hospital.' My mother's house appeared to me confiningly neat and ineptly contrived. She went in for that style of interior decoration which ought, given the evidence, to have induced epilepsy in its profusion of optical effect. A confusion of conflicting patterns on floor and wall. On the floor, autumnal patterned Axminster carpet. Patterned, my mother said, because it wouldn't show the dirt, but since our activities were restricted to those which would not create dirt, there was never any dirt to show. Cleanliness dominated our domestic lives, as I remember the Hoover factory—that imposing period piece—dominated the outer reaches of London. Displayed behind me on the wallpaper, which my mother called 'contemporary' (meaning to denote thereby that its design was non-representational), was a more than adequate collection of bas-relief china ducks. 'A goodly bloody third of the transatlantic migration,' Jonathan Goldman called them once in years to come, by which time they had become smart kitsch.

'It wasn't very polite of you to stay on when you knew the baby was coming,' my mother said. Mothers never believe that you know how to respond to your friends. They are so concerned that you shall not go friendless through this life that they become over-protective in this respect.

15

I never again went to bed with John Millet, though I went occasionally to the theatre with him. Sometimes he brought along a rather pretty solicitor with whom he had goings on, and sometimes he brought Jane. Jane would leave Jacob and Jonathan to mind the children, climb out of her wellingtons and threadbare jeans, and clothe herself with indifference in a dowdy two-piece more suitable for prison visiting. It only served to underline her remarkable good looks. It was always great fun to be on the town with her. In spite of the age difference, Jane superseded most of my friends and became my foremost giggling companion. I spent quite a lot of time at her house. Once in the ladies' loo at the Purcell Room she tried on my mascara.

'Say, why do you think he likes to ask us out together?' she said. 'It's like a polygamous marriage, isn't it, without either children or Jacob. What a soothing fantasy.' I laughed, not realizing in my inexperience, of course, quite what an assault on her identity and peace of mind Jacob constituted. Or quite how difficult it was for either of them to kick against the idea that the loveliest of women born were born for loveliness alone.

Once, she turned to me from the passenger seat of John's car and said, 'Roger wants your address, Katherine. Some cover-up nonsense about needing you to buy a book for him. Could it be that my lovely boy is fond of you?' I caught my breath in the darkness and said nothing.

'Send him my address too,' John said. A remark he would never have made in Jacob's presence, and one which Jane clearly found quite alarming.

'One move in that direction and I'll send my Jacob round to

break your jaw,' she said, over-reacting, perhaps. John laughed at her. 'I mean it,' she said. 'He's damned good at making fisticuffs. He didn't grow up in the Mile End Road for nothing, you know, with all those disgusting Moseleyites. Your nice sanded floor would be a mess of blood and teeth.' John laughed again.

'I'm teasing you,' he said. 'Your Roger is too intense for me in any case. You've got yourselves a genuine little neurotic there between the two of you, haven't you?'

'Take me to the railway station,' she said.

'I'm teasing you,' he said.

'Take me to the bloody railway station before my breasts become engorged,' she said.

At Victoria station I got into the vacant front seat. John Millet drove me home. I said nothing, having been disturbed by his unaccustomed malice. John Millet had, I believe, set me up in the first place to threaten Jane, who enjoyed his attentions, and to compromise Jacob, who had taken on the woman he might have taken on, had he but had it in him to face the ensuing mess of human life. It had certainly not been part of his design that his latter-day quattrocento should end up in the arms of Jane's son, whom he had last seen at fifteen. Perhaps it had slipped his mind that children grew. He never, in any case, liked the idea that Jane had Jacob's children.

In their house the Goldmans had a small edition of the Shakespeare *Sonnets*, bound in red leather, which had a pointed little message on the flyleaf directing one to Sonnet 87. Sonnet 87 is the one that goes,

> Farewell thou art too dear for my possessing
> And like enough thou knowest thy estimate.

It had been given to Jane as a wedding present by John Millet. I found it one day on the bathroom floor, where it had been left by Jonathan, who was by then using it as part of his 'A' Level English course.

16

Roger's handwriting was a shock to me. I had until then made the assumption that all superior people were acquainted with the necessity that calligraphic characters were parallel, thick on the down-stroke and joined by upward angles of forty-five degrees. Roger's handwriting was small, inconsistent in its slope and difficult to read. I therefore revised my opinion to the effect that Roger, as the pinnacle of superior man, had licence to make his own manners and that his handwriting was the mark of his magnificent disregard for the standards of the world. The truth of the matter was simply that Roger had lousy, undistinguished handwriting. It was a thing he was no good at.

Roger, in his first letter to me, said that he was helping to teach maths in a country high school in a Nissen hut, and that in addition he banged out hymn tunes every morning on a piano which gave him the horrors. There was no felt left on the hammers, he said, and there was too much Christianity about. The buses had no springs, but carried you into town and slung your bicycle on the roof it you were lucky enough to have one. Everybody insisted on sharing bananas with you on bus journeys. Neighbourliness, he said, drove him mad. The houseboy, who came with the house, drove him mad too, he said, taking hours to scrub with steel wool at a few aluminium saucepans which he could polish off in minutes. The same despised menial, he said, got insulted if you washed your own shirts and chose instead to scrub at them with blocks of blue mottled soap because he was so used to white employers crabbing at him about the cost of Square Deal Surf. There were mangoes more profuse than people, more wonderful than Christianity, and he would bring some back for me. He had forgotten to take his transistor radio and he needed it, he said, to prevent the possibility of conversation with the people who shared his house. 'Provincial English bores,' he said, who thought that progress was making 'the whole world like West Hartlepool.' They drove him mad. Everything drove him mad. I loved him for his commanding snobbery.

'I want to tell you that you sing well,' he wrote. 'Also that I hope John Millet is no great friend of yours.' As a result of this curious letter, which I re-read every hour, I struggled to improve myself by looking up West Hartlepool on the map and resolving from then on to wash my own clothes which, until then, my mother had always washed for me. My mother, unfortunately, manifested herself as a person as possessive of her territory as Roger's houseboy.

'When you have your own house you can do what you like,' she said, insufferably, denying me access to the washing-machine. When I complained to Jane about this high-handed dismissal of my rights, I found, understandably, that her perspective on the matter was different.

'Any place where somebody else does the washing can't be all bad,' she said. 'Do you know, Katherine, when my twins were born I screwed out of Jacob the right to use disposable nappies only to find that the bloody things didn't work.'

I wrote back to Roger, telling him warmly how sorry I had been to go without saying goodbye. I told him, in order to recreate the moments of our togetherness, that I believed the piano to be the Holy Ghost's revenge for his insults in the black-berry bushes. I told him that I had been to a concert with his mother who had tried on my eye make-up in the loo and what a smashing lady I thought her. That my term had begun and that I had had the great joy of spending my book allowance. That I had covered all my clip-back files in Florentine wrapping-paper out of pure joy, and sharpened all my green Venus pencils. That I found it all delightfully unlike school and that Jacob was a terrific hit with the students, being a very racy and lucid teacher. John Millet, I assured him, was a very casual friend who occasionally took me to the theatre. I wished him many happy evenings escaping the sound of steel wool on tin and speculated upon whether or not my letter would be delivered to him by a runner who would carry it, mud-stained, in a forked stick.

'I have been singing on my way from the underground station because you praised my voice,' I wrote. 'Tell me what I should sing.' Thinking back, I could probably not have written him a more annoying letter. Had he not already decided that he was in love with me the correspondence would have ceased right there. I had mocked his irritation with the piano and with the houseboy, when he was a young person who wished his aversions to be treated with respect. I had committed the folly of praising his parents. I had exposed myself to my high-minded crusader as a young person seeking after venial delight: I wore eye make-up and covered my notebooks—those symbols of plain living and hard thinking—in gilded wrapping-paper.

Roger's next letter, written in fury, said that somebody had just stolen his violin. I was not to tell his parents, he said, because Jacob would storm about the expense of replacing it, being a tightfisted old bastard, and he wasn't going to be abused behind his back. He would rather I told his parents nothing at all about him, he said, because he would sooner not have his affairs talked about. He then advised me to buy myself some folk song scores in Cecil Sharpe House and to sing those. He wrote, rather witheringly, of the school he taught in, that its object seemed to be to push the pupils into clerical jobs in government offices and the result was terrific grinding emphasis on the three Rs and on respectability. The students were conforming and deferential to a man, he said. There was nobody in the place like his brother Jonathan.

'Everyone polishes his shoes,' he wrote in disgust, with an assumption that this obsolete custom had been dead since the demise of National Service. I gave up polishing my shoes forth-with, and committed the additional folly of seeking out for Roger, in the Victoria and Albert Museum, a postcard of a Stradivarius violin which I sent him with my commiserations. I also confessed that musical scores were not much more to me than tadpoles running up and down stairs, since I had never learned how to read them, and that I had got a wonderfully high mark for an essay on a priori knowledge, which was a great

61

feather in my cap since I thought a priori was the kind of word reserved for people who gave talks on the Third Programme and that I never expected to be one of the people who knew what it meant.

Roger replied to the effect that what he wanted, if I was going to send him photographs, was a photograph, please, of me. He had got the violin back, he said, but without the bow. He enclosed a money order and instructed me to go to Wardour Street and buy him another one, which I did, feeling as unequal to the task as I might have done had I been sent out to buy a packet of contraceptive sheaths from a male hairdresser. I despatched the bow to him, feeling that it would never arrive; that somebody would acquire it along the way and use it to shoot rabbits. It had not occurred to me until I made this purchase how similar a violin bow was in appearance to the other kind. I also sent him a photograph of myself taken at the Vanessa Bell chapel by John Millet.

Roger's embroidered butterfly fell into my lap from his next letter, and also a photograph of himself. His letter said that he loved me. Would I please wear his butterfly, which the house-boy was in danger of scrubbing into oblivion. That was, if I felt I could return his feeling for me. If not, could I pitch it in the rubbish bin and tell him so immediately?

The photograph was a delight, since until then I had reconstructed him only out of Jane's smile and Jane's eyes. But the elements of beard shadow and youth were not there. And also not those elements of zeal and righteousness, which made me fall at his feet. He was depicted standing—brown as a hazelnut, in most un-English sandals—beside his Nissen hut with some of his pupils. All of them sharply defined in the bright light. Behind them a tangle of vegetation without haze. The students posed rather formally, unused to being photographed. Straight ties. Products of a mission school education which Roger despised. Roger, with his hands in his pockets, was smiling slightly, with a degree of controlled impatience, as though he were about to give the photographer a lecture on the correct use of the light meter.

I kept his photograph slid into the frame of my dressing-table mirror. A little white-painted plywood thing with curtains around the base. A relic of more youthful tastes.

'You wouldn't know he was Jewish,' my mother said, 'would you?' She said this by way of complimenting me on the quality of male I had at last reassured her by pulling in.

'He isn't Jewish,' I said irritably. 'You're only Jewish if your mother is Jewish.' My mother looked at me knowingly, almost sympathetically, understanding that I wished to deny any stigma attached to my young man. She hadn't lived in north London for so long and not learned that if you were called Goldman you were a Jew.

'I've got nothing against Jews,' she said. 'It's such a pity he has to be in Africa when you could do with his company. Aren't there enough blacks for him in England?'

17

I wore the butterfly pinned to my book-bag which caused Jacob, with whom I shared the library lift one day, to remark innocently that the young these days seemed curiously disposed to lepidoptery.

'My boy has just such an insect tacked to his jeans,' he said. 'He doesn't write to us, you know, the little bastard. Jont is in receipt of the odd letter from time to time, so we have no reason to await the black-edged telegram.'

'Perhaps he's busy,' I said. Jacob looked sceptical.

'Schoolboys running amok in foreign parts. Roger and his like are defined as "Aid to Developing Countries," ' he said, with caustic amusement. 'It's your taxes and mine, Katherine, pays for this piece of neo-colonialism.'

'I don't pay taxes,' I said. Jacob laughed.

'In that case it's only mine. He tells Jont that he plays hymns on the piano every morning. Is that part of the export drive, Katherine? Christianity and Commerce hand in hand? First sell the Protestant ethic and then sell the rest? The poor child has had his violin pinched, it appears. Hey, Katherine—have you ever had mumps?'

'Yes,' I said. 'Why?'

'Annie has mumps,' he said. 'You wouldn't like to come down and support my suffering wife, would you? As you will appreciate, the quality of life is somewhat reduced for women when there are sick children and suckling babes in the house. The babe has a stuffed up nose and needs to be fed every ten minutes. She has to let the nipple go to breathe, you see. Not much goes down at any given time.' Jacob was always explicit in these matters. 'It's dehumanizing for women,' he said, 'this incessant nurturing of sick children.'

'I'll come tonight if you like,' I said. 'I'm going home after this. I'll get some things.'

'Bless you, my dear,' he said. 'The wife enjoys your company. I don't mean to have you scrubbing floors, you understand?'

We caught the train together that afternoon where Jacob, having gallantly paid my train fare, offered me the choice of the *Guardian* or *New Society*. I chose *New Society*.

'Terrible rag,' he said apologetically. 'Cooked up by the kind of chaps who need fifteen-hundred-pound research grants from the Social Science Research Council before they can tell you the way to the nearest brothel.'

'Really?' I said. I had never read it before. 'Why do you buy it, Jacob?' He smiled. According to Jane he was addicted to newsprint in any form. If there was none about he would search through old chests in the hope of finding that the drawers had been lined with the previous year's *Hampstead and Highgate Gazette*. He read the *Guardian* like a practised commuter, folding it longitudinally into eight-inch lengths. He read the business page, which even now is a thing I use only to wrap vegetable peelings, but Jacob always liked to know the enemy.

One of the first things I did when I got to the Goldmans' house was scrub the kitchen floor with washing soda crystals, while Jane played picture dominoes with Annie and breast-fed Sylvia at the same time. Jacob, who had so effectively articulated for me the dilemma of the captive wife, had, of course, locked himself in his study with a thermos flask of coffee and a nice fat biography of Rosa Luxemburg.

'If my sons have any sense they'll marry girls like you,' Jane said to me. 'I could no more bring myself to scrub that floor than fly. When I got married, Katherine, I would let Roger's cot sheets and nappies pile up in the bath and then go out and grumble over Jacob's mother. She was an absolute brick to me, Jacob's mother. Spoke almost no English, which was a great advantage, of course. She always accepted me without question. Such a pleasant change she was from my own crowd. Even the coming of the first male grandchild brought not a word on the subject of genital mutilation.' I paused in my scrubbing to contemplate the advantage of this foreknowledge —this evidence of Roger's unassailed foreskin.

'There she was in her pokey little flat, hoarding Nescafé and dark chocolate among her underwear,' Jane said. 'Husband missing, presumed dead, surrounded by the bigoted British proletariat. Not a bad word to say against anybody. It's no wonder Jake is so very nice. I've never liked people much. Leaving aside Jacob and the children, there's a half-dozen people in this world I care for, not much more.'

I scrubbed the floor for her, being honoured to be one of them.

'She's a knitter like you,' Jane said. 'Not of your class, you understand. She used to knit Rogsie nasty little matinée jackets out of unravelled jerseys, the sweet thing.' I had recently knitted Rosie a mini-dress in broad horizontal stripes of candy pink and orange which had won her heart utterly and which she frequently pulled, wet and smelling, out of the laundry basket, because she wouldn't have it plucked from her. Jane had then asked if she could employ me to knit, in secret, a large black pullover for Jonathan to have at Christmas.

'Because he would love it so much,' she said, 'and he would look so sweet in it, don't you think? He imagines that he will look wonderfully sinister.' Jonathan in a black pullover, I considered, would look like the God of Thunder with a migraine. Because I loved her, I refused to accept more than one shilling the ounce for undertaking this project. It was sweated labour if anything was.

I babysat for the Goldmans that night, while they went to the cinema, because Jonathan had something on at school. He returned at ten, burning up with anger because the headmaster, who had asked him to submit a poem for a competition, had then turned down his consequent offering as unsuitable.

'I'd lay my head on the bloody block,' he announced to me, 'that if I'd copied out the fucking "Scholar Gypsy" and handed it to him as my own, he'd have had it. I reckon these stupid fucking headmasters get their jobs for being on their fucking knees in church every fucking Sunday and twice on fucking Good Friday.' I was in the playroom carefully transcribing the rough

66

draft of my essay onto lined foolscap with margins on either side.

'Jesus, aren't you neat?' he said. 'Isn't your writing beautiful?' He was still talking to me when his parents came home, to whom he relayed his somewhat subdued indignation.

'Can I see it?' Jacob said of the poem. Jonathan pulled it out of his trouser pocket. The poem made Jacob laugh appreciatively.

'What did you stand to win then, Jont?' he said.

'A hundred pounds,' Jonathan said.

'Make me a copy and I'll give you a fiver for it,' Jacob said.

'Okay,' Jonathan said. 'Hey, Jake, look at Katherine's essay. Isn't it neat?'

'I know what her essays look like,' he said.

'But it's her writing,' Jonathan said persistently. 'Isn't it beautiful? Isn't it sensational?'

'It's women, Jonathan,' Jacob said. 'Women write like that. That is the way middle-class women write. Search me how they do it. The only man I know who writes like that is John Millet.'

'Don't you visit this bigotry on my children,' Jane said.

18

Jacob's mother appeared that weekend, with her grey hair, set like the Queen's, and with her handbag full of Suchard chocolates which she produced like treasure for the children. With the help of German war reparation she had made the climb to Golders Green and appeared to ask for no more. Rosie behaved very shabbily with her, I remember, squirming away from her kisses and grabbing the loot. She embraced me, smelling genteelly of 4711. She called Jonathan 'Yonny' and, since her eyesight was failing, had him read to her from some weighty Teutonic version of *Woman's Own*. Jonathan read the German to the manner born because accents were a great talent with him, but the content got him down.

'Jesus wept,' he said after a while, 'I can't go on reading this crap.'

'No asides please,' Jane said. 'Read it, Jont. It's good for your soul.' Grandmother offered Jonathan another chocolate, smiling upon him benignly and taking no offence.

'It's all right for you, isn't it?' Jonathan said to Jane. 'You can't understand it. It's about the Shah of Iran's ex. It's fawning bullshit about a fascist's wife who can't have bloody babies. So what? That makes less dictators, doesn't it?'

'You wait till it's your wife who can't have a baby,' Jane said. Jonathan threw his eyes impatiently to heaven, before guzzling his chocolate and sportingly continuing with his text. Later that day I went for a walk with Jacob and Jonathan, during which Jonathan enacted the episode for his father, catching his grandmother's speech and gesture with astonishing and wicked accuracy. I remember that the three of us cackled treacherously along the hedgerows, with great enjoyment, feeling, for that moment, comfortably together. Jake's mother was the daughter of a butcher. She had married above herself into the Berlin intelligentsia. Jacob produced, as we walked across the field, a childhood memory of his maternal grandfather telling him not to block the shop window.

'Stand avay from ze vindow, boy. And let ze people see ze sausages. And let ze sausages see ze people.' I am very fond of this anecdote. I told him then that my father had been a green-grocer. He probably knew this anyway, from my university application form. Jacob said, very sweetly, that it accounted for the bond between us, that we had roots in the petit bourgeois trading class. I think this may have been true.

I thought about Roger almost all of the time. I put the thought by while I wrote my essays, read or slept, but in between para-graphs, at the ends of chapters, and as I turned on my pillow towards dawn, I would fix my mind again upon his appearance and gesture. It gave me energy and inspiration, that quiet romanticism. I did some very good work that year. The tax-payer's money was not mis-spent upon me.

19

Roger telephoned me from Heathrow Airport the day he came back from Kenya, and appeared at my mother's door two hours later. I saw him from the landing window before he rang the bell, and made my way sedately downstairs, containing a surge of youthful joy. And there he was, fulfilling my every tremulous expectation, tossing dark schoolboy hair from his eyes, smiling dimples from bronzed cheeks, travelling light in every sense, being suspended above geographical and social involvement.

'Your doorbell is in the key of D Major,' he said. My mother's doorbell was one which played a snatch of the Big Ben chime. Welcoming, but nonetheless pregnant with suitably petit bourgeois implication, it was called 'The Harmonious Chime.'

'It's not my doorbell,' I said defensively, 'it's my mother's.' We began as we went on. Roger representing, with his arrogant febrile grace, what seemed to me an awesome accumulation of high breeding. Me, breast-beating and struggling to improve myself. King Cophetua and the Beggarmaid. But I noticed only that Roger's light blue eyes showed themselves to quite startling effect in his delicate brown face. He had in his left hand two duty-free Johnny Walker whisky carrier bags bulging with freckled mangoes, and all for me. He had argued zealously with customs officials to get them through and had succeeded, because conviction can move mountains and Roger had conviction in no small measure. I believe that Roger would have put his hand in the fire rather than bow to false gods, at that time.

Roger ate my mother's chocolate cake with a schoolboy appetite which charmed her and told us that he had spent the three days before his flight lying on a beach in Mombasa. He pulled photographs out of an overnight bag, stuck with East African Airways luggage labels, of Arab dhows and market stalls. He had a photograph of a rickety little Asian hotel with a tin roof and a verandah. The hotel was signposted 'Bond Street Hotel, Piccadilly,' and bore an enamelled hoarding advising one to drink Coca-Cola ice-cold. They depicted another world which he had slowly come to enjoy. When he had finished at Oxford, he said, he would go back to East Africa and teach. It embarrasses me to confess with what innocent suburban promptitude I began to build into my scheme of things the unlikely prospect of becoming a schoolmaster's wife on the slopes of Kilimanjaro. I would peg up sun-bleached terry napkins on a line which fluttered among burgeoning hibiscus bushes, while Roger stretched long legs and paused in his perusal of exercise books, covered in brown wrapping-paper, to contemplate, contentedly, his satisfactory domestic situation.

'My family thinks I'm arriving tomorrow,' Roger said. 'I'll spend tonight in Golders Green with my grandmother.' The announcement opened up for us the delightful prospect of being on the loose in the metropolis for one whole day.

'Is she expecting you?' my mother said. Roger shook his head.

'I'll telephone her a bit later.' he said.

'But your parents,' my mother said incredulously. 'Won't they be at the airport tomorrow to meet you?' That was what one did. One met people at airports. Particularly one's kith and kin.

'My parents?' Roger said. 'No fear.' Roger's parents would more likely have expected him to earn the train fare home, or to leg it with the help of the Ordnance Survey map and a little 'O' Level Geography. For my mother this rather confirmed that the Goldmans, who had in the first place been irresponsible enough to have had six children, were now as neglectful of them as was to be expected. She sighed, displaying the merest hint of vicarious pique.

We walked, later, on Primrose Hill, Roger and I, and pressed our faces and limbs inexpertly together in the privacy of the wooded verges.

'I love you,' Roger said. 'I missed you. I thought about you all the time.'

'Me too,' I said.

'You're so lovely,' Roger said. I remember that as he said this I was too much aware that I had on my cheekbone a small rash of pubescent spots, partially obscured with medicated cake make-up, and that I was humbled before his perfect brown skin.

'I can do you the Coventry Carol on the descant recorder,' I said. 'The two flats and the one sharp.' Roger smiled and kissed me rather clumsily on the mouth, causing my earring to fall off into the grass.

At the top of the hill Roger initiated a game which we played with sunlight. We stared into the sun, then covered our eyes with our fingers and described the patterns on the retina. Endlessly repeating cones and vibrant amoebae in tones of red and green. Then he talked about Oxford. Roger loved Oxford. It was the place where he had spent his childhood holidays, away from his quarrelling parents. His grandfather who, inconceivably, persisted in refusing to harbour Jane, had always been perfectly willing to harbour Jane's children, provided his wife made the arrangements for their visits. Roger's perception of this person to whom Jane referred as 'the old Gothic Horror', was of somebody who played three-legged races with one in the fellows' garden and allowed one to try out his pipes. Oxford was a place of magical cobbled lanes which led to the sweet-shop. It was a place where tea came with strawberries before the peal of bells for Evensong, where Grandmother, in a Pringle sweater and thick stockings, took one to watch punters from the bridge over the High Street, and where one went through doors into secret gardens with high stone walls. He never came to see it as a place afflicted with too much trad and old stones. He was not, as I was, embarrassed by the idea of privilege. He described to me with an almost holy joy the journey he would make from the railway station, past the litter and grot beside the slime-green canal, past the jail and on into St Ebbes towards the ample splendour of Christ Church.

'You can come and see me all the time,' he said. 'I'll show you the bridge where Jont and I had spitting competitions.' In the contemplation of Oxford's sweet privilege we confronted our awakening selves. Roger slung his leg rather daringly over mine as we reclined on the grass.

'Think of a fate worse than death,' he said. It made us both laugh briefly, excitedly, the melodramatic phrase and the reality behind it. Roger had used it with a sure intuition to cover, thereby, the awkwardness of our inexperience.

I had visited Oxford for the first time that summer and only briefly. I had driven with Jane to deposit Rosie with the grandparents for a week. They had moved by this time from their college house among the cobbled lanes to a comfortable Edwardian structure northwards of the town centre, set in a garden full of plum trees. Through the garden gate one could see, in the back garden, a sundial held up by two stone putti agreeably covered in lichen. On the way Jane had told me that her father kept a collection of antique Japanese swords in his study.

'A very nasty collection of old knives for killing people,' she said. With a sudden crazy panic I had watched Rosie walk towards the door of a house full of knives.

20

Roger was what my mother called a 'character.' This was largely because he laced his shoes with string. As time went on and she began to suspect that he would never buy me an engagement ring, she became rather hostile to him and conceived the idea that he laced his shoes with string to annoy her, and also that he was slightly unhinged.

'I don't deny that he's very clever,' she said, 'but clever people are very delicately balanced.' The implication, intended to be flattering to myself, was, of course, that I was not clever and therefore quite sane. Cleverness was not something she hoped for in her daughter. Prettiness was what girls required, and I was quite pretty enough, though I became less and less so in her eyes as I strove to please Roger, who let it be known that he disliked the clink of silver bracelets on the wrist and preferred unpainted faces.

Roger laced his shoes with string because he couldn't bring himself to go to Selfridges like other people when he needed anything. He almost never bought anything new. He was like Jane in this respect. When Jane or Roger needed anything they went to the Oxfam shop. They went to jumble sales, auction sales, and shops selling the leftovers of deceased estates. Roger, who had never, for instance, been a Sea Scout, went about for a long time in a cast-off Sea Scout jumper which he occasionally wore inside out. It bore a Cash's name-tape which said 'John Venables.' He wore what must have been one of the first calligraphically emblazoned T-shirts. It said 'Mark' across the front, which caused his father to remark wittily (to Roger's annoyance) that he had 'a mark on his shirt.' I found myself once wondering morbidly in the face of Roger's recycled size

74

fourteen shirts whether size fourteen necks were mysteriously more vulnerable than most to deaths on the road or untimely terminal illness. How was it otherwise that the shops he frequented were so full of them?

Being a believer in works of reference, Roger had duly acquired us an antiquated sex manual by this process of ferreting in yesterday's meat. We found that it said, among other uproarious bullshit, that the semen of the young Aryan male was sweet-smelling, like chestnuts, and that the aureola surrounding the female virgin nipple was rose pink, but darkened to brown with increasing sexual experience. This wonderful book proved to be an endearing ice-breaker for us in a potentially awkward area, since it detailed various love positions so excessive in their rococo extravagance that we fell giggling into trying them out, zipped up as we were in our chaste corduroy jeans. Most of them involved unlikely entanglements with chairs and overhanging table tops. It allowed us to believe, by contrast, in our own urbane suavity in these matters.

Roger and I, let me confess it, never altogether got it right in bed, though we enjoyed the comforting proximity of flesh on flesh. It was never much different from PE classes at school, I found, and left me similarly sweaty, exhausted, and sneaking glances at my watch to see how much longer it could possibly go on. Roger once caught me in the act of looking at my watch and took offence, being an arrogant and insecure young man. I had not yet realized that somebody as beautiful and clever as Roger could be as morbidly riddled with inadequacies as the next man. I was a rather hesitant person myself with a different collection of self-doubts. Thinking back, I realize that I had instinctively built my inadequacies into my public persona, in the hope that thereby I could bestow upon them the dignity of a presence. Roger was different. Readers of Pogo may remember that Pogo's friend Albert kept a 'Down with the Gummint' shout in a bag in the cupboard. When you opened the bag it said 'Up with the Gummint' because the shout was heavily disguised. Roger kept his inadequacies in the cupboard and when you got at the bag it issued forth statements of withering omnipotence.

'Sex ought to be no more than a routine and necessary

function,' Roger said later that day, as he scratched his dandruff over his mathematical hieroglyphics. He had such a beautiful neck. 'Like blowing one's nose,' he said. Roger, in his fierce instinct to protect himself from criticism, could leave one feeling like a dropped noserag.

We made each other very happy sometimes, I think. Because I was always a little in awe of Roger, I often cast myself in the role of entertainer for him, talked a lot and told stories against myself to make him laugh, never dreaming that he would store these up as ammunition against me. Roger quite often made me feel like the yokel in Shakespeare who concludes, in the presence of eminent personages, that 'remuneration' is the Latin for three farthings. I played the part for him, regaling him with slices of my non-U childhood, my delicious orgies of Enid Blyton, my unrelieved childhood diet of the Bobbsey twins and the frivolous Mam'zelle in her curl papers, who quailed at the sight of mice. Of bad golliwogs and whimsical spankings, of lacrosse sticks gathering in the hall as the hols came to an end. I painted disloyal portraits for him of my mother in her emerald crimplene trouser-suit, reclining in her fringed garden seat with the latest Nevil Shute. I told him that my uncle collected George Formby records. I meant thereby more, I think, to indulge a comic sense than to ingratiate myself, but that, ultimately, was its effect. I had, after all, read books as a child, unlike his sister Rosie who, like a lovely barbarian, did nothing but jump and run.

21

I was a disappointment to Roger in the matter of Symbolic Logic. He was more academic than I could ever have been. I often felt, during my time in Jacob's department, that somebody would unmask me for a fraud. Each decent essay mark came as a new surprise to me and a temporary reprieve. It was a feeling not unlike the relief of waking to find that one has only dreamt it. That one has not in truth walked down the High Street in one's grubby vest on Saturday morning. I had been drawn to Philosophy for no other reason than that it seemed, after the solid pragmatism of the greengrocer's shop, to be elevated by a marvellous uselessness. It was the subtlest kick in the teeth I could deliver to my mother and aunts who saw me enshrined as the director's personal secretary. Having embarked upon it, I found it often crazily high falutin'. Jacob, who thankfully had his feet so firmly on the ground, was, of course, my grand exception. Because he taught so well, because he was not above making it perfectly clear that he had a political ideology which directed his approach, because he had roots in German history and intellectual life, these things enlivened a lot of what he said. When he talked to us about Kant, for instance, he made it seem as controversial as if the postillion had just delivered the stuff into our hands from eighteenth-century Koningsberg. He would pick delightful energetic holes in Marxist epistemology for us with the licence of the converted. Since most of us leaned towards the left, we loved him in his critical analyses for never giving comfort to the right. Then came the business of Symbolic Logic.

I had been taught mathematics at school by the games mistress who did it on the side and did it badly. Mathematics, she said, was 'exercise for the brain.' All I ever saw was sums with the numbers taken away. I never saw that system glowing with the beauty of pure reason which Roger saw. I was confirmed in my arty bias against it in the war of the two cultures. I liked the things of the heart. How could I therefore enter into a relationship with a's, b's and x's? It was manifestly true, also, that the girls from my school who went off to university to do sciences were those who couldn't compete with men for places in History and English. I was, therefore, a humanities bigot. Scratch me and I still am. Only because Roger's beauty and high culture took my breath away, did I forgive him for his nasty fluids in jars and his collections of fossils chipped from the walls of old quarries. Then all of a sudden, in the middle of my arty education, came propositions expressed in the language of the games mistress.

'I hate it,' I said to Roger, of the p's and q's, the following weekend. We were lying on the grass on Port Meadow watching sailing boats weaving between the ducks.

'I'll explain it to you,' Roger said. On the back of his William Byrd, which he had in his pocket, he wrote, 'If p then q. Not q . . . so not p.'

'If all bread were sliced bread,' Roger said, 'we would have no need of a bread knife, right?'

'Except if you spread jam with the bread knife,' I said. A thing he always did. Roger ignored me.

'We cannot do without the bread knife, so not all bread is sliced. Okay?'

'Okay,' I said.

'You are required to express this as 'If p then q. Not q therefore not p,' because symbols are more use to you than the specific examples of the bread and bread knife.'

'Yes,' I said, because I loved him, though for me all that mattered was the bread, glowing in a bag labelled Mother's Pride. As the afternoon wore on, Roger liquidated not only the bread, but also 'if,' 'then' and 'not.' The sliced bread had become bracket p hook q close bracket stroke q turnstile stroke p. The jam was nowhere. The strokes had to do with falsehood, I remember. They denoted that, within the proposition, was an odious damned lie. We classified propositions in rows of ones

78

and zeroes. An hour later I got lost off in the axiomatic method.

'If a binary constant is flanked by a propositional variable,' Roger said, 'then the scope—' I noticed, at that point, that a small boy had caught a fish.

'He's caught a fish,' I said. Because Roger was, at that stage, still in love with me, he didn't get nasty.

'Katherine,' he said, 'what use is your philosophy going to be to you without maths? You'll be like an architect with no engineering. Trust that father of mine to take you on with no maths, the shallow buffoon.' I had not considered my usefulness. The only use I had for myself was in pleasing Roger. I had dimly begun to notice that men students were different. That they thought about careers and research grants, while I thought about cultivating a range of accomplishments to gratify a grade A husband.

'Not all of it is to do with p and q,' I said, which was perfectly true.

'What isn't is an obsolete mish-mash of malignant demons and morality,' he said. His quarrel was with Jacob not with me, but, because he was slightly paranoid, he saw me often as Jacob's emissary.

'Mathematically, you are like a person who pre-dates the invention of the printing press,' he said. 'I have to go and sing.' Roger sang in the cathedral choir. He went off, summoned by bells, like somebody, one might almost say, who pre-dated the theory of evolution. He began to teach me algebra that evening in the waiting-room of the railway station—and left me shamed by my incompetence. I got on the train feeling uneasily that Roger would prefer not to make love to a woman who had an emotional block about substituting signs for concepts.

22

Roger was a great success at Oxford. I do not mean that he became a professional undergrad who took up oars and organized summer balls, because he didn't, but having been rather lonely and rather resented at school as haughty and precocious, he found recognition in Oxford's less philistine atmosphere and time-honoured elitism. Given his family background he had none of the common grammar school chips on his shoulder in the face of that great concentration of ex-public schoolboys. His tutors fraternized with him as a man who was going places. He loved the ancient music, in spite of its interweaving with the Church, which he professed to despise. Admittedly, such men of God as one encountered in Oxford appeared much too sophisticated to concern themselves with the mere naivety of belief. I perceived Christ Church as a place dominated by the temporal presence of Cardinal Wolsey. To my vestigial Methodism, wrapped latterly in the cloak of Jacob's Marxism, this appeared very shocking, that the churchmen should be the king's men, creating and transmitting an ideology of control to the ruling class. I also didn't care for the ex-choir school boys, clad in their Harris tweed, with whom Roger played the violin at weekends. I like people to defy stereotypes and these lived up to them. Roger considered it a churlish irrelevance to speculate upon their voting habits, when they made up the stuff of decent string quartets, but it got on my nerves to listen to their in-group Oxford talk. It was the era of student revolt, after all, and they talked, instead, of being 'up' and 'down,' of reading in the 'Bod' and pedalling down the 'High,' of 'handshake' and 'Ninth Week.' I never got used to people being 'up.' Up what? Up a bloody pole, like Simon

Stylites? And 'don' is a word I couldn't use. I found it embarrassing. My teachers were teachers, not 'dons.' Jacob was never a don. A don to my mind evokes a person more than commonly incompetent at boiling an egg or tying a parcel. A person combing cobwebs out of his hair. A person brewing up magical green sparks in the potting-shed with batty conviction. Dr Faustus. A person always in mortar-board and horn-rims crashing eternally through the dean's cucumber frame. I took to reading breakaway Trot newspapers to provoke Roger's musicians as I hung around among the music bags and overcoats, waiting for Roger.

'Is that prescribed reading at the LSE?' one of them said to me once.

'I'm not at the LSE,' I said. This same character once observed, hilariously, to Roger that, 'Just because I believe in God, your girlfriend thinks I'm Bolshie,' which, even Roger admitted, was highly amusing.

Only once during my visit to Oxford did I meet a truly delightful man. I met him on a wall near the science buildings where I was waiting for Roger. An Australian graduate student in mathematics, he was, called Donald O'Brien. The son of a policeman, I discovered, descended from an Irish convict labourer.

'You attached to this here Uni?' he said. His terminology delighted me in its unbowed colonial assertiveness and made me laugh. I told him that I was not.

'They don't on the whole breed them like you around here, if you'll pardon the liberty,' he said. I confess that this blatantly chauvinistic remark pleased me, since Roger had recently found a female piano accompanist from Dartington Hall with upper-class vowels and dowdy clothes like Jane's whose presence reduced me to panic. I think I always knew that Roger would, in the end, abandon me for some Roedean-educated bishop's daughter who played the harpsichord; for some second cousin of the Huxleys who dissected frogs. It made me clinging and vulnerable.

'It beats me,' said my Aussie, as we watched the oncoming drizzle, 'why nobody thought of turning this place into a penal colony and exporting the British populace en masse to

Australia.' The idea was logical in its simplicity. It caused me to acknowledge—perhaps for the first time—the uses of the mathematical mind.

'Do you not like Oxford?' I said.

'Sure, I like it,' he said. 'It's a real place. Leaving aside that the colleges are like boarding-school, the women are either non-existent or ugly as sin, and the colonial Mafia like me talk about nothing but beer and pissing. The movies, I hand it to you, are a bit of all right. You can't sit around in the rain, baby. Come and have a drink with me.' I missed my chance with him. I passed him up, being as resolute as the unspotted Lucrece, that nobody but Roger should ever know whether or not I bore a mole upon my breast. I remember thinking with affection as he left me that he made 'can't' rhyme with 'ant.'

23

Roger told me, on one occasion, that I laughed too much. There were other things I did which caused him displeasure. I read *Vogue* magazine and I did my knitting in public. These were badges of female subjection which Roger attempted to eliminate in order that I might go forth as his brave and equal consort. All of it was little more than a punitive desire to scratch my face with briars. I laughed too much. 'Especially at Jake's jokes,' he said.

'You should try not to,' he said. 'It encourages him to perform.' I was too much in love with him and too young to perceive him as an absurd and petulant Hamlet, screwed up with sexual jealousy where Jacob was concerned. Refrain tonight, as it were, and that shall lend a kind of easiness to the next abstinence. It seems obvious to me now that Roger who had been allowed by his mother, in the initial shock and loneliness of her marriage, to believe himself more important to her than anybody else, was more than commonly beset with the fantasy that she belonged to him. It did not help, of course, that Jacob went in for biting his wife's neck sexily in public or for making after-dinner conversation of the state of her post-natal cervix. Jacob would come in off his commuter train and get his hands up Jane's jumper as she stood about making toast for the children's tea. Having got over my surprise at this, I did not find it offensive or unattractive. I found it rather sweet. Also that he would quite blatantly invite her upstairs sometimes in the middle of the afternoon. It helped me to accept the difficult fact that one owed one's existence to one's parents' coming together. It helped me to think more charitably of my parents' demure twin beds with their matching candlewick spreads. It helped me to acknowledge that passion might go on even under candlewick. Even with the Eno's Fruit Salts on the table between the beds.

'He's like the bloke in the Cloggies,' Jonathan once said cheerily to Roger, as Jacob was engaged upon feeling up his wife over the sink. 'He never stops raping her in public.' Jonathan seemed not to notice or care that Roger swallowed hard and began to examine his fingernails.

Jonathan was a mystery to me. Roger evidently admired and respected him. Jonathan, unlike me, could read *Vogue*, *Beano*, or any damn thing he liked without incurring Roger's disapproval, and a lot of the time he did. For Jonathan was powerfully streaked with anti-Culture. He alternated between the most god-awful vulgar comics full of blood and lust, and avant garde forms of highbrow literature. He was the only person I had ever met who had read *Finnegans Wake*. He had read *The Tin Drum* in German. He almost never uttered a sentence without saying fuck. If I had been his mother I'd have been moved to wash his mouth in carbolic soap. It was not at all that Jane had no control over her children, but she seemed not to mind it. I could see that he was very nice with his little brothers and sisters, and that he had a brazen childlike innocence himself at times which contradicted his more menacing characteristics. On the occasion of his seventeenth birthday, for example, he telephoned me to say he was having a birthday tea and would I come. It materialized as the most delightfully innocuous occasion, to which he had invited his two best schoolfriends, his entire family including his German grandmother, and me. Jane had made him a birthday cake which Sam and Annie had iced for him, and Rosie had done the writing with an icing forcer. He insisted on its having candles. The children sang to him in paper hats:

> Happy Birthday to You
> Squashed tomatoes and stew.
> Bread and butter in the gutter
> Happy Birthday to You.

It could have been made by Elstree Studios. Roger would never have submitted himself to the indignity. His presents—his John

Williams record, his subscription to *Private Eye*, his wonderful equipment for murdering river fish—all came wrapped in flowered paper with ribbon bows and tags. After tea there was a treasure hunt with clues. Hard clues for us older people devised by Jacob in the style of *The Times* crossword puzzle, and more charitable clues for younger people, which Rosie said were easy-peasy-Japanesy. Having been at a loss as to what to give him, I gave him a *Magic Roundabout* bell for his bicycle with Zebedee on it, because it was cheap. As it turned out, it fell in very suitably with the regressive nature of the occasion, pleased Jonathan no end, and was the envy of Annie and Sam. Also, I suspect, of Roger, who wouldn't admit to it. I would never have presumed to have given Roger such a piece of Japanesy tat.

24

For more than six months Roger enacted a convoluted charade with his parents where I was concerned, and said he didn't want them to know that we were involved with each other. He didn't want his parents invading his private life, he said. The result of this was that I was required to keep my visits there to a minimum, which was difficult, since Jane asked me fairly often to visit her. I declined to visit them at Christmas for this reason, even though she asked my mother to come too.

'We're going to have a super time,' she said coaxingly. 'I've just bought a whole blue Stilton cheese, Katherine. It's enormous. And my mother has filched an entire crate of the old boy's best claret for us and sent it down by rail. Go on. We'll sing some lovely old carols and make Roger play for us. Roger would love it if you came.'

'I have to go to my aunt's,' I said, feeling puny and dishonest.

'Oh, Katherine,' she said. 'Go on. Jake is so much more bearable at Christmas if I bring in an outsider. If you don't come he'll crab on at us about the expense and the singing and wish us well over the fast like a great killjoy. I need you to come.' It was ridiculous.

When I did succumb to invitations, or when Roger deemed it acceptable for me to come, he kept himself rather remote from me, which I could not but find unnecessary and rejecting. Being blessed, as he was, with parents who, unlike most, would not have raised an objection to him having his girlfriend in his bed, he chose instead to bed me on bits of grimy sacking in the farmer's outhouse or in the cycle-shed on a plastic mac, with my vertebrae grinding into the concrete. As a fundamental human need, warmth takes precedence over sexual urges. In both of these locations I was colder than I have ever been in my life.

'I love you,' Roger said, as I eased the butt end of an old Dutch hoe out of my shoulder blade. If Roger could have screwed me on a bed of nails he would have done it.

There was the time, one warm spring day, when he wouldn't come to the sea. He had to work, he said. I sat in the back of the car, therefore, between Jonathan and Rosie, missing him terribly, enduring the scufflings of Sam and Annie who were in the luggage space of the Goldmans' sizeable estate car exhuming Ladybird books from among the debris on the floor and arguing over ownership.

'Think of a game,' Jane said from the front seat. She had Sylvia on her lap. Jonathan had a game which Rosie knew too.

'You take imaginary pot shots at passers-by,' Jonathan said, 'and you score points on a scale between one and ten.'

'Yes,' Rosie said excitedly, 'and you get ten for old ladies in wheelchairs and eight for old ladies with a stick.'

'There's a correlation between decrepitude and high scoring?' Jacob asked.

'And also if you're black,' Rosie said. 'You get ten for a black person who's old, even if they aren't in a wheelchair.'

'There's a correlation also between stigmatizing ethnic attributes and high scoring?' Jacob asked. 'Is that right?'

'That's it,' Jonathan said.

'And able-bodied pinkoes are consequently hardly worth aiming at?' Jacob said.

'Right,' Jonathan said. Jacob shrugged. Mock despair.

'Far be it from me to repress you with the Liberal Conscience,' he said. 'Carry on.' The game broke down at a pedestrian crossing, when everyone claimed to have aimed the first shot at an aged crone in a red wig who was wheeling five toothless pekes across the street in a pram.

'Can you stop this, chaps?' Jane said. 'I find it moderately disgusting.'

'Tell me,' Jacob said, 'do you discriminate within the category of decrepit black persons? For example, between people of African and Asian origin?'

'You get more for Pakistanis,' Rosie said. 'We do it on the bus to swimming.'

'Good God,' Jacob said. 'Do you by any chance also get a bonus for a Jew?'

'Don't be silly,' Rosie said. 'You can't tell Jews. They just look like ordinary people.'

'Like what sort of ordinary people?' Jacob said. 'Like ordinary black people, for example?' Rosie growled impatiently. She had not much inclination for sociological analysis.

'You're so stupid, Jake,' she said. 'Why are you so stupid?'

On the pebbles where we stripped to our bathers, I discovered that Jacob's chest hair continued black and copious over his shoulders and all the way down his back. It grew in tight curls along the breast bone and straightened out over the shoulders where it lay in smooth two-inch lengths. I stared at him surreptitiously, like a kid sizing up a hunchback.

'Say,' Jane said, who had noticed my gaping, 'you really are most immoderately and unnaturally hirsute, aren't you, my husband?'

Roger, when I got back to him, was engaged upon modifications to his home-made stereo equipment.

'I love you,' he said.

There was the Saturday afternoon when Roger wouldn't take me to the pictures. Jane and Roger had spent the morning over the *Spring Symphony* while I minded the little ones. I enjoyed it. The worst they did, after all, was to blob finger paint on the kitchen floor, which was not going to bother anyone, and Sylvia ate paint which was reassuringly labelled 'non-toxic.' I enjoy children's paintings. Sam, I remember, painted a series of snappish crocodiles with zig-zag teeth, and Annie a 'female onion tree.'

'Only the girl ones grow them,' she said. 'These aren't the kind that grow under the ground.'

'Janie,' Jacob said over lunch, 'how is it you play the piano all morning and leave this poor young woman to care for your children?' Jacob was neurotic about Jane's piano-playing. Perhaps he couldn't bear to have her involved in something other than himself, or perhaps it turned him on to the point where he couldn't bear it.

'*My* children, are they?' she said, bestowing her winning smile upon him.

'Damn it, Jane,' he said, 'I've got work to do. All I know is you ask the child to visit you and then you use her like a domestic.'

'I really do not think that I need you to advise me on how to behave towards my friends,' Jane said. 'Katherine is a childless young woman. Child-minding is not her whole life. It makes a pleasant change for a person in her situation to care for children for an hour or two. They're nice children, aren't they? What's the matter with them?' Jacob stared at her sceptically.

'Jacob, for heaven's sake,' she said. 'She hasn't anything else pressing to do. Ask her. Don't make use of her to get at me.'

'Katherine, where is this tin-pot university of yours that gives you nothing to do?' Jacob said to me. 'If you've got nothing to do, you should be enjoying yourself.'

'I *was* enjoying myself,' I said. 'I like your children.'

'I like my children too, but I also know that they are boring and irritating,' he said. 'Roger, take the girl to the pictures. Let's find out what's on. Get me the paper, Sammy. The local one. It's on the bathroom floor.'

'I'm too busy,' Roger said. 'I'm seeing my tutor on Monday.' Sam returned with the newspaper, holding it in damp crumpled lumps. It hung in his arms like a dead bird. Jacob took it and bashed it into shape with a vengeance.

'Thank you, my sweet boy,' he said. Jonathan leant over Jacob's shoulder and read delightedly from the front page of the local rag.

'BLAZE FAMILY IN KITCHEN FIRE SHOCK,' he read, sending up the prose. He and Jacob fell about sharing a favourite joke.

'Ah, yes,' Jacob said. 'Our friends the unfortunate Mr and Mrs Blaze. Another shock for them. I wonder they aren't catatonic with shock by now, eh, Jont?' Rosie and I giggled girlishly. Jane smiled indulgently. Only Roger was unamused.

'What's funny?' Annie said, agitating to be included. 'Tell me what's funny.'

'Somebody's house has burned down,' Roger said. 'Ask Jake

why that's funny.' Jacob ignored him. He scuffled resolutely through the small ads for farm machinery and bay gelding horses, past the wedding pictures and the furniture shops advertising sales.

'Now then, Roger,' he said, '*Women in Love*. Just the thing for Katherine. A film of *Women in Love*. Lots of heavy breathing among the bracken. Take her, Roggs. Don't be such a snotty bloody tiresome swot.'

'He's not a swot, Jake. He's merely interested in the work,' Jane said.

'I know,' Jacob said. 'I know. He can nevertheless take this presentable young woman to the pictures, can't he? Work tonight, Rogsie. Down some black coffee at midnight.'

'I cannot think that Katherine is a young woman who needs to have you tout for her escorts,' Jane said.

'Oh, for Christssake!' Jacob said impatiently. 'Jonathan, you take her.'

'Neither Katherine nor Jonathan has a driver's licence, Jacob,' Jane said, 'and Katherine doesn't cycle.'

'Then you'll very sweetly get the car-keys, Janie, and run them into town,' Jacob said.

'I won't, as it happens,' Jane said. 'This has nothing to do with me, or with Katherine. You are simply becoming manic in the face of a project.'

'Jont,' Jacob said, 'can you drive that bloody car?'

'Sure,' Jonathan said.

'Jacob,' Jane said ominously, 'he hasn't got a licence.'

'And tell me, Jont. Can you park the thing?' Jacob said.

'Of course,' Jonathan said. 'Jane knows I can. She taught me how to do it.'

'Jacob,' Jane said, 'he hasn't got a licence. Will you stop behaving like a teenage delinquent?'

'Take her,' Jacob said.

'If Katherine will come with me,' Jonathan said. I had never seen him so decently humble. Jacob clapped a hand impatiently to his brow and sighed.

'Katherine,' he said sarcastically, 'will you go with my son to the pictures? You don't have to marry him, you understand? Just to sit next to him for an hour or two.' I tried not to explode with laughter, because Roger was suddenly passing me messages of black intensity with his eyes.

'I'll go,' I said. Roger got up and walked out. The dark indigo patch on his jeans, where he had removed the butterfly, was glaringly obvious to anyone with eyes. I knew immediately that Jacob knew whose butterfly it was that I had on my book-bag.

Half of Jonathan's grammar school class appeared to be at the cinema that afternoon judging by the craning of necks which went on to verify that it really was Goldman there, in the flesh, with a glamorous bird they'd never seen before, and to establish exactly what it was he intended to do with her once the lights went out. Somebody graciously hurled a paper ball at me, which bounced off the front of my shirt. Jonathan, having acquired a bag of popcorn, slouched stoically in his seat until his neck disappeared into the collar of his reefer jacket and did nothing, other than offer me popcorn, which I refused. One could have heard a pin drop as the men wrestled naked before the fire. Even with the text behind me, I was convinced that one of them would fall in. They looked so vulnerable with their absurd, pendant genitalia and bald buttocks. They had none of the nobility of wrestling stags. There was a nice homosexual mime at the end which reminded me of John Millet.

The other half of Jonathan's grammar school class was hanging loose on the town as we came out.

'Hey, Goldman,' one of them called bawdily as we moved off, 'what have you got that we haven't got?' Jonathan glared over his shoulder.

'Charm,' he said ferociously.

'Serenade her, Jonathan,' one of them said, below the belt, in a mimicking falsetto voice.

'Get lost,' Jonathan said, in his manly baritone. It occurred to me then that, among the indignities Jonathan had survived as the child of cultivated and arty parents, he had evidently survived having to sing male alto at school.

'You didn't have to go to the pictures with my brother,' Roger said when I got back. 'I don't believe that you love me.'

25

The day Roger gave me up for his pianist I had spent two hours waiting for him in a draughty hall where he was rehearsing the King of Hades in Monteverdi. It was within days of my final exams. The three of us went thereafter to the Science Museum, where I caught my destiny in the innuendo of ganging up. While his young woman gave her attention to a showcase of limestones, Roger diverted me onto the upper floor landing beyond the skeleton of the hanged man. The thing was as efficient as a premeditated putsch. Exorcising his own guilt, no doubt, and uneasiness, he made me a careful articulate pyramid of my shortcomings, which was anything but kind. It said, in short, that, weighed in the balance, I showed up trivial. That I covered my notebooks in Florentine wrapping-paper like a Girl Guide on a nature trail, that I cared more for knitting than logic, that I made a brazen virtue of all that was unfortunate, vulgar and semi-educated in my own history, that, frankly, my mother's plaster ducks left him feeling ill, that I fondled my earrings while he, Roger Goldman, played the violin, that I laughed too much, that in that very Science Museum I had, that very day, spent the bulk of my time admiring the stencil designs on the iron vaults, 'as if,' he said, 'as if the place were housing an annual craft exhibition run by the Women's Institute.'

I think that before he turned and walked away from me I said that I was sorry. In this life there are those that apologize and those that do not. I am a person who says sorry if a passer-by stands on my foot. I thought, first, crazily, that I ought to tell him that my mother's ducks were china and not plaster; that my mother, whose chocolate cake he had not disdained, was my property to criticize, not his. Then, as the tears spilled in silence down my face, I thought that I would do anything, anything to get him back. That I would do algebra in sackcloth for the privilege of touching the hem of his hand-on Sea Scout jumper. Suddenly, as I saw him reach his showcase of limestones, my only thought was to get my stuff from his room and go before they came back to it; before Roger could encounter the disfiguring squalor of my tears, and to go quietly, without fuss. I was no good at rage and indignation. It had never been encouraged in my house. I had never told my parents, for example, to fuck off, or thrown garlic bread across the dinner table. These things were not licensed in my house. I did not pursue the option, therefore, of following Roger across the floor to his limestones and dismantling his personality, as he had done mine. Of screaming at him, gratifyingly, that he was an arrogant and joyless youth, rejoicing righteously in the fate of the damned; scrambled, punitive, and jealous. Might we have hammered out something and moved on together? Perhaps not, though I will never know. Perhaps all Roger's words said nothing more than that he wanted his pianist in his bed, not me. Perhaps I was always more in love with him than he with me. To this day I cannot watch Roger Goldman shake hair from his eyes without some pain. He is an absurd, abiding, adolescent passion, which I resolve by being seldom in his company.

In Roger's bedsitting room I took down from the cupboard the travelling bag with which he had come back from Kenya two years before. Into it I stuffed my mother's whistling kettle, which he had on loan, my two patchworked sofa cushions with which I had adorned his room, and an Aran sweater of my own making which we had shared. The routine petty division of property. In the train I registered over and over, through a film of tears, that the bag still bore an East African Airways luggage-label on which was written, in block capitals, R.J. GOLDMAN. It put me in mind of the laundry basket full of old wellington boots. It evoked for me, vividly and painfully, an image of Roger at the kitchen table in the Hamlet hat, raising his eyes for the first time to encounter mine. It made me, quite simply, want to die.

After that, the nights were the worst. In the daylight I

occasionally talked the thing over with a girlfriend or in my own mind, working my misery into a rational shape which gave an hour's relief. But alone, at the end of the day, the painful fact of Roger was still there, impinging like the appalling and sudden scream of brakes. Sometimes I did not sleep at all. Twice on these occasions I tiptoed downstairs and sat wrapped in a blanket on a tree-stump in that rigid little suburban garden, watching distant inky clouds blow across the moon, watching the relentless progress of each one towards its own disintegration, as it crossed the moon, into dispersed and tortured fragments. I cried a lot, but only to myself. I telephoned the speaking clock in the small hours for the sound of a voice.

'At the first stroke it will be four forty-two and ten seconds,' said the voice. 'Peep, peep, peep.' I never telephoned Roger. I slipped politely and obligingly out of his life without a word of recrimination. Once, at a news-stand, I went so far as to buy for him a picture postcard of a snarling female tiger, feeling that in that creature's rage I could take some vicarious, impotent stand. I never posted it. I wrote my final exams in an almost indifferent stupor, drugged up on purple hearts, wondering what Jacob would say to me if I failed. It had ceased to matter to me for myself. Wondering would the British taxpayer rise up, with just clamour, for the return of his money? After that I did what I hadn't done for a long time. I telephoned John Millet and told him.

26

John Millet's house in Greenwich can be approached by rail from London Bridge. The trains rumble over the roof of Southwark Cathedral, where Geoffrey Chaucer lies buried, and lure one with the emotive promise of Rochester, Chatham and Gillingham at the end of the line. It was the romance of the platform announcement which gave me the idea of going away. John was lunching with a friend upon German wine and onion quiche made, of course, by himself.

'We didn't wait for you,' he said. 'You were rather vague about your plans.'

'Sorry,' I said. 'I look terrible, John. Don't look at me.' Because I knew appearances mattered to him, I felt that I was an affront to his aesthetic senses. John smiled quite kindly.

'Boyfriend trouble is only temporarily disfiguring,' he said. 'Sit down. Alex,' he said, 'Katherine.' He handed me an engraved hock glass containing chilled wine. A great pleasure to have in the hand.

'Katherine is embroiled in a poor little tottering affair with Jake Goldman's son,' he said. 'Remember Jake? My neighbour in Belsize Park? Stunning wife. Beautiful eyes. Yes?' He made a fluent cosmopolitan gesture, drawing a circle in the air and lightly kissing his fingers. An ironic, romantic, harlequin gesture. His friend had taken off his suit jacket and was sitting in his waistcoat and pinstriped shirt sleeves.

'I never met him,' he said, 'but I remember the woman. A handsome, tired young woman, with a mewling toddler.' John gestured again, spreading his hands to denote, with resignation, the condition of mortality which besets us all.

'The "mewling toddler" is now the cause of Katherine's

scorbutic pallor,' he said. 'We are none of us getting any younger, Alex.'

That afternoon we walked alone along the waterfront, he and I, to the naval college where he expanded upon the decorative use of symmetry in wrought iron.

'I thought I might go to Rome,' I said.

John lent me a book called *Italian without Toil*. It came with a set of records. Then he wrote letters on my behalf to two of his friends, employing, in my interest, his stunning left-handed writing which Jacob had previously slandered. He gave them to me to post.

'Cheer up, Katherine,' he said. 'That pretty little Goldman is not the only man in the world.' I replied with simple commitment that he was for me. John, having given me a glass of brandy, sat opposite me for an hour or so and sketched me as I sat on his sofa, chronicling, in brown chalk, a phase of my unhappiness. Then he got up and ran a bath. He came back and handed me a large porridge-coloured bath towel. To resist would have seemed gauche. It was when he entered the bathroom to get me out, had wrapped me in the towel, with my arms pinned to my sides, and propelled me towards his bed, that I remembered the spanner.

'Jacob says—' I said. I was not going to tell him about the spanner. Merely to gabble nervously, to break the dignity of his hypnotic magic, that Jacob had said—as he had in a light moment—that John slept in black sheets. John put his index finger over my lips.

'Shshsh,' he said. And very quietly, very strangely, I thought, he said into my ear, 'You will say after me, "Jacob is the butcher's grandson." ' I found this so perverted, so bizarre, so ridiculous, that I pulled away from him in ungainly, childish confusion and scrambled clumsily for my clothes.

'I think I hate you,' I said.

In the train I opened the book. *'Non e difficile l'italiano per un francese,'* it said, encouragingly. 'Italian is not difficult for a French person.'

27

Three weeks later I stole like a thief into the Philosophy Department to return some books. I had no plan to wait for my results, but simply to shake the dust from my feet and light out for the territory, as Huck Finn says. John Millet had set it up for me to teach in a language school in Rome and to stay with friends of his until I found my feet. I had been avoiding Jacob like the plague, but I ran into him in the vestibule on my way in.

'I've been avoiding you,' I said.

'And how is that?' he said. I talked very fast, sounding very unbalanced, I suspect.

'I didn't mean to write you so much drivel,' I said. 'None of you. I mean, feel free, all of you, to throw my scripts into the fire. Well, you haven't really got fires, I suppose. The waste-paper baskets will do. I'm not really all that much of a skive, Jacob, it's just that it wasn't a good time for me. As a matter of fact, it's still not so good. It's, well, a crisis, Jacob. I was having an emotional crisis. That's it. It's not good for people when they're writing exams. I'm sorry.'

'You look like the back of a bus, sweetheart,' Jacob said candidly. 'What the hell is the matter with you? Your face looks different. Are you pregnant?'

'No,' I said. 'It's pimples, Jacob. Like people get when they're upset.' Jacob smiled.

'You're a sweet child,' he said. 'You're a funny child, do you know that? I was a crazy, bright, fatherless child like you once upon a time. I like you.' We repaired to the coffee machine where I was, all the time, jumpy and slightly manic. I got my head in the way as he bent to get the cup out for me.

97

'Careful I don't spill it on you,' he said, to jolly me along. 'You might get a swollen head.'

'I've got one of those already,' I said.

'Yes and no,' he said. 'I'll tell you what I've been doing this morning, shall I? I've been interviewing my seventh case of pre-menstrual depression. Perhaps that's what's wrong with you, Katherine. You're pre-menstrually depressed. Why haven't you come to see me about it? You're in a minority of two or three. I thought that the entire female student population wrote exams in a state of pre-menstrual depression these days. Or so they all tell me after the event.' I got a little uneasy sometimes with Jacob's male-oriented jokes. I didn't altogether know what he was saying.

'Perhaps they could all get pregnant before the exams,' I said sarcastically.

'Perhaps,' he said. 'In truth, Katherine, pregnancy is, in my admittedly limited and vicarious experience, a very favourable time.' Was he saying that he wasted his time on the education of women when biology pulled them more effectively in another direction?

'Do they want you to bump up their marks?' I said. I am a person who has been known to approach him, after the return of an essay, with the request that he lower the mark for the following reasons, which I then conscientiously enumerate for him.

'Sure,' he said, 'all the time. In my day such women students as there were didn't have this female trouble. I tell you this, Katherine, I don't pretend to understand the present.' I suspected him of saying that he understood the present perfectly and wished to take a snipe at the first rumblings of reviving feminism. I had a sound hunch that, for Jacob, this was a manifestation of middle-class female parasitism, spreading false consciousness in the class war. (Jacob was, of course, the first always to put his hand in his pocket if one was collecting for the cleaning ladies' strike fund.)

'What's the cause of these crises, then?' he said. 'It is not, I hope, that son of mine who causes you these crises?'

'Just the one,' I said. 'That's all. One crisis, Jacob. I expect you know about it anyway. That we're not together any more.'

'Don't imagine that Roger tells me anything,' he said. 'In any case, he's climbing rocks in Wales. Anything I can do about it? Bang your heads together, perhaps?' Oh, Roger, with your rope and spiked boots, will I never see you again? Will we meet as polite strangers in polite sitting rooms?

'Oh, no,' I said hastily. 'Nothing. Mutual consent. You know. Let's not even talk about it.' Jacob nodded, understanding that there was nothing he could do.

'We must have a talk about your future, you and I,' he said. 'What do you think of doing with yourself? What do you imagine a degree in philosophy equips you for?' I eyed him shiftily, not wishing to make the approach.

'Are you saying I'll have a degree in philosophy?' I said. 'Because you don't have to pass me, you know. I mean, I know this isn't a charitable institution, Jacob. I didn't come here to try and get you to give me a degree, you know. I don't think that you ought to feel that just because you think I'm deserving—' Jacob laughed.

'Stop this, Katherine. You know that I know that you're a bright young woman. Are you telling me you don't know you're a comfortable upper second? Come now. I am aware that for reasons which I cannot fathom you are completely neurotic in this area. Not so? We neither of us can win. Whatever I tell you will simply lead you to believe that my judgement is impaired.'

'But Jacob,' I said, 'have you actually *looked* at my scripts?'

'Course I have,' he said, 'I and my colleagues. Even if the external examiner decided to have you for breakfast, you're a cert, my lovey. Find something else to worry about.'

'I'm going to Rome, you know,' I said. 'I'm going to teach.'

'Good God,' he said. 'Has John got anything to do with this?'

'Not really,' I said.

'Does that mean yes or no?' he said.

'It means only insofar as I asked him to help me,' I said.

'To teach what?' he said.

'English,' I said, 'to foreigners. Well,' I said, attempting a joke, 'they won't be foreigners, will they? Not in Italy. I'll be the foreigner.' Jacob looked both concerned and unamused.

'Come home with me,' he said. 'Let Jane put you to bed, for heaven's sake. Sleep on it.' I could not face the thought of entering his house, to give in under the influence of kindness.

'I want to be on my own,' I said, 'I really do.' Jacob had manifestly not slept much of late either, but then this was a perennial affliction of his.

'To speak true, it's not much fun at home at present,' he said. 'Jane is behaving like any other pressuring bloody bourgeois parent with poor old Jonathan. She's driving him away. I've been watching her at it for days on end. She fancies that he should sit the Oxford Entrance Examination. I'm not against it, you know, but she can't make the child do it. He has decided in consequence of her nagging to take himself off to Europe.'

'To do what?' I said. Jacob shrugged.

'God knows,' he said. 'You know Jonathan. He's a flower child. He wants to walk the Pyrenees. Doss on riverbanks. Scrounge. Earn pennies at a street corner with that bloody flute. He says, right now, that he will never come back. Do I believe him? For myself, I don't give a damn for the Oxford Entrance Exam. I don't care if he takes himself to the Huddersfield Poly or the Labour Exchange. People as bright as Jonathan don't need degrees, after all. Jane, of course, thinks differently. People always do who haven't been through it themselves. It's all surrogate gratification for her. What concerns me is, will I ever see that boy again? Will I ever know if he's been kicked in the head in a gutter somewhere?'

'Won't he come home when he's hungry?' I said, inadequately. 'The way he does when he's fishing?'

Jacob was no longer thinking of me. He was thinking of his favourite child. For is there not a pity beyond all telling hid in the heart of love, as Yeats says? Yeats, W.B. That brother of the more famous Jack as Jacob once called him. Do not the very stars threaten that beloved head?

'Well,' he said, suddenly, briskly, 'I'm sorry to hear that you're having these, these . . .'

'Crisis,' I said.

'To be sure,' he said, 'just the one. If you are determined to go, you'll absolutely come down and say goodbye to Jane, eh? She'll miss you. Rosie, I may say, will be prostrated with grief.'

'I'll come,' I said. 'You must know that I'll miss you all terribly. Jane has been very important to me, Jake,' I said, tears welling in my eyes. 'Tell her—tell her that her kitchen has been my other university.' Jacob laughed.

'I will,' he said. I fell upon his hairy chest and cried like hell. Jacob kept patting my shoulder.

'If you're in trouble ever, you'll reverse the charge on the 'phone?' he said. 'It's an easy thing, Katherine, to pick up the 'phone, eh? And reverse the charge?'

'I'll remember that,' I said.

'Good,' he said, 'and don't you let any of those Catholic bloody foreigners grind you down.'

When I next saw Jacob the hair on his chest had turned completely white.

28

I made an effort to appear at my best for Jane. I had washed my hair and turned in early with a tranquillizer, washed down with a glass of beer. I painted my face for her and caught the train, secure in the knowledge that Roger wasn't there. He was climbing rocks in Wales. I bought her a present in the flower shop in the High Street. A little indoor palm tree in a pot. Jane herself was certainly not at her best that day. I entered to find her crabbing unreasonably at Sylvia, who had wet her pants. Jonathan, who came into the kitchen to make cheese doorsteps for himself, ignored her very pointedly. As she had once said to me, she was not 'one of those insufferable people who does it all right.' She did not, surprisingly, seem all that concerned over me and Roger. She had other things on her mind. Roger had told her nothing much and had seemed cheerful enough, she said, and I was determined to pose the same. Roger had always made a point of being thoroughly undemonstrative with me in the presence of his parents in any case. She said, a little wistfully, 'That's it then, is it? It does seem a shame, Katherine. But you cannot, of course, think of pleasing me. I will not hear a word against either of you. I'll miss you terribly. Jonathan, will you bugger off, please?' She clearly couldn't bear to have him in the same room. Jonathan turned very slowly and looked at her, daggers in his eyes, and said nothing.

'Katherine is going abroad,' she said. 'She's got herself a very nice job. There's a moral in that, somewhere, which you might pick up.'

'Piss off,' Jonathan said to her. 'Where are you going, Katherine?'

'Rome,' I said. 'I got some Italian money today. Can I show

you my Monopoly money?' I pulled out of my purse my wad of wonderful lire. We gazed at them, the three of us. Jane started suddenly with new inspiration.

'You wouldn't stoop to bribery, would you, Jontikins?' she said. Jonathan, who had relaxed over the banknotes, returned to his hostile stare.

'It'll take you a lot of fucking Smarties to get me to write that exam, lady,' he said.

'I was thinking more of something like six hundred pounds,' she said. 'Stay and write the exam and I will give you six hundred pounds. You could have a better time in Europe with money, you know.' Jonathan left the room, but suddenly he was there again.

'You haven't got it,' he said.

'I'll borrow it, won't I?' she said. 'I'll tack it onto the mortgage. Useful things, mortgages.'

'I want it in writing,' Jonathan said. 'I don't trust you.'

'Okay,' she said. 'Have seven. It's only money, you know. Give me some paper.'

'Jesus, Ma,' Jonathan said, climbing down, 'I don't need it in writing. I don't need seven hundred pounds. Give me four.'

'Have six, Jont,' she said, 'and have it in writing. Don't get soft on me.' She wrote it down and signed it. I couldn't believe it. Jonathan put the note in his pocket.

'I make three conditions,' she said firmly. 'Come back next October and give Oxford a try. Send me a postcard every eight weeks, and don't get anyone pregnant.'

'I'm not stupid,' Jonathan said.

'As if I don't know that,' she said. 'Why do you think I'm making all this fuss over you? But someone has yet to prove that bright young men are less capable of impregnating women.'

'Don't imagine I'm going to surround myself with pissing infants, like you,' he said.

'You, Jonathan,' Jane said with emphasis, 'you were the only one of my children who consistently peed into my wellington boots and *don't you forget it*.'

After that she and I said goodbye. We both cried a little. Her

103

gardening gloves were lying on the table. She picked up one of them to mop her eyes and gave me the other.

'Here,' she said, 'have it for the train.' I took it, knowing I would treasure it like a relic of the cross. Within the week I had packed my hand luggage into Roger's hold-all and boarded a train for Europe.

29

As we drew into Milan one of the two nuns in my train compartment fainted with the heat. She was revived by her companion with the help of two men in sweaty vests. I had never been in a train compartment before with nuns. No more with men in sweaty vests, and the Northern Line seemed light years away. The carriage was like a Daumier carriage. It had more in common, perhaps, with Roger's third-world buses than with anything I knew. Nothing in my experience had prepared me for the visual impact of the countryside, for a landscape of vines and olive trees. When I later read, in D. H. Lawrence on Tuscany, that one expected Jesus to step out of the landscape, I thought Yes, exactly so. There were no slivers of mousetrap cheese enclosed in triangles of Wonderloaf to be had upon the station platform, only some rather biblical loaves and bottles of wine. The unfamiliar typeface on the newspapers jumped giddily at me from news-stands as I endured the terror of changing trains.

On the Rome train I shared a compartment with a respectable matron who scribbled postcards and asked me the date. John's language course had taught me all kinds of stuff suitable to bizarre and remote eventualities. It had taught me (for example) to say that I had not, alas, read Dante because 'what with my dear wife, my mother-in-law and the seven children' I had not 'felt the need of it.' In the face of a simple question I could only mumble and panic. After four week's toiling I had, like the sorcerer's apprentice, forgotten the words. In addition, I had yet to make the shattering discovery that nobody in Italy, other than myself, wore a mini-skirt.

John's friends lived in Trastevere. To enter it is to enter a world which starts with the Romans and ends with the Baroque. Unfamiliar human density in the narrow cobbled streets, no curbs to distinguish traffic from pedestrian. My taxi hooted its way through football games which divided to let us pass. Footballs which bounced off twelfth-century church walls, pasted with election posters and daubed with aerosol slogans. And above the footballs and the posters and the slogans, rising in bright array of antique gold mosaic, the saints looked down on the fountain and the square and the bar and the buzzing Vespas.

We stopped outside the apartment building where I saw, to my astonishment, that *Vogue* was taking a photograph. The cameraman had posed, against the crumbling sepia walls of the tobacco shop, against a backdrop of picturesque urban poverty, a collection of extravagantly coiffed model girls wearing silver tentacles on their heads and silver sandals on their feet. They were dressed, from shoulder to hem, in sun-ray pleated gossamer and were being gawped at, impassively, by an old woman in black crêpe seated behind them on a wooden café chair on the cobbled street.

The apartment, like all the best apartments, was on the top floor, rising airily with its new green shutters above the rotting vegetables and discarded fish-heads of the street. I approached it by means of a prodigious flight of barren stone steps and walked in through the open door, treading ceramic tiles underfoot. The Signora, my hostess, was one-time English. Her name was Leone Bernard. She was in the bath drinking whisky. One of her man friends was sitting in his clothes upon the bidet.

'*Cara*,' he said to her, 'you must trim your pubic hair. I will not rape a woman who looks like Archbishop Makarios.' I stopped momentarily in my poor suburban tracks, thinking Wow! The sophistication of it! Over the past years I had got used to Jacob being graphic, but Jacob was never smart. He had no aspirations towards becoming a man-about-town.

'It's John's little *Caterina*,' said my hostess, her voice a boozy croak plucked somewhere from Noël Coward. '*Avanti*, my dear and welcome. Get her a glass, Oliver. My God, but aren't you young?' she said. 'And gorgeous,' she added, assessing flesh by pound and ounce. She wore her hair knotted prettily on top of

106

her head and strands curled damply in the nape of her neck. Her head, as she talked, turned frequently from front to side as she presented a contrived but nonetheless alluring right half-profile. I took the glass, thinking nervously for a moment of the white slave trade. I'm not much of a boozer even now. When people ask me what I will drink I have a strong urge to say Cherryade, please. Stone's Ginger Wine is my only serious tipple.

'If you have crossed Italy in that skirt,' she said with emphasis, 'then I think you are game for anything. You'll have to take us out, Oliver.' With commendable good humour did Oliver put aside his thoughts of rape for another day and take us to lunch. Leone was nothing if not commanding. She reminded me often of those little girls in the junior school who told you not to wear your shiny pink dress to the party because they were going to wear theirs. And you didn't wear it, even though you had got your own dress first and it wasn't fair. And then you went on being flattered when they chose you first for their side in games.

I have a blurred, heady memory of that lunch and of picking my way to the restaurant, whisky-drunk, through narrow streets in unaccustomed heat; of bees around flower stalls, of suckers on fried octopus legs and the sound of Leone's voice on the windless air.

Leone had learned her voice at Cambridge in the nineteen-fifties. She was the daughter of an unmarried kitchen maid and had got a university place very much against the odds. But she had left it a year later in disgrace: a botched home abortion had caused her to pass out, theatrically, in a pool of uterine blood on the floor of the dining hall. She had terrific, mannered style, and wore the most marvellous clothes, which she flung shamelessly at the ironing woman, who laboured half the day in Leone's kitchen, wearing her stockings rolled over bulging veins, bow-legged and smelling of old sweat. A part of me was highly susceptible to Leone's style. I am in general susceptible to style. Style is what attracted me to John Millet. I have that within which admires the well-plucked eyebrow and the well-hung lithograph almost as much as the well-turned sonnet. I am a reader of glossies—archetypal fodder for the *Habitat* catalogue. Like Leone I have always understood these things as the cues to social mobility. That is why Jane Goldman was, with her indifference to them, like a breath of new air for me. But if, like Jane, you have been to school with girls who marry merchant bankers it is no doubt easier to jack in the trappings of privilege in the face of a decent alternative. Jane saw things very straight. She had no need of Jacob's Marxist reading group to understand base and superstructure. Given the choice, Jane would far sooner have consumed the well-hung pheasant than been the owner of the well-hung lithograph with which to impress the neighbours. Come to think, she had made a point of not having neighbours. Her self-esteem was not bound up with what she owned. She could 'live off the land,' as Jacob said in jest. 'Upper-class buggers,' as he put it, 'are not slow to learn the lessons of guerrilla warfare.'

Dear Jacob, how easily one could miss the benefits of his lunatic sanity! If Jacob had met Leone Bernard he might, I reckon, have conceded grudgingly that she had better legs than Marlene Dietrich. She appeared to me a wonderfully spirited parasite. She visited beauticians and she bought shoes. Her major pleasures were spending her husband's money and bedding his friends. And she would talk so disloyally about the poor chaps afterwards that I soon could not look at the Bernards' friends without knowing which was obsessed with anal sex and which had what she called 'potency problems.'

Two mornings a week, Leone went out to buy food. She called this 'doing the marketing.' Something to do, I believe, with the high proportion of Americans which made up the Bernards' expatriate smart set. There was never much marketing to be done, since a great deal of eating out went on, but Leone and I—until my job began to take up my mornings— would each of us take a ludicrously small but picturesque basket into the Campo de Fiori where Leone would buy flowers and figs and present charming half-profiles to the Bohemian young men who hung about on the statuary. I would wander in and out through the little rows of specialist food shops, glorying in the ornate and gilded packaging, and the wrappings adorned with facsimiles of medals won at food fairs in the eighteen-nineties, or displaying neo-classical profiles of Victor

Emmanuel the Second. There is none of that Sainsbury's lower-case restraint, that deliberate suppression of graphic *joie de vivre*. Leone would push her way to the front in a bakery bursting with its pretty star-shaped loaves and buy an *etto* of biscuits. We would pass butchers' stalls displaying rows of spongy, pink, inflated lung, pegged to clothes lines over the counter. I remember that once the brevity of my skirt caused two paunchy market vendors to gesture heartily to each other with unmistakably phallic aubergines, after which, for a while, I wore Leone's clothes. Later I made my own. The old woman in black crêpe was my home landmark. She was always there, planted on the curb on her café chair. She sold black market cigarettes, Peter Bernard said.

Peter was Leone's husband. She had acquired him, or rather, had stolen him, from a previous wife in Southampton, where he still had two children. Leone had gone to Southampton to consult a psychiatrist. She had been sent there by a person she referred to, off-handedly, as 'my haberdasher.' She had married the haberdasher after leaving Cambridge, because he was rich and Leone liked to live as high as possible. She was damned if she was going to append herself to anyone who would need to work nights to pay her debts. She had met Peter in a coffee bar. After six months of bogus visits to the psychiatrist, the haberdasher had one day thought to telephone the consulting-room. In the ensuing show-down Peter left his wife, who subsequently threatened to kill both herself and the children, and the haberdasher began attending a Japanese martial arts class, with a view to killing Peter. All of them ended up on the couch of the same Southampton psychiatrist—except Leone, that is, who had discovered she had a taste for high drama and was therefore feeling fine.

Peter had once worked with John Millet and the connection took them to Rome. In spite of the money he had inherited from his dead mother and his admirable parade-ground stance, Peter had the look of a man weighed down by alimony and exile. He wore his Christopher Robin hair over a face incongruously lined and had a horror of being recognized for the straight man he was. For Leone needed him to be avant garde. She was wedded to her life on the piazzas, feeling the chic of rubbing shoulders in the summer with Sartre in a bar; of catching brief glimpses of Sophia Loren stepping into a motor car. So Peter, who, without her, might well have been the kind of man who spent weekends happily repairing the brake-linings on his Morgan or putting together plastic model bi-planes with his kids in Southampton, had cultivated instead a series of advanced poses the most embarrassing of which were nudity and communal bathing.

I ought to explain that the Bernards' bathroom was in any case conducive to impromptu happenings. Things came to a head in that part of the apartment as they had in the Goldmans' kitchen. The bathroom had no door. It gave access to both kitchen and balcony and was got up not merely for bathing. There was a record player and a pile of *New Yorkers*; trailing plants and abandoned whisky tumblers; a glass orb filled with Mediterranean sea-shells and an elegant, high-glazed, pedestal fruit dish, piled high with a pyramid of French soap lemons. Peter would come in from a squash game, therefore, and hang about lighting cigarettes or soaping one's boobs, parading his male equipment, all the while, at eye-level. He was, I think, attempting to get even with Leone who, having first wrecked his marriage, gave much of her creative energy to destroying him in public. But it suited her a treat, in fact, to have him preening nude before me. She pushed me at him until I felt like a stage housemaid. Black suspenders and fishnet could have done no more for me, nor a saucy flick of the feather duster. It gives me goose-pimples even now to think of the Bernards. They were like people locked together in hell.

During the weeks I spent there, Leone Bernard, beautifully dressed, carefully made up, smelling always of *Antelop*, bore down upon me with a greedy, controlling urge which unnerved me a little. She spoke to me in English, peppering her talk impressively with Italian phrases which she pronounced with theatrical perfection, lingering exaggeratedly upon the double consonant and stressing the penultimate syllable to absurdity. She evidently relished to a degree the idea of me as a young person disappointed in love and began to remove for me thereby even the comfort of the emotion's validity, leaving me feeling like the heroine of a melodramatic operetta. Most nights

110

I cried myself to sleep behind the open, shuttered window of my tiny bedroom against a soothing blur of sound from the restaurant below, with its tanks of clams planted out each night upon the cobbles. '*Specialità*,' said the notice, '*Zuppa di Pesce*.' Somebody had crossed it out to read, '*Zuppa di Gatto*.' I have always liked cat soup.

I bore with it, I believe, not only because at first I had nowhere else to go but because I was resolute in the determination to make my way in a place where there were at last no mothers or aunts to undermine my anonymity and because I was still too much in love with Roger to care what happened to me. I was also quite dizzy with the look and the feel of a place whose textures never staled. Though most of my life consisted of catching buses to work and discovering how grindingly wearing it was to earn one's living along with the rest of humanity, I nevertheless wrote repeatedly to Jane Goldman telling her effusively that it was all happening. Jane wrote back hasty scribbled postcards giving me, with a certain ironic flair, the view from her kitchen sink. After a while our correspondence petered and died.

30

As painful as I found Leone Bernard, so equivalently, I found
my colleagues a pleasure. A fortuitous collection of young
British teachers, all of them living from day to day, without
sickness benefits or holiday pay, some tied by Italian boyfriends and girlfriends, some by the evident advantages of the
Roman life-style over what they had known in Bradford and
Tottenham. They were both my escape route from the
Bernards and in the long run the most loyal of friends. Their
range of knock-knock jokes exceeded even Rosie Goldman's. I
moved in with one of them, who had had the good luck to find a
tiny flat near the Spanish Steps, over a bar, where we quenched
our thirst on tumblers of frozen black coffee on hot days and
bought slabs of pizza for breakfast. The art of dressing myself,
without guilt, in fantastic clothes came back to me; of hanging
jewels in my ears and of blowing a week's earnings upon sea
green crêpe without being answerable to Roger Goldman for
the excess. On the rebound from Roger's puritanism, I had a lot
of men. I do not much like voyeurism among other people's
heavy breathing, so I will only tell you that with not one of them
did I descend to the floor of a bike shed and that nearly all of
them were married. Unmarried men in southern Europe have
mothers. Strong, frank matriarchs, who nose one out as a subversive within minutes, who make perfectly clear the reality
that their sons will not make injudicious, long-term attach-
ments with bookish, unconventional, Protestant women:
women who have no reputable dowry and insufficient deference for the art of home-made *fettuccine*. So who am I? I asked
myself. Am I that despicably suburban young woman,
interested only in knitting and personal adornment, whom

112

Roger Goldman saw fit to cast off? Or am I that dangerous emancipate, steeped in Plato and febrile subversion? In short, I avoided the wives as they walked out with the children in the parks.

Only once did I think, absurdly, that I saw Roger Goldman. I pursued the illusion feverishly through the streets, clutching to myself my sturdy brown paper bag full of grapes and wine and buffalo milk cheese, until I shook with exhaustion and went home shattered and tearful knowing that I would, at a nod from that snooty bastard, yield up the whole seductive edifice. All that booze and cheese and crumbling sepia. All that unwonted credit one got for being blonde. All those times when, flitting by in my brassy tart's earrings and my high-heeled shoes I had caught, without desert, the reverent accolade, 'Madonna'.

31

My mother came to see me twice. She came by air and stayed with me in the cubby-hole on the way to the shower cubicle which passed for my bedroom. She insistently begged me to come home. She could see no reason for my feelings for the place. And no more could I, in my youthful ignorance, see why she was less than euphoric at the prospect of dossing in my cubby-hole for two weeks on end, in a flat above a bar, in a town where the natives never go to bed. She saw no reason why the food came as it did. She saw no reason at all, she said once over a plateful of squid, why the locals couldn't eat 'ordinary' food like people in England. You couldn't drink the coffee and you couldn't toast the bread. It was stale by lunch-time and it had no insides. Only crusts.

Then she wrote to me suddenly from Hendon to say that she was getting married. Her letter was both extraordinary and revealing to me. She was planning to marry an assistant bank manager from Dorset, she said, and she hoped that I wouldn't mind. I wondered by what right I ought to mind. She felt free to do so, she said, since I had grown up and left home and appeared not to need her any more. She had only once before considered marrying again but, as I might remember, I had taken against the gentleman and she had felt that she ought to put me first. I was stunned to discover that I had wielded this kind of power over her. I recalled that when I was twelve there had been a man who had called at the house a good bit, whom I had vocally disliked for the profound reasons that he had blown his nose over-politely at table, almost burying his head under the cloth, that he had worn bow ties, and that he had made a point of carving meat with a formidable show of expertise. That my mother had decided against re-marrying on the basis of these youthful aversions filled me with horror. With what contained resentment had she thereafter washed my clothes and brought me my cocoa and custard creams in bed? And what kind of reciprocal sacrifices were, in consequence, required of me? Pish, I thought, as I went my way, stamping firmly on guilt.

I went to her wedding and played out, for an hour or two, my mother's fantasy: her desire to see me as a reflection of the best of herself. I enacted a charade in a tasteless navy two-piece with yellow saddle-stitching and a yellow shirt which tied at the neck, feeling like a perfume lady in John Barnes. I bore the castrated smut which emanated from the best man's speech. I gave her my love and hopped it, an extravagant and wheeling stranger, belonging nowhere. I was, in addition, about to lose my rights to the cubby-hole over the bar. My flat-mate's boyfriend had designs upon it.

32

There is the whiff of low cliché about airport romance, but let me confess to it. I fell in love with a man at the airport after my cheap return flight.

The aeroplane was crowded with Italian boys returning from a summer camp in England. They fell into the arms of their parents at the arrivals lounge—all but two of them, who appended themselves to me. Two well brought up little boys, clutching duty-free perfume for mother and looking in vain for a welcoming parent. I waited with them on the steps outside in the sunlight. The disinherited among the blessed. All around us lovely, smothering mothers were asking their offspring concernedly how often they had changed their socks.

Enter Michele, half an hour late, swearing wonderfully, built like a cart-horse. Somebody had stolen his wallet and his keys, he said. He couldn't drive home. The police would, as usual, do nothing, he said. He had not a kind word for the children, whom he ignored, other than to abuse them impatiently for wasting the *signorina*'s time. I volunteered the money for the bus into the city. We took the bus to the Cinecittà, where we took the underground to the Termini, where we took a taxi to his one-time wife's apartment to unload the children. Then we took a taxi to his apartment to collect his spare keys. He lived not a million miles from Leone Bernard, and the black-market cigarette lady was visible from his window. He had, upon the marble floor, a sparse collection of stark, punitive wire chairs, chairs that Marinetti might have dreamed up in a futurist vision. Then we took the bus to the Termini, where we took the underground to the Cinecittà, where we took the bus to the airport, where we found that whoever stole Michele's car keys

116

had now stolen the whole car. Michele, who, like most Italians, expected nothing from the police except ignorance and brutality, cast injudicious doubt upon the fidelity of the policeman's wife. It raised the level of aggro to a pitch where the fuzz went off in rage. Then we took the bus to the Cinecittà, where we took the underground to the Termini, where we took a taxi to his apartment and made love in his unmade bed.

Afterwards we sat in the wire chairs and drank red wine till the restaurants opened. Michele was an engineer. He was also that very wicked thing, a landlord. He could just possibly have a flat for me, he said. Like this one, for example. But this one, I said, is where he happens to live. *Non è vero*? He could move out, he said, and about time too. The Communist Party posters across the street disturbed his peace of mind. Michele was that doubly wicked thing, a landlord and a middle-aged black-shirt. Jacob would, doubtless, have had a niche for him somewhere among the rungs of decadent capitalism. The apartment, I said, would be too expensive for me. I was a badly paid teacher of English. *Non importa*, Michele said. He would halve the rent. In return I could teach him English. Michele never, of course, had the slightest intention of learning English. He was merely concerned to involve me in a relationship of feudal obligation with regard to his property. The first and last lesson took place that evening in the *ristorante* in the neighbouring piazza, where Michele showed his white teeth and asked me how you said in English *stracciatella*. I told him that on the whole one didn't. One said Heinz Cream of Tomato. Twiddled egg soup, perhaps?

33

Michele never moved out. We shared the flat on and off for the next six years. He was an explosive, authoritarian mad guy. A crazy, backward-looking romantic with right-wing views and left-wing friends. A believer in the past. A past which hung like a tapestry of noble lords and dignified peasants, of which he was neither. It was the kind of society, ordered and static, that would have had a man like himself clapped in irons. The stones of the city sang to him. To stand with him on a night upon a flood-lit ruin was to espouse religion. Wrapped in a sheet first thing in the morning he looked like Hadrian. But that can be one of the delights of Rome, that in one morning's shopping you see five senators, two Michelangelos and enough quattro-cento to nourish John Millet for a decade. Everywhere you go nature is imitating art. In spite of our proximity to Leone Bernard, the contact ceased. Michele, after having been the subject of ten minutes of that lady's attention, dismissed her as 'the English whore' and that was the end of the matter. He always gave the orders.

I ought perhaps to be more decently apologetic before announcing that I co-habited with a fascist. I cannot imagine that I would ever have done so in England. In my first few years in Italy I had certainly ventured upon a greater ideological range than I would have done at home. It wasn't my country. The issues were not mine and I hadn't sorted them out. I was quite as happy bowling down the autóstrada in the back of a lorry singing the 'Bandiera Rossa' with communist university students as I was comfortable, metaphorically speaking, in Michele's fascistic armchairs. The only factor informing the varied ideologies of all the men I knew, was anti-clericalism.

118

There was not a one among them who would not pull from out of his hat—whichever one he wore—at least a dozen foul anecdotes pertaining to the Pope's prick and the Pope's nephews. The violence and cynicism of this was at first quite extraordinary to me, given that in England religion is no more to people than the daily school assembly, thick with hymns which roll God around in anthropomorphic euphemism. Religion is a fringe activity which doesn't impinge. Nobody tells you jokes about the Archbishop of Canterbury's deranged sexual habits, or brings the house down by fantasizing about male prostitutes behind the door of the lav in Lambeth Palace. Superstition is older, after all, more universal, more seductive than Christianity. Michele couldn't throw away bread, because it was unlucky. We hoarded it in mouldering sacks in the vestibule and referred to it politely as 'the bread for the ducks.'

My mother, when I told her about this years later, couldn't believe her ears.

'Fancy a man being afraid of a bit of bread,' she said. Proper men, north of Calais, are never afraid, are they? The presence of a black cat among them never causes a jam of Fiats.

Michele didn't drive a Fiat. He drove an open-topped MG. This was not because he was an Anglophile—far from it—but because he was an oddball who liked to be different. It was a piece of understated showing-off which I found most appealing. He gave me to understand, from time to time, that it was the cross he had to bear, to have an English girlfriend. A barbarous Anglo-Saxon, who had yens for Marmite and sponge pudding in tins which we bought at the English supermarket. A woman from a race only partially subdued by the Roman conquest who did her hand-washing in the bidet. He would stand over me and make me douche before he took me to bed. The English didn't bathe, he said. Coal in the bath. Knickers in the bidet. He behaved, in his small English motor car, in a most un-English manner, bawling 'cretin' and 'whore' to anyone, regardless of sex, who crossed his path. When he finally sold that little car, he did so in the dark to a gullible young English tourist and refused to give him his money back when the thing fell apart the next day, as Michele knew it would. Michele, though he looked like a Roman emperor, was in truth a Venetian. Like

119

most typical types, he was misleading. He was, as I have mentioned, married. He didn't like watching women turning into mothers, he said. Mothers were interested only in cough syrup and pasta and illness and baby-talk. Never in Dante. Not that Michele ever read Dante, which was of course much too saturated with religious implication for his taste, but he liked a proper deference for national sacred cows. One could not live with a woman who talked only about pasta and babies, he said. Michele was a man of diminished responsibility. That was part of his charm for me. I could recall a time when I had stood beside my mother in the kitchen watching her peeling potatoes and haranguing her the while on the poetry of Wilfred Owen. I remembered reciting 'Move him into the Sun' while she muttered discouragingly about the bad bits in the spuds. Admittedly, Michele was about to turn forty. He was no schoolboy. But a part of me was still in tune with his frustration. I do not myself feel comfortable with the statuesque proportions women assume as they ladle out soup, as if they are making huge complacent statements about the sanctity of their limiting female offices. A part of me, out of sexual loyalty, wanted to scream at Michele that if he had spent more time on the pasta and baby-talk himself, his wife might have had more time for Dante: that with her husband, her mother-in-law and the two children, she had not, as it were, felt the need of it. But I didn't. Michele was not much fun in disputation. He did not care for the finesse of debate. If one said, for instance, making polite conversation over the newspaper. 'It says here, Michele, that red wine is wine made from grapes with the skins left on, and white wine from grapes without,' he would give the idea no quarter. He would not offer one polite, tentative doubts. 'Red wine, red grapes,' he would say with devastating finality. 'White wine, white grapes. *Imbecille.*'

He treated his children in a way which at times made me feel ill. They had developed a reflex to duck whenever he made a flamboyant gesture in their direction. We collected them, on the occasional Sunday, from their apartment in the gentle suburb. Two little boys in ties, with their hair combed down with water. Michele would receive them, of course, in sloppy shorts and Japanese flip-flops. He would exchange brief words with his wife on the doorstep, slouching and scratching rudely at his arse. He would make no effort at all to entertain his little boys, and on one occasion gave them a football but couldn't be prevailed upon to take them out to play with it. When the younger child resorted, tentatively, to kicking it indoors, Michele hit him on the temple with the back of his hand and caused him to stumble painfully upon the Meccano which was strewn upon the floor.

'*Basta!*' he said. The Meccano had been bought by me, Papa's *Inglese* fancy woman, to give them something to do. 'Have you said thank you to Caterina for this thing she has bought for you?' he said. 'Why don't you play with it?' Play boy play, thy father plays. I found the episode an obscenity. He would make them do sums in the car. *Aritmetica* to exercise the brain. It brought me out in a sweat. He had the habit, regrettably common in Italy, of loving babies—other people's babies. He would babble like a demented crone over an infant in the piazza and volunteer to have the barman warm its bottle. He had no time for anyone between the ages of eighteen months and sixteen.

34

Michele was convinced that I was having affairs with every man I spoke to, regardless of age, nationality or presentability. The male teachers in the language school were his prime suspects and were treated in consequence to inexplicable displays of insulting, silent hostility. I learned, thanks to Michele, that there is no need ever to embrace one's man's quarrels, that there is no need ever to apologize for somebody else by virtue of one's co-habiting with that person. If I had not learned this I would have crossed swords with half the planet.

He went so far as to suspect me with women too. He came to pluck me out one evening from my friend Janice's flat, where we were sewing together using her machine. I was very fond of Janice, who taught with me. She was a plain, rather mouse-coloured woman of middle age who was cursed with a bad, acne-marked skin and was not altogether happy.

'Why,' Michele said in the car, 'why are so many English women lesbian?' I assumed this to relate to some item he had absorbed from the gutter press, because Michele had a remarkable, innocent susceptibility when it came to the gutter press.

'Name me five,' I said. Sometimes I considered myself a lot brainier than Michele.

'You spend your evening with Janice,' he said. 'How does it feel to go to bed with a woman?' I thought he was, quite simply, out of his mind.

'You should know,' I said.

'Is it because the woman is too ugly to find a man that you do this for her? Or do you want to be a man, my Caterina?' he said, pityingly. 'You are lacking in important respects.' I found this so absurd, not to say distasteful, that I could not take it seriously. I

122

thought he was soliciting for praise. Praise for his maleness. Thank you, Michele, for your male crotch which no Meccano can simulate. Remembering Jake, I said that we used spanners, Janice and I. This was a mistake, because he believed me, I think.

Once, only once, Jonathan Goldman came to see me, en route for Greece. Unhappily, I missed him. A grown-up Jonathan, who had sat resolutely in the flat for an hour, weathering Michele's hostility. And who was this Goldman? Michele demanded. This Goldman who saw fit to wait a whole hour in the flat? I got quite wild with excitement, thinking Roger had come to see me. Roger Goldman in Rome and coming to see me.

'Where?' I said, with undisguised fervour. 'Where is he? I have to see him.' Michele, delighted to be vindicated in his suspicions, presented me with a note. A note scribbled by Jonathan under Michele's searching eye. It gave an address and telephone number in Athens and went as follows:

Kath,

I came to leave you a million pounds but sadly you were out. Now you ask me how I found you in this town where all the streets appear to be called *Senso Unico*? I crossed the Tiber by the Ponte Garibaldi and asked in French for a gorgeous *Inglese*. Your man thinks I'm here to steal the silver and looks as if he means to throw me to the lions.

'Phone me in Athens sometime.

Jonathan G.

'And who is this Goldman?' Michele said again. 'This big English Jew who waits for you a whole hour in my apartment, and wants to be telephoned in Athens?'

'He's the younger son of my philosophy professor,' I said. Michele looked infinitely sceptical.

'*Credo*,' he said, nastily. It had ceased to bother me that Michele didn't believe a word that I said. It gave me the liberty to lie whenever I chose.

For all this I never felt that Michele was crushing me. He didn't attempt to warp my soul or manipulate me the way Roger had done. I make an analogy, I hope not unforgivably, with *The Taming of the Shrew*. It has always seemed to me about that play that it is not the terrible, delightful Petruchio (unscrupulous chancer that he is) who warps and crushes the girl, but the dreadful combination of that goody-goody sister, who warps her with feminine wiles, and that hidebound, favouritizing father, who tells her to go ply her needle and grovel for a husband. They are the ones who knock her about. After them, life with Petruchio is a day out from a sadistic nunnery. He and she are equal in high spirits. And how does he tame her? He makes her kiss him in the street. He makes her enact the hilarious burlesque of embracing a strange old man and calling him a sweet young virgin. Tame girls don't kiss in public and embrace strange men. He gives her scope for a comic talent, he is no more a respecter of orthodox behaviour than she is. At the end of the play she is not tame, she is the wench with the wit to win her old man's bet for him. They leave Padua a few hundred crowns richer, thanks to her. I do not wish to whitewash the issues. The play is about wife-beating. The colour it comes only half offends me. Michele played Petruchio-style mating-games with me all the time. It only half offended me. The rest was terrific fun.

There was the time he drove in the wrong direction to a lunch date. I told him. I said the Thingummies didn't live there any more. Michele, inevitably, approached the challenge in the spirit of who is driving, him or me? I answered provokingly, in English, because Michele, thanks to me, had by then the crudest rudiments of that tongue.

'Michele', I said between my teeth, 'you make meestake. *Beeg* meestake.'

'No meestake,' he said. 'Caterina, you meestake.'

'I say you meestake, you big slob,' I said.

'*Allora*. Meestake, eh?' he said, challengingly. He stopped the car without warning, in the middle of the road. Around us a crescendo of blasting horns. 'Meestake?' he said.

'Yes,' I said. He got out of the car and sauntered to the sidewalk, where he made as if to enter a pizza shop. I couldn't drive the thing to the side of the road, so I got out and joined him on the sidewalk where we fell laughing with delight into each other's arms.

'*Andiamo*,' he said. We jumped back into the vehicle and drove like hell, before the *carabinieri* descended upon us.

'Meestake?' he said.

We never got to our lunch party because the sex was better at home.

35

The year I turned thirty I got pregnant. I forgot to take a contraceptive pill. We are all of us so well acquainted with this kind of error in the post-Freudian era that I might as well confess to it immediately and save myself the trouble of constructing my defence. I am indeed an only child who never had anything to cuddle. I had a cat, I say, feebly. I even accept that much of the sleeping around I did, when it wasn't directly to spite Roger Goldman, had to do with the urge to nurture and be nurtured and not all that much to do with the pleasure I got from the act. It was not until I met Michele that I discovered sex as something seriously worth staying at home for. It took me over half a decade to discover what Jane Goldman had obviously found out in one night. That, to quote her, sex was 'unexpectedly jolly.' Jonathan Goldman once told me a terrible schoolboy joke about the rabbi and the priest in the train compartment exchanging confidences. They both confess to having broken the taboos of their religion. The rabbi has eaten pork. The priest has had sex with a woman. The punch line is perfectly obvious, and thanks to Michele I discovered, as the rabbi observes, that sex is better than pork. This discovery was so delightful to me that we were almost never out of bed.

But I digress. I got pregnant. I had no hope of hiding the fact since Michele was wont to watch my ovulation like a hawk. I told him as soon as I suspected it. Michele had a habit of downing nasty egg nog stuff for breakfast in the belief that this was beneficial to his health. It was in effect raw *zabaglione*. He choked on it. Having recovered, he bawled wonderfully colourful oaths at me. He had a way of rolling composite insults which involved casting doubt on the virtue, not only of one's female relations but upon the holy Mother of God and the Pope's great-grandmother. In short, he was not pleased. He added his only English insult to the rest and called me a 'beetch'. I began to giggle nervously when he said 'beetch,' because it made me think of the seaside. Then I hopped it before he resorted to physical violence. He was very nice to me when I came home that evening, which I ought to have known was suspect. He embraced me very sweetly and kissed my hair.

'*Come stai?*' he said solicitously. I said I was, frankly, bloody scared of him, that's how I was. He made some sweet gentle love to me, after which he went so far as to quote me some old Tuscan poetry and to tell me I was the most pure and beautiful of women. He had a present for me, he said. He got up and brought it to me in an enormous bag from the Via Lombardia. Jesus. It was a mink coat. There was something inept in this, I couldn't help thinking. I couldn't say to him that nothing could be calculated to make one feel less pure and more like the pro-verbial kept woman, more like the landlord's moll. The coat was, of course, a bribe. I said thank you very much. Michele had a plan. We would take a week off from work, he said, and go to London, where we would have the foetus aborted in a good private clinic. These things were easy in London, not so? Then I would show him London. Nice for me, eh? To see London again. And to show it to him, as he had shown me Venice. He got quite spritely on the idea. He could be as phoney as plastic daffodils at times. London was beautiful, was it not? he said. What he knew about London was Buckingham Palazzo and the Horse Guards. He combined this with his own belief that the women in the British royal family rode horses all the time to give themselves orgasms. (Their blokes couldn't, of course, being without chins and other attributes. Unlike himself. Michele, with his imperial jaw and his well-bedded English girlfriend.)

I took a shower. When I came out I told him, in trepidation, what I wanted. I said that I wanted him to take the coat back to the shop and to give me the money, and that I would use it towards paying for my antenatal care. The effect was astonishing.

'Come with me,' he said. He took me in one hand and the

127

coat in the other. We went down the street and across the square. By the time we reached the black-market cigarette lady he was holding my arm behind my back like the bouncer at a Working Men's Club. He gave me the coat.

'Give the coat to the *signora*,' he said.

'You're crazy.'

'Give the coat to her.'

'*Signora*,' I said, 'my boyfriend wants you to have this coat.' In English I said, 'Michele, will you stop breaking my arm, you big fucking yobbo?'

'Tell her your boyfriend especially wants her to have it,' he said.

'Tell her yourself,' I said. 'I'm not going to insult an old woman. Do it yourself, you crude bastard.' Michele performed on my arm what we used to call 'Barley Sugars' in our infancy. A subtle and agonizing twist.

'*Signora*, my boyfriend especially wants you to have it,' I said, like a parrot.

'*Grazie, signore*,' she said, without emotion. Not to me. To Michele. He was the one dispensing the goodies. She couldn't miss the coercion. Then he marched me home, delighting the neighbours. Wife-clobbering, to catch the eye of the groundlings.

I watched him pack a few things. He packed them into Roger's hold-all. I saw him take a good look at the label. It still said R.J.GOLDMAN. He stuffed a few of his clothes into the bag and opened the zip pocket to throw in his shaving stuff. Then he pulled out a letter, which must have hibernated in the bag those ten years or more, and gave it to me.

'Goldman,' he said, reading the envelope. '*Ciao*, Caterina. Now you may go to Athens and sleep with your English Jew.'

'Michele,' I said as he got to the door, 'I only once before went to bed with a man who smoked French cigarettes, like you. But he was a homosexual.' Michele didn't blow a fuse, as I thought he might. Perhaps I had hoped to provoke a cathartic explosion and have him make it up to me. Perhaps I was crazy enough to imagine it was worth it to me to spend the next ten years watching Michele clip my child over the head with the back of his hand, shouting '*Basta!*' and making it do sums over breakfast.

Perhaps I was simply proving to myself that I had claws to show. That nobody was going to walk out of my life into a sunset of limestones no more and do so with impunity. He approached me, scrutinizing my face wistfully and tenderly with his marvellous brown eyes, and held my chin for a moment between his thumb and forefinger.

'*Ciao, amica,*' he said.

Jonathan's letter had evidently been written to Roger twelve years before in Kenya.

Rogsie,

Don't fret about your fiddle. Try a comb on paper. Didn't Mozart stoop to a glass harmonica? Here's to make you homesick. Mother has bought Rosie a 'cello. She won't get her knees around the bloody thing and is throwing herself all over the floor in hysterics. Annie has got the mumps, which makes you impotent if you catch it. Ma has spent the morning wringing her hands over the prospect of Jake's balls and mine placed in jeopardy. That's when she isn't using them to pull out her tits and feed Sylvia, who is a right tit-freak if ever there was one. The bloody bathroom smells of curdled baby shit and chlorine bleach. The headmaster refused to submit my poem because 'tis, as I told you, about lust. Speaking of lust, we have the delectable Katherine in the house again, writing her essays in beautiful italic script and scivvying for Jane. Jesus, I'd pawn the Holy Grail for an hour up that woman's skirt, wouldn't you? It's time we had some women, Rogsie. How many Green Shield stamps does it take to hire them? And can one be sure that they aren't traffic wardens in disguise?

If we do not meet again in this life, dearest Brother, I trust we will meet in the next.

Love and kisses

Jont.

Since I was already feeling vulnerable, the letter made me cry a little for my lost youth. Michele did not evict me and neither did he leave me high and dry. He fetched his chattels from the apartment when I wasn't there, and deposited one million lire

129

in my bank account. I do not think that any of it was any easier for him than it was for me. Once or twice I saw him afterwards, when I was pregnant and bulging, in the company of a very small, delicate Libyan girl who walked like a ballet dancer. Out of respect for him, I think, I kept out of his way.

36

I loved being pregnant. I felt very well. During the first few months I enjoyed carrying the fact around in secret. I missed Michele something chronic. I was not miserable, as I had been when Roger left me. My own violent frustration at his absence even amused me at times. I lived up to the most compromising of male chauvinist stereotypes—I missed him in bed. I was the lady who needed servicing. I didn't want anybody, mind, I wanted him. But I survived. Janice was absolutely irreplaceable to me. She threw herself with unconcealed enthusiasm into the project of preparing for the baby. She uncovered an entire network of people with cots to dispose of and nappies to hand on. She acquired squeaky pink elephants and books on how to handle childbirth, brought out in English by the National Childbirth Trust. Together we went to the flea market and found an old pram. We made fitted cot sheets in apple green and navy, and knitted woolly caps and arty baby bags. I made a quilted patchwork lining in a Moses basket, which was a thing of great beauty. As I began to bulge conspicuously I provided entertainment for some of my neighbours, for whom I had gratifyingly changed from being the glamorous mistress of the *signore* of means to being the loose foreigner with a bun in the oven. I didn't mind too much. I even, after some audible speculation about my condition, brazenly told a group of housewives on one occasion that we had pulled it off on the autostrada doing 90 kilometres an hour.

Near where I lived was the beautiful old church of Santa Cecilia. Often, as I passed it, I thought briefly of Roger who, being a music wallah, had always made a thing of St Cecilia's Day. On this particular St Cecilia's Day, I was sitting wrapped in a loose coat in the Piazza di Santa Cecilia listening to the music emanating from within and knitting baby clothes. I was two months pregnant and without external evidence of the fact, but an old man stopped before me, saw what I was knitting and said, babbling absurdly, 'Knitting on the day of St Cecilia! Your child will have bad luck.' He tottered off like the bad fairy, the old fool. People don't leave you alone in Italy. There is no privacy.

I was sitting in the cinema with Janice next April when I began to give forth copious gouts of blood. This was not at all like the blueprint. Before I knew it I was on a mobile hospital bed being strapped up to machines and pumped with drugs. I thought, rather wistfully, as somebody shoved a suppository up my anus, of Jane Goldman puking into her antique jug and subsequently giving birth in her pretty brass bed with Jacob to hold her legs while she pushed the baby out. I wondered, as I tried to breathe around contractions, why I had a continuous, screaming ache in the back. I was all politeness and control, which seemed to amuse my attendant doctor. All around me were the sounds of Roman women enacting the vocal melodrama for which they had been reared.

'Come look at this, Claudio,' he said at one point, calling a passing colleague into the room and indicating me on the bed. 'Good, eh? It's another race, no?'

Nothing I had read, useful as it was, had prepared me for the degree or duration of pain. There was some mistake about the state of my cervical dilation. The baby came too early and then could not be delivered without forceps. There followed a great deal of injecting and hacking at my pelvic floor. The baby was female and instantly removed, having been diagnosed as suffering from mild inflammation of the lung, which required intensive care. We stayed in the hospital for over two weeks, where my internal stitches went septic and where I was told I would subsequently need some repair work on my cervix. I was provided with an expensive space-age machine which expressed my breast milk for the baby. Finally I went home in a taxi with my lovely baby in the Moses basket. It was the happiest day of my life. She had been so initiated into the hospital routine that she cried for food exactly every four hours. I could have set my watch by it. I had lovely enlarged boobs which leaked milk every time she cried. The pull of the toothless infant mouth on one's nipple is highly erotic, I discovered. It induces ecstasy. The little hand on one's breast and the tiny piggy gruntings are a delight. When she was a month old I wheeled her out in her flea-market pram, to the horror of the populace who considered her pram grievously lacking in flounces because most Italian prams are a jungle of festoons and lace. She looked hilariously like Michele and not at all like me. I called her Simonetta, after Botticelli's lady with whom he had been in love. When she was five weeks old she slept through the night. I was so proud of her, when I woke at six, aching with milk, to find that it was morning that I went to smother her with praise. The baby was dead.

Janice and the doctor were very nice. They came immediately. The doctor was at pains to emphasize that it was not my fault. That it happened sometimes and they didn't know why. He stayed for quite a while and Janice stayed all day. I became hysterical and said I wanted to bury her under the geraniums on the roof outside my bathroom. That the body was mine and oughtn't to be removed. I found to my cost, over the next few days, that to bury the bastard child of a foreigner is no easy matter and requires a lot of standing in queues. The bureaucracy, which had always seemed baroque, had become macabre. After that I went to pieces. I didn't know what to do. I tried 'phoning Jonathan in Athens, but got nobody on the line who knew what I was talking about. In that way in which, inevitably, one is attentive to people who are geographically close and inattentive to the remote, I had years before stopped communicating with Jane Goldman. I now remembered Jacob saying to me that it was an easy thing to pick up the 'phone and reverse the charge. It was not an easy thing at all. The telephone exchange, after repeated enquiries, insisted that the Goldmans' telephone number did not exist.

I returned to the hospital after the baby died to have my cervix patched up. Janice must have told Michele because he came white-faced to see me the day before I was to leave. I say with gratitude for his sensitivity on this occasion that he did not bring me presents, buy only himself. It hurt unbearably to have him there.

'*Santo Cielo*,' he said. 'These things that have happened to you.' He sat beside the bed, having kissed my cheek, and he took my hand. His presence caused me an uncontrolled and painful flood of tears which ran coldly into my neck and my hair.

'The baby was a girl,' I said. 'She was so lovely, Michele. I've never loved anything so much in my whole life. Never. Not even you.' I wept into my neck. 'She was my friend,' I said. He was quite evidently affected by the sight of my grief and his involvement in it.

'Come back to me,' he said, 'dearest Caterina. I will make you another baby.' He was crying too, though not so copiously. A rather tactless nurse that morning had told me I would probably never have another baby.

'I want that baby,' I said, 'not any other.'

'I want to be good to you,' he said. 'Please. Come back to me.' I loved him all the more for his obtuse romanticism, for he touched in me that yearning for the once-upon-a-time when hearts were brave and arms were strong.

'I never left you, remember?' I said. I even smiled at him a bit. 'You always were good to me. Thanks for the money,' I said. 'Is it dreadful for me to say that it's not actually enough? Janice gave me all the money she had, but I want to pay her back.' He wrote me a cheque on the spot to give her, and said he'd see to the rest. I felt extremely uncomfortable. He was well off but he wasn't a millionaire, and the baby had been my indulgence.

'*Stupida*,' he said. It cheered me up no end. 'Is it possible that I can love you so much?'

'You can't come back to me because you've got another woman,' I said. Michele shrugged indifferently. What is a woman, after all, if not expendable in the face of another one you like better?

'I've seen her,' I said, trying to smile. 'You'd better not try any rough stuff on her or you'll break her in half. Have you given away any fur coats lately?' Michele smiled.

'*Allora*,' he said, 'I come for you tomorrow. We learn by making mistakes.'

134

A meestake, Michele? You admit to a meestake?

'I'm going to England tomorrow,' I said, rejecting him horribly. 'My mother is coming for me. Goodbye, Michele. Get that girl of yours sterilized.' Though I turned my back on him, Michele wouldn't leave until the nurse threw him out.

Janice had telephoned my mother on the day I went into hospital. She got on an aeroplane as soon as she could and came to take me home. She was very decent to me and didn't moralize. I knew that in her eyes, I had gone on a predictable and unnecessary downward slope, from homosexuals and Jews to married foreigners. I sat about in her house, noticing with relief that the ducks had moved with her to Dorset, and reading back numbers of the *Reader's Digest*. They all left me feeling that if cancer didn't get me then germ warfare would. I couldn't revert with any ease to the role of dependent daughter and seeing Michele again had not been especially good for my peace of mind. I tried repeatedly to write letters to him. I felt I owed it to his concern to tell him where and how I was, but the letters collapsed, always, into tear-stained wallowing. I noticed that my mother on one occasion found it embarrassing to answer a neighbour's question about what my baby's name had been. I called her Simonetta Janice out of recognition for Janice's kindnesses to me.

'For me she will always be Janice,' my mother said in reply.

Because I did not sleep very well, the GP gave me sleeping tablets and also anti-depressants. Then after a couple of weeks he sent me to the outpatients' clinic of a local mental hospital to get me through the day, which I was finding not impossible but not easy either. It could be that this was a mistake. My mother drove me there in the morning and back again in the evening. I could see that she was terribly worried about me. It made me humble and apologetic. I began to do terrific post mortems on my past. Roger kept coming back to me. I cried all over the shrink one day, in a fit of regression, that if Roger Goldman had only gone on loving me my life would have been different and better. They put an awful lot of junk on you when you're down, do psychiatrists, I discovered. They have enormous sway with you, not only by virtue of their expertise but because when

135

your self-esteem is low you gratefully receive any analysis of yourself, no matter how unfavourable. Every two days I was interviewed by the psych allotted to me, who seemed to have had all the humanity trained out of him. He kept his distance in a most demoralizing way, as if he felt familiarity with me would give me a hold on him. Heaven forbid, I might ring him up at home or greet him in the supermarket. Loonies bearing down upon him during weekend outings with the wife and kids. He told me, to my horror, that I was, he thought, incapable of love. Instead of throwing my coffee in his face, I took it to heart. Perhaps it wasn't love that made me sleep in Michele's night-shirt when he had stayed overnight in Florence, or cry into the telephone at four in the morning when Roger left me. And the baby? Perhaps that wasn't love either.

'All your relationships have been constructed in defiance of your upbringing,' he said, as though this necessarily made them invalid. What was normal was not to defy one's upbring-ing. It was to enact the whole bloody roadshow as scripted by one's aunts and grandmothers. When I wasn't with the psych I was with the occupational therapist, together with half a dozen very sad middle-aged housewives and three depressed adolescent girls. There was one man among us, unattached and silent. We wove wicker edgings around rather tasteless tea trays displaying chocolate-box pictures of poodles and knitted up string into dishclothes. After lunch we slopped our uneaten marrowfat peas and Miracle Whip into the pig bins. If Michele could have seen the hospital food he would have sworn, by the Pope's foreskin, that the English were more uncivilized even than he had hitherto conceived.

37

I spent my thirty-first birthday listening to the radio news in the bin. I was knitting up the dishcloth string at the time and beginning to feel a little better. A little less desolate. The radio announcer addressed an eccentric remark to me.

'Now we have a humanist's despair before the News,' he said.

'Did you hear what he said?' I said.

'A few minutes to spare before the News?' said the occupational therapist. The radio announcer had obviously said it only to me. There is a comfort to be got out of feeling that you are completely crazy. You feel that you have hit rock bottom and you have no fear that you are going to fall. You can only rise. Or maybe just stay there taking in the view. *Down and Arise I Never Shall.* Also, you can make a fuss. I am no good at making a fuss, as I have said. But when you're crazy it's legitimate. That's what loonies do, isn't it? Fuss. That morning I began to split hairs over the dishcloth string instead of knitting it up like a good girl. At first I said that if she gave me a safety-pin I'd do her a dishcloth with a cable-stitched border. When I got no response to this, I unravelled the thing in an exhibitionist manner and announced that I was bloody well going to knit hats with the string instead, and sell them in the King's Road.

'Right on,' said the occupational therapist.

'Aren't the mentally ill supposed to have any taste?' I said. 'Why wicker edges around these simpering dogs? Couldn't it at least be Gainsborough?' I gestured towards the trays. 'What about us loonies with arty pretensions?' I said. 'And aren't most people here in the first place because of all this trays and dishcloth stuff? Else why are we all women? The kitchen sink and the idea of service? If you want to make us better, put us in a

137

charabanc and take us to the theatre.' I remember that one of the depressed housewives muttered that I was a hussy, but that the occupational therapist broke into a generous smile.

'Knit anything you like,' she said. 'I don't somehow think that you need me any more.'

That afternoon I saw the psych. He observed, as a result of my unwonted jauntiness, that I appeared to waver dramatically between arrogance and humility. As if I couldn't have told him that ten years before.

'My IQ is 98,' I said, to be cheeky. 'I tested it with that Eysenck paperback when I was sixteen.' This is true. I did. My score was 98. The psych laughed.

'Your IQ is more in the region of a hundred and forty,' he said. Jesus Christ, I thought. Here's a man of science who thinks I'm brainy, the bloody fool. I had read in the local paper a week before that my very same psych had given a paper to a conference on whether or not Queen Boadicea had been a transvestite. The sure mark of a fool.

'I do not think that I need to see you again,' he said. I shook his hand.

> Lord dismiss us with thy Blessing
> Those who here will meet no more.

My mother's husband suggested that evening, as a birthday treat for me, that we dine out. We had a lovely British gorge upon gammon and tinned pineapple in the Berni Inn, with Irish coffee for afters. It was a Saturday night. I remembered that R. J. Goldman had always declined to go out with me on a Saturday night, because that was the night when the lower orders had time off to polish their fingernails and hit the town, which was, in consequence, too crowded for him. My mother told me over the coffee that a small insurance policy which my father had taken out for me had just matured.

'He made it thirty-one, because he naturally assumed that you would be settled with a family by thirty,' she said, 'and growing children are a great expense.' One has to allow one's mother the odd aggressive aside. An unattached, childless out-patient is no sort of daughter to have. The policy was worth three hundred pounds, but it made me feel like an heiress. I had been going about with permed, greasy hair and in shapeless jerseys, but it came to me then that I had the inclination to go and blow the whole lot on clothes.

I woke from a very funny dream that week. Jacob Goldman had written me a reference for a job as nanny in the Gulf States. I saw the headed college notepaper and the Germanic handwriting, clear as day. He had written as follows:

Katherine Browne is an admirable young woman with a small inherited income and a small inherited brain.

The swine, I thought. Damn him! Hadn't the psych said that my IQ was around 140? I woke feeling that I had to get him on the 'phone. The dream was so much with me that I told my mother about it at breakfast, with a certain righteous conviction.

'But he didn't say it,' she said, 'you dreamed it.'

'I don't care,' I said. 'It's none of his business whether he said it or not. I'm going to get him on the 'phone.'

'I think that's a good idea,' she said.

I got no proper tone from the Goldmans' number in Sussex. The directory enquiries confirmed for me again that the number didn't exist. I railed at my mother.

'Perhaps they've moved,' she said. Perhaps they've moved! Foolish woman. The Goldmans don't move. I move. They stay there in Sussex providing me with a rock upon which to prop my insecurities.

'Why should they move?' I said. My mother shrugged.

'I moved,' she said. 'Sometimes people do.' Well, so she did. She, a creature of fixed habits, who could only wash dishes from left to right. But where would they go? Then I remembered the Northern Line and the Everyman Theatre.

'Hampstead,' I said. 'Mark my words. They've moved to Hampstead.' The directory enquiries told me that the number of subscribers residing in NW3 under the name of Goldman ran into pages. Would do.

'Professor,' I said. 'Could you try Professor?' There were two Professors Goldman J in NW3, but one was Joel and the other was Julian.

'Try Dr,' I said.

'There are hundreds of them,' said the lady at the switch-board. She read me out, at my request, the numbers of the first half dozen. I took them down. They were all very kind and took time off from fixing bones and teeth to answer the telephone. I gave up in despair. I found my mother in her kitchen and stormed at her.

'The place is full of them,' I said, angrily. 'The whole of Hampstead is full of bloody Jews.'

'Well,' my mother said, venturing to tread on marshy ground because I had opened the gate, 'frankly, nobody else can afford to live there these days.' I got hysterical almost with laughter and embraced her as I hadn't done in years. A great surge of warmth as we were united, uncompromisingly, by a burst of gut anti-Semitism.

'Why don't you try the University?' my mother said. This was an excellent idea, which I had been too agitated to hit upon. I tried the department.

Jacob's secretary wouldn't give me the telephone number. I almost screamed at her.

'He's left emphatic instructions with me that he is not to be telephoned at home,' she said.

'I'm an old friend,' I said. 'I haven't seen him for ten years.' She told me to try the next morning, when he would be in the building.

'I'm sorry,' she said.

'Well, put me onto Dr Hunt,' I said. He was the Symbolic Logic man.

'Who?' she said. They had all, no doubt, moved on to chairs in Leicester, or fellowships abroad. Departed and left no addresses.

'Please give me the number,' I said. 'I promise you he won't mind.'

'Professor Goldman said nobody,' she said, getting heated. 'Not the Queen of Sheba offering her body.' Wouldn't he? I put the 'phone down in rage. Then I telephoned Roger's grand-parents' house in Oxford. The number had come back to me, all at once, over the decade. Roger's grandfather was, in times past, wont to pick up the 'phone, which stood on his desk, and bark 'Fitz-Whatsit' into one's ear, but on this occasion a woman answered. A woman with a rather high, rather girlish voice.

'Sally Goldman here,' she said. Godalmighty, I thought, there's another one of them. Seven children. What must John Millet be saying about it?

'Excuse me,' I said, 'I wonder if you can help me. Are you connected with Jane Goldman at all, who used to live in Sussex?

'I'm her daughter-in-law,' said the voice. 'I'm Roger's wife. To whom am I speaking?' For a moment I think I couldn't speak.

'My name is Katherine Browne,' I said, feeling like someone come back from the dead. 'It's possible that you've heard of me. I'm a friend of Roger's parents. I'm trying to trace them.'

'I know exactly,' she said. 'We even have a photograph of you somewhere. Jane and Jacob would love to see you, I know. You must 'phone them at once.' She gave me the number.

'May I take your number?' she said. I gave her my mother's telephone number. She couldn't have been nicer.

'They're in Hampstead,' she said.

Bullseye.

Then it was no time at all before I had Jacob on the line, blasting my eardrum with his glottal stops.

'Katherine?' he said. '*Katherine?* Where the hell are you?'

'In Dorset,' I said. 'Why aren't you in the telephone book, Jake?'

'I'm ex-directory,' he said. 'Did you have any trouble finding me?'

'I've had a nervous breakdown over it,' I said, which was not altogether untrue. Jacob laughed.

'Sorry, my love,' he said. 'The idea is that I stay home some days and write without getting interrupted, but my secretary gives my number to every Tom, Dick and Harry who sees fit to ask her for it, while nice people like you are put to all this trouble.'

'She didn't give it to me,' I said. 'I couldn't wring it out of her.' There was a sober pause.

'Blame me,' he said contritely. 'I told her just yesterday that I'd fire her if she gave it to anybody. Anybody.'

'Including the Queen of Sheba flogging her body,' I said. Jacob laughed again.

'That's right,' he said. 'Why can these wretched women not use a little judgement?' Something in my early childhood must be answerable for the fact that I find certain forms of male chauvinist piggery such a turn-on.

'It could be that they're traumatized by overbearing employers,' I said.

'When are you coming to see me?' he said. 'Today? Tomorrow? Why have we not heard from you since God knows when?' I arranged that I would catch the train the next day, be in Hampstead by lunchtime, and stay over for a while. Left at the Everyman, left and left again. I was also longing to see North London.

38

It is very soon apparent to me that the Goldmans have experienced a delightful financial step up, not to say a change in lifestyle. Their charming new maisonette in Hampstead, tall and thin, built into existing house backs like a mews, has climbing geraniums at the cobbled front doorstep and a speaky thing, which you talk into before the door unlocks. The ground floor is all garage and laundry. Above, from whence Jacob comes to greet me, is a long narrow living room, lined with two large cushioned sofas fitted into piped chintzy covers. Plants hang and trail from a wall of glass which overlooks the back gardens of substantial Victorian town houses, rich in Galt climbing-frames and pretty garden furniture. Beyond that is Hampstead Heath. The floor on which Jacob stands is sanded pale and gleaming. Somebody has dry-cleaned the Persian rugs which Rosie once dragged through the mud and which now lie on the floor. But Jacob, who greets me with open arms, is the greatest surprise of all. His blackhorsehair eyebrows and wiry hair have turned an elegant silver white. My first response is to think that he is got up for a play.

'God, Jacob,' I say, 'you look amazing.' We embrace emotionally.

'Let me get a look at you,' he says, after a moment, and holds me out at arm's length. 'You look the same,' he says.

'I don't,' I say.

'Very well, you don't,' he says. 'You look better. You were red eyed and pimpled when you left. Now you are a woman of the world.' I laugh.

'And you, Jacob? How are you? How do you manage to

143

intimidate your students these days, without your ferocious eyebrows?'

'I retire in five years,' Jacob says. 'I'll be an Old Age Pensioner. An "OAP," Katherine, as the sign says outside the cinema—"Children and OAPs half price." It happens to us all. Even you, sweetheart.'

'I hope I'll be an OAP with such lovely white hair,' I say. 'And how is Jane? Where is Jane?'

'Jane is in hospital, as a matter of fact,' he says, 'recovering from a hysterectomy. A small growth. Nothing to worry about. She's better. A week ago she looked like a corpse hanging on a glucose drip, but now I can see that she looks better every day. You'll stay, won't you, and come with me to visit her? She'll be more than delighted to see you again. She was always very partial to you, Katherine. There's not many people get the seal of approval from my wife, as you may remember. You have to talk into my left ear, Kath. I've had some trouble with the other one.'

'It's such a pleasure to talk to you, Jake,' I say, swapping ears. 'Either ear is a great treat for me. Is she really all right?'

'Fine,' Jacob says. 'She's fine. My poor old mother died, you know. Just a month or so ago. Upset us both a bit. She was uphill work for Jane mind, so perhaps it's for the best. Her eyesight was gone, you see. There's not much left when you can't watch the telly any more.'

'No,' I say. 'I'm sorry, Jacob.'

'Coffee,' he says briskly. The kitchen shares the first floor with the living room. An open slatted staircase runs through the middle of the house to the floor above.

'Golly, Jacob,' I say. 'What a four-star, Double O Seven kitchen you have. This is not the Goldman kitchen as I remember it.' Jacob's kitchen has double sinks and a waste grinder into which he pitches the coffee grounds. He has a dishwasher under the workboard and an extractor fan above it. Some Edward Lear watercolours which used to hang awry on the stairs have been beautifully mounted and hang against a wall of brown cork wallpaper. There is a very nice Brecht poster from the German Democratic Republic framed in alumi-

144

nium over the breakfast table. The Windsor chairs have been bleached and waxed.

'Why is it all so clean?' I say. 'This is very bad for my nostalgia. I always thought dirt was a principle.' Jacob laughs a little and shrugs.

'Dirt is in a sense a principle, isn't it?' he says. 'One doesn't want to have one's wife on her knees chasing dirt. One wants to put the needs of one's children before the needs of one's possessions. One doesn't want to bow down to wood and stone, you know, like the heathen in his blindness. My children are grown up. You want me to tread fish fingers underfoot forever just to please you, Katherine?' I like him as much as I ever did. Having him in a new setting makes no difference at all. It only lends novelty.

'Do you miss your house in Sussex?' I say, casting off with ease, myself, that great symbol of hard-won domestic security. What is it but wood and stone?

'No,' he says with certainty. 'That was always my concession to Jane. Now this is her concession to me.' He is five minutes' walk from the Hampstead Everyman, but the neighbourhood is too salubrious for Coke tins in gutters and very nice too.

'Doesn't Jane miss the garden?' I say. He shrugs it off.

'Who needs to garden that much?' he says. 'It was a device she had for escaping the children. That's my belief. A way of demonstrating to them that she was busy. She gardens a bit on the roof and all over the window-sills, as you see. You can't close the blinds without knocking the bloody things down, but that's Hampstead for you, isn't it? The gardens are all full of furniture and the houses full of plants. She's playing the piano most of the time these days, before the arthritic joints get her. And learning German. We were in the GDR together last year. It bothered her not talking to people. So that's what she's doing. She's thriving, is Jane. No need to bother your head about her. I recommend it to you, Katherine. The post-menopausal phase. She enjoys it. So do I. For five years now I've been screwing her without making her pregnant.' It makes me smile, thinking how Jacob always felt impelled to put his house guests in the picture with regard to his sexual habits. I can't resist the temptation.

'You mean old guys like you can still do it?' I say.

'We do our best,' he says. 'I shouldn't be depressing you. I expect you are in the middle of all that breeding. How many babies have you got, my child? And where are they? Why have you not brought some fat little Italian babies with you for me to show my wife?'

'Haven't got any,' I say.

'And how is that?' he says. The nosey bastard.

'Because I'm a socio-gynaecological disaster, Jake,' I say, trying to be flip. 'I had one baby that died and a man that upped and left. The last of many. I'm also a little buggered up around the cervix. I'll tell you about it in detail if you like because I know how you like private parts, but I'm warning you I'm very likely to cry.'

Jacob gives me my coffee in silence and we take it through to the living room and drink it on one of the sofas.

'Well, well,' he says. 'Poor Katherine. When?'

'Eleven weeks,' I say. 'That's when the baby died. The man left when I got pregnant. She was five weeks old, the baby.'

'Jesus, child,' he says, 'eleven weeks? That's yesterday. Well, cry. You have things to cry about.' I get by with a quick controlling sniff, a swallow and a blink, wondering why the shrink never had the humanity to say that to me. That I had things to cry about.

'You've covered the Lady Gregory chair,' I say. 'The Celtic Twilight chair. I like to do that kind of embroidery.'

'*Ach*, yes,' Jacob says carelessly. 'Jane found a humble young woman who undertakes these things.'

'Like Little Dorrit,' I say. Jacob smiles at me.

'What a girl you always were for the apt literary reference,' he says. 'I ought really to have turned you over to the Little Dorrit crowd when you came to me all those years ago. I suspect you never had much enthusiasm for abstract reasoning.'

'It's a showy habit I've got,' I say. 'To be always quoting poetry and stuff. Some of us use our brains, and some of us use our memories.'

'Not at all,' he says, 'it's charming. You were always charming. Remember that day you came to see me? Apple for teacher. Sixpence for Oxfam. "Of course there's sex in *Emma*." I telephoned Jane as soon as you left, you know, and told her about you. It was right up her street. "Have her," Jane said. "Grab her before some place like Girton gets her." '

'Don't embarrass me, Jacob,' I say.

'Best legs I interviewed that year,' he says. 'It *was* your legs I was interviewing, wasn't it? Do you remember that remarkable purple mini-dress? Oh Katherine, child, a dead baby. For God's sake, what happened?'

'Don't know,' I say. 'I thought she was having her first night sleeping through. I went to congratulate her.' I stuff the corner of one of Jacob's sofa cushions into my mouth to muffle my oncoming choking gasp. 'Oh Jesus God, Jacob. It was so bloody awful.' Jacob has an arm around my shoulders for a good while, saying nothing.

'It gets better, you know, as time piles up,' he says eventually. 'Last year, in Berlin, I walked the streets. No trouble. Even the one I'd lived in.' It is the first time he has ever made a reference to that particular loss to me.

'You'll be surprised,' he says. 'One day some kind and sensible man will come along and give you another baby.' I don't like to tell him that I can probably not have another child.

'Are you here to stay,' he says, 'or just visiting?'

'I don't know,' I say.

'Stay,' he says. 'Get yourself a rest. Get a nice job somewhere. East Finchley, that's the place to be. Some nice place like that.'

'You mean, and find a nice English husband?' I say. Jacob laughs, admitting to it.

'Why not?' he says. 'A nice reliable English husband.'

'You're the only one of those that I know,' I say, 'and you're a foreigner. I turned thirty-one last week, Jacob. I'm too old.'

'Happy birthday,' he says. 'Yes, I can see you're getting wrinkles, but they're very nice wrinkles. What is life but a progression from pimples to wrinkles, but for the getting of wisdom?'

Jacob's books line the walls from floor to ceiling. In superior panel-backed shelving it is all there, as of yore, plus additions. The long runs of academic journals, the *New Left Review*, the prison notebooks of Antonio Gramsci, Isaac Deutscher on Trotsky. All the German heavy stuff, the metaphysics and lots

147

of lovely poetry. I think of Jacob as a great reader of poetry, having seen him once hurl his Heinrich Heine deftly across the room at Rosie's head when she knocked over his coffee with an ill-timed cartwheel; having seen him in a deckchair of a Sunday, reading *Paradise Lost* and call it 'relaxing'.

'Did Jane find a humble young woman to make your bookshelves?' I say.

'A man,' Jacob says. 'Rosie's boyfriend. One of Rosie's many boyfriends. Rosie's men are all either carpenters, brickies, plumbers or bloody floor-layer's apprentices. She has a strong proletarian bias in her choice of men. She also prefers them to be black. I don't know what's the matter with that girl. She's prettier than is good for her. Too many options, I think. Is that your trouble too, perhaps?' Of Jacob's children, Rosie and Roger were always the only really pretty ones. It amuses me to sit opposite Jacob's rows of revolutionary books and listen to him grumbling about his daughter's working-class leanings.

'And Annie and Sylvia?' I say. 'What's with them? Do they like brickies, too?'

'Annie is a sensible young woman,' he says. 'Annie is a great comfort to my old age. Sylvia, of course, is a child. Annie sculpts at the art college in Hornsey. She lives with a collection of nice youngsters in a house with hazardous floorboards. They work very hard. They eat a lot of brown lentils. They make a lot of love. She's a splendid girl, my Annie. Big. Not one to accost in a dark alley. She keeps all these damned chisels in the bib pockets of her overalls.' He gestures in the region of his chest. 'She's taken herself to the Women's Self-Defence class, has Annie. She knows how to kick a man in the face.' He points proudly to an object on the floor. 'That's a thing of Annie's,' he says. A life-size clay head, it is, by the plate-glass window. It has a spider plant growing out of its hollow cranium. 'That creature with the green hair.'

'And Sylvia?' I say.

'Sylvia is thirteen and goes to a boarding school,' he says.

'Boarding school?' I say in disbelief. Lacrosse sticks in the hall. A vision of Mam'zelle in the curl-papers. 'You send your daughter to boarding school? What boarding school? Mallory Towers?'

148

'Bedales,' he says without shame. 'She likes it. She gets on well there. The comprehensive seemed to be doing her no good.' He catches my eye and laughs. 'My head for the block, is it?' he says. 'Quite right. More power to the axe-man. Do you know, Katherine, Roger won a scholarship to one of these filthy public schools once. Jane set it up when I was too busy to pay any attention. She has this bee in her bonnet about music. She wanted him to get more of it. I refused to let the poor child take it up. I had both of them united against me in fury for days on end. Neither of them would talk to me. I got enough black looks from that blue-eyed little Mafia to make me expect ground glass in my coffee. It didn't shake me. One is so high principled in one's youth. I made the little bastard pedal off in his cycle clips to the local grammar school every morning.' I laugh in spite of myself at this cheery and wholly unrepentant account of patri- archal tyranny, I suspect because I get pleasure from the thought of Roger being stuffed in the eye.

'Shame on you, Jacob,' I say. 'You were always a pig to Roger.'

'*Ach*,' Jacob says. 'He didn't know how lucky he was. He was a sweet looking kid, my little Roger. Put him in a surplice and he'd have had half the Upper Sixth up his backside.' Jacob, who is in general well acquainted with the ways of the Enemy, is unshakeable in his conviction that not much goes on at public schools other than cold showers and buggery in the choir stalls.

'But here I am,' he says, 'spending my own money on send- ing this pampered baby of mine to Bedales. Roger was, at least, deserving of an elite education.'

'Bedales is different,' I say comfortingly. Jacob is amused by my tactfulness.

'Don't be kind to me,' he says. 'It's the acceptable face of privilege.'

'What I want to know is, how do you pay for it?' I say. 'I mean, pardon my asking.'

'I get paid too much,' he says. 'All this money and no expenses. I'm a landlord, of all things, Katherine. People pay me rent for the house in Sussex. Jane had an old aunt who died and left her a house in Cadogan Square. Nice old creature. Full of advanced causes from Yoga to nude bathing. The house of

149

hers, it more than paid for this place, of course. I'm planning to sell the Sussex house in a year or two and buy a garage for my Sam. He likes to fix cars.'

'Fix cars?' I say. Another proletarian bias.

'He appended himself to a motor mechanic in Brighton when he was sixteen,' Jacob says. 'The chap sends him off on day release courses to the college of FE. He's a nice kid. Disturbingly sane, however. Always knows where he's going. The only one in the family, other than Roger, who knows how to get the back off the washing-machine. Now then, Katherine, are you hungry? Shall I wine and dine you somewhere?'

'Somewhere really Ritzy,' I say, 'since you're so rich. I've been working hard these years, Jake. I've spent ten years teaching in a language school. I'd love some glamour.'

'Glamour you always had,' Jacob said. 'Direction you had less of. Yes, come along, sweetheart. Let's eat elegantly. Bestow on me some lovely vicarious glamour. It's not a thing my wife goes in for, as you know. The wretched woman has refused for thirty-odd years to pierce her ears for me. What do you make of a woman like that?' I laugh.

'I might get used to you over the waste disposal unit,' I say, 'but never to Jane with pierced ears.'

'Tell me, child,' he says, as we walk down the street, 'why did you never marry that boy of mine? Suddenly you were off. Like a bird. Might it have been a satisfactory alternative, do you think? A north Oxford wife? Pedalling off to the Bodleian in the rain to take the master his reader's ticket? Lots of jolly children at Phil and James or Pip and Jimmy, or whatever the hell that damned school is called? Not for you, perhaps, but I always thought that you cared for him. Did you not, in fact, care for him?'

'He wouldn't have me, Jacob,' I say firmly. 'Why do you pick my brain? Why don't you ask Roger?'

'Roger has never really talked to me, to tell you the truth,' he says.

'I take it he's still in Oxford?' I say. 'He never went back to Africa?'

'He's still there,' Jacob says. 'Bright lad, Roger. It suits him, Oxford does, I think. He got a very good first, you know. Instant

150

college fellowship. He researches in the Mathematical Institute.'

'I spoke to his wife on the 'phone,' I say. 'She gave me your number. How long has he been married?'

'Couple of years,' he says. 'Four, come to think of it. A nice young woman. A proper wedding in the college chapel, my dear. Rather lovely, as a matter of fact, these Christian rituals. He's taken to the Church, in recent years.'

'The *Church*?' I say, with my soul in tears for my bold iconoclast. My Roger, who lobbed defiant stones into the sea. My Roger, who put down the Holy Ghost so effectively at the age of six.

'Oh, yes,' Jacob says, 'and sings in the choir, of course. So you see, he got the surplice after all.' The image of Roger on his knees is an obscenity to me. I almost cry.

We eat in Hampstead. Lots of veal and cream and stinky cheese. Jacob smokes foul smelly cigars over coffee in place of his foul smelly cigarettes in an effort to stave off the decay of the flesh.

'Now tell me about Jonathan,' I say. 'Did Jane ever get him to Oxford, or is he still walking the Pyrenees?'

'Yes, of course she did,' he says. 'She bribed him. With my money.' He laughs. 'I'm still paying it off, as a matter of fact, on the twenty-five year mortgage. Modern languages. Another first, I may say. A family tradition, the Oxford first. Perhaps Oxford gives them away.'

'Perhaps you've got very bright children,' I say. 'Crumbs, Jake, you could paper your bathroom with first-class degree certificates.'

'No, no,' he says modestly. 'Only those two. The rest of my children are not that way at all. Jonathan isn't academic either, for that matter, he's just highly intelligent. The whole damn thing was a waste of his time. It simply delayed his going to Europe.'

'And where is he?' I say. 'I got a letter from him once which suggested he was in Athens.' Jacob smiles indulgently because, as always, Jonathan can do no wrong.

'In Kilburn,' he says, 'living on the dole and writing a novel. He can't throw it off, I suspect. It's my guess that he likes it too much to let the publishers have it. Yes, he spent some years in Athens. He came back here two years ago with a Greek child bride and a lovely dark-eyed baby. The wife, not surprisingly, upped and left for home after a couple of months, taking the baby with her. She couldn't adapt. Lunacy, the whole thing. Typical Jonathan. He had got the child pregnant. A student, she was, in the school he was teaching in. Father a well-off shoe manufacturer. He spent some time living with her people but couldn't survive it and brought her to London. A nice bourgeois merchant's daughter in need of a solid, dependable husband.'

'You make her sound like me,' I say. Jacob throws up his eyes in disbelief.

'Anything less like you would be hard to imagine,' he says. 'You—apart from being slightly crazy—are a traitor to your social group, Katherine, I'm happy to say. Like Jane. Like all of us, come to that. It's my belief the poor sweet boy was too nice not to marry her. He was received into the Greek Orthodox Church for the purpose of marrying her. The whole damn thing lasted all of eighteen months.'

'They're a churchy pair then, your two older sons,' I say, thinking to myself, Wouldn't he, wouldn't Jonathan screw around and get schoolgirls pregnant, the little swine.

'I'm very fond of that young man,' Jacob says, 'as you may remember. Perhaps you ought to take him on.'

'Jesus, Jacob, why don't you offer me Sam as well and be done with it? Why not Sam? What's wrong with Sam?' I say, getting rattled. Jacob enjoys it.

'Sam is too young for you,' he says, 'and Sam is too straight. Have Jonathan.'

'I'll tell you this, Jacob,' I say, 'I've had enough of your sons. To coin a phrase, right now I need your Jonathan like I need a hole in the head. I'd sooner have the one you've got lined up for me in East Finchley.'

'You'll like Jonathan,' he says. 'Jonathan will surprise you.' If there were not still a degree of deference in my relationship with Jacob, I would kick him under the table.

'Nicely brought up Greek women don't drop their knickers for anybody, after all, do they?' he says. It is such a long time since I've heard anyone say 'knickers.'

On the way to the hospital, Jacob begins to set me up in a job. His publisher needs a copy-editor, he says. Should it be my good self? He is due to see his publisher in ten days, he says.

'I'm not a copy-editor, Jake,' I say, 'I'm a lackey in a language school.'

'You can turn your hand to it,' he says, 'you're a literate woman.'

'Daughters at Bedales, jobs for the boys,' I say. 'I haven't lived in Rome for ten years without getting to know corruption when I see it.' Jacob raises his eyebrow.

'Get along with you,' he says. He is driving a very nice new Volkswagen Golf. 'You're man enough to accept a little honest graft, aren't you?'

39

In her hospital ward, Jane has Jonathan with her. He is in the
process of replenishing her illicit supplies of Guinness and
sneaking out the empties.

'The Mum's Ruin,' he says, with reference to the empty
Guinness bottles which he transfers to his left armpit. He takes
my hand across the bed. 'Katherine,' he says. 'It's been a long
time.'

'Yes,' I say. It is an absurd and omnipotent but very common
response to be surprised that people grow and change when
you are not there to observe the process. For this reason,
Jonathan's appearance at least is indeed a surprise. I find both
that, and his bearing, highly prepossessing. This is perhaps
because my tastes have evolved. He wears his wild hair clipped
poodle-wise in two-inch lengths all over his head. It could be
mistaken for a fashionable perm. The look has caught up with
him. This is the age of the unset frizz; we grew up in the age of
the undulating curl. Jonathan has squarish steel-framed glasses
which interrupt the inquisitorial power of his great nose and he
wears a small thick well-cut tortoiseshell moustache. He has
about him the same confident ease but carries it with greater
subtlety and wears cleaner clothes.

'My dearest Katherine,' Jane says. She invites me to sit beside
her on the bed and inches up cautiously, clutching at her
abdominal scar. 'I may look decrepit but I'm absolutely fine,'
she says. She kisses me, and I her. In her dowdy NHS glasses,
leaning on the iron bedhead, her hair streaked with grey, she
looks, as always, miraculously beautiful. 'What a lovely surprise!' she says. 'Oh, Jake, where did you find her? You got lost.
And to have you visit me with your dowry in your hair. What a

tonic you are.' I have plaited gold beads into the ends of my hair, which is longish and crêpe. I sit with her, loving her as much as always.

'Look at my companions,' she says after a while, in a conspiratorial whisper. 'This sweet young thing here on my right has been forced to have her tubes tied by her husband. Him in the army boots. He refuses to have a vasectomy, of course. She's twenty-one. That one is a martyr to her vaginal prolapse and she can't wear a diaphragm because she's allergic to rubber. The old lady there has just returned from a three-day ordeal with her legs up in stirrups being treated with radiation for uterine cancer.' I regard this by now as a typical Goldman conversation, and feel cosily at home with her at once.

'I've got some plastic surgery on my cervix for you,' I say invitingly, closing the decade of our long separation. Jacob and Jonathan glance at each other with ironic implication, seeking mutual support as aliens in a world monopolized by female complaints. Jonathan smiles.

'I'm getting out of here before I get lynched,' he says. 'I need tea.' He kisses Jane's forehead. 'Goodbye, Ma. Jake, I'll wait for you in the canteen. Katherine, come and have some tea with me. There's a slop house on the premises.' In the corridor we pass the trolleys and the stink of meths. Jonathan, whose adolescent belligerence has evolved into a certain bold charisma, evokes glances from some comely nurses on the way. He steers me with a comfortable, brotherly arm into the canteen. In the other hand he has a plastic carrier-bag containing Guinness bottles.

'I hope you still have Zebedee on your bicycle,' I say.

'I don't,' Jonathan says with feeling. 'Some dirty swine pinched that bell from me in my first term at Oxford.' At the counter we pick up some dark brown tea and Jonathan rises to doughnuts.

'I'm rich today,' he says, 'I've just got my first publisher's advance. Six hundred pounds.' I associate him recurringly with sums of six hundred pounds.

'Good Lord,' I say, much impressed. 'How do you feel?'

'Like a person who is about to buy an electric typewriter,' he

155

says. We sit at a formica-topped table displaying pools of slop and the odd abandoned yoghurt carton.

'Drink up,' he says cheerily, when I get a little snooty over the tea. 'It's guaranteed to put hairs on your chest.' I laugh, at no more than the unstated and amusing fact of our physiological difference.

'What do you expect of your tea then?' he says, smiling at me. 'Ice cubes? Sprigs of mint?'

'Yes,' I say.

'Where've you been? Italy? All the time? Just come back?'

'Yes,' I say, lying a little. 'Yes, yes.'

'How's tricks, Katherine?' he says. 'How are you?'

'Ravaged,' I say, protectively mock-dramatic. 'Don't ask me. I've just been through it all with Jake.'

'You look marvellous,' he says, 'but then you always did. You graced my boyhood fantasies as a thing of pendant shiny objects and pale gleaming hair.' He makes me laugh.

'Have you seen Roger?' he says.

'Nope,' I say bravely, 'not in ten years. Only thing I see from time to time of Roger's is that embroidered butterfly patch he gave me from his bum pocket. It turns up now and again in my workbasket.' Jonathan pulls a face.

'Etherized, I hope?' he says. 'Impaled on a pin.' He gestures with a teaspoon, grinding it into the formica. 'You ought to know that Roggs keeps his bifocals in his bum pocket these days. He sat on them not long ago, the silly bugger. He's got them all taped together with Sellotape.' He gestures again to indicate the makeshift repair.

'Jake says he goes to church,' I say. 'Is that a malicious fabrication?'

'Not a bit of it,' Jonathan says. 'All week he's in the Mathematical Institute, is Roggs, trying to devise ways of measuring Infinity, and on Sunday, there he is in church, on his knees before the Unknowable. Isn't it wonderful what Oxford does for people? They get to know more and more about less and less. He's a dear chap, I have to say, for all that.' It occurs to me that Roger's Christianity could be a gigantic act of aggression towards Jacob, but I don't want to sound like the

156

Tavistock Clinic or anything. Psychs are not my favourite people.

'Perhaps he goes for the plainsong,' I say.

'Time was when he went for the plainsong, Kath,' Jonathan says, 'but now he goes for the hard stuff. The Body and the Blood. It's the real McCoy with Rogsie, I assure you.' Rather successfully, he takes the pain out of the thing for me. I never heard anyone call the transubstantiation the real McCoy before, though I am accustomed to irreverence.

'He's very generous with it,' he says. 'Made me his child's godfather. A little archaic do around the font. He knows I intend to be an altogether secular godfather, of course. I deal in ice-cream and treats, not in the word of God. None of it could really surprise you, Kath. Didn't he always behave like Savonarola?'

'Bloody Jiminy Cricket, more like,' I say, provoked a little by Jonathan's indulgence towards him.

'Oh, come,' Jonathan says reproachfully, 'you can't mean to be so nasty.'

'He used to wear that hat,' I say, 'that dead grandfather's hat. That morbid Hamlet hat.' Jonathan is clearly delighted to be reminded of it.

'The hat,' he says, 'exactly so. A Hamlet hat. "Lay not that flattering unction to your soul that not my madness but your trespass speaks." '

'Other way round,' I say, 'else it doesn't make sense. "Not your trespass but my madness speaks." '

'Right,' he says. 'He's a poor, sweet, loony Jew. File him away. I expect you have. He was never all that nice to you.'

'He couldn't cast me off without unloading blame,' I say. 'He made me a devastating heap of my iniquities. All nice and sym-metrical. Everything, Jonathan. You wouldn't believe. How I'd disappointed him reading *Good Housekeeping* when I had a brain to feed. How I was hick enough to knit.' Jonathan grins.

'I did try laying him a bet once, that you'd knit your own graduation robes,' he says, 'but Rogsie was not amused.'

'I don't want to hear a word in his favour,' I say. 'He was a pig to me, your brother. He made me feel like Mrs Weetabix. I was so under his spell I believed him in a way. He buggered up my self-esteem. I didn't have his advantages, did I? He got me where I was most vulnerable and all because I wouldn't dress like a kibbutznik for him.' Jonathan laughs.

'Don't be humble, Kaffrin,' he says. 'You've no cause to be humble. It might comfort you to know that the last time I saw Roggs he was making a violin from a paper pattern. Cross-legged, he was, on the floor, like the Tailor of Gloucester. He's Mr Fixit, is Roggs. He makes little red lights go on and off on the cooker for his wife. It's like Star Wars in there. You know that he's married, do you? A sweet Christian wench, part-time Maths tutor for the Open University.' I pull a sour face, to cover the fact that I find this threatening.

'Don't let that trouble you, Kath. It's a putting-out system for dons' wives. It isn't the big time.' Jonathan has inherited Jacob's ability to air a good prejudice without inhibition.

'Is she flat-chested?' I ask, because, to my shame, this is important to me. Jonathan can obviously not believe what he hears.

'What?' he says.

'Is she flat-chested?'

'No,' he says. 'Did you want her to be?'

'I am sorry to say that it would have been a great comfort to me,' I say.

'Good God, Kath,' he says, 'the woman is an innocuous parsonage-educated school marm with pretty boobs. Since she troubles you so much, I will be good to you and tell you that she wears a crucifix in her cleavage.'

'Thank you, Jonathan,' I say, 'that's a big help. A crucifix in the cleavage is more hick than knitting, isn't it? Don't you think so?'

'I confess it's not a great turn-on for me. It says to me, I know you want them, but I have committed them to Jesus. It mixes the sacred and the profane in a manner which doesn't excite me.'

'Yes, exactly,' I say.

'Sally wouldn't see it that way,' he says. 'She's not devious. She's just a nice little Maths bod. She's not a creature of subtle charm like you.'

I find Jonathan's brazen and extravagant compliments rather enjoyable.

'Are you married, Kath?' he says. 'Are you committed?' I reach instinctively for signs of commitment around the cleavage but I have none. Neither cleavage nor commitment. Jonathan notices and tries not to smile.

'No,' I say, 'why?'

'Because I'd like to chance my arm,' Jonathan says. 'I fancy you. I always have.'

'Rubbish,' I say. Listening to Jonathan talk has left me slightly high. It is like watching somebody relentlessly winning at ninepins.

'It's the truth,' he says. 'From the moment you walked into my parents' house wearing those sexy fantastic shoes, I said to myself, Jesus, Goldman, you were born too late.'

'What a shameless, filthy liar you are, Jonathan,' I say, but I enjoy the game. 'This is all complete rubbish.'

'It's not rubbish,' he says. 'Roggs had the advantage over me, didn't he? He was older, and turning your head with his pretty face and cultured talk. Always impelled to improve your mind, he was. If it wasn't Thomas bloody Morley and the broken consort, it was the chemical elements or some other damn thing. You wouldn't even come fishing with me, that day. You chose to listen to Roger playing Stravinsky.'

'I was scared of you, Jonathan,' I say, blushing foolishly. 'You were a very bolshie, menacing adolescent. I must say that I noticed how you pined and gave up eating for me.'

'Did you want homage then?' he says. 'Yellow stockings, cross-gartered?'

'Not on those butchy rugger legs of yours,' I say. Jonathan casts an eye over a section of grey sock protruding below his trouser hem.

'Oh, come on, Kath. Tell me at least that you know I'm no mean Philistine jock.'

'Of course I know,' I say.

'Rogsie was the one who played rugger, you know,' he says. 'I was the gentle arty one who wrote poetry. I wrote a poem about you once, for a competition, but the Head wouldn't have it.' I enjoy this flirting over doughnuts and tea. The last time I did it was in the Tate Gallery with John Millet.

'How is John Millet?' I say.

'Dead,' Jonathan says. 'Lung cancer.'

'*Dead!*' I screech hysterically, for my nerves are not yet quite what they should be. I keep my Valium in a little tin box with my initial on it which Rosie once gave me when I visited the Goldmans at Christmas. Jonathan is puzzled, even a little alarmed, by the vehemence of my response. Protectively, he puts a hand over mine on the table.

'Nothing and nobody lasts forever, Kath,' he says, watching me carefully as my tears fall. Sensing that he is kind, I pour out to him my sadness and my loss, dripping tears and snot onto the formica and wiping my nose crudely on the back of my hand. He does nothing but hears me out, as I tell him of my overwhelming urge to carry the little creature out under my coat and bury her in the geraniums; of the standing in queues and signing things, the listening to bureaucratic telephones ring; of my months communing in the evenings with the bulge; of the strong urge to hold and possess something after the jarring and violent assault on the cervix.

'The man left before the baby came, you see,' I say.

'Was that the man I met?' he asks. 'I called once, remember? But you weren't there.'

'That was the man,' I say. 'He was nice. He was reasonable. He'd just seen too much of it already.'

Jacob approaches us unnoticed.

'Feeling lachrymose, Katherine?' he says suddenly, a little too heartily perhaps.

'Leave her, Jake,' Jonathan says.

'The poor child has been mixed up with Catholic foreigners. Has she told you?' Jacob says.

'Leave her,' Jonathan says again. 'Tell me what Jane's consultant says.'

'He says four days and he reckons she can come home,' Jacob says. 'But what's this Jane tells me about your book, Jont? You actually bunged it in?'

'The money is nice,' Jonathan says.

'The whole thing is absolutely marvellous,' Jacob says, 'and very much as you deserve.'

'Not so,' Jonathan says modestly.

'Well,' Jacob says, laughing, clapping him on the shoulder, 'if it's not what you deserve that's even better. Good for you, Jont. Most of us merely cough in ink. You've done the real thing.' He takes out a bunch of keys and removes one which he hands to me.

'Have a house key, my dear,' he says. 'Don't let her disappear, Jont, will you? Take care of her. I must do some quick chores in the department. Shall I see you chaps at home?'

'Thanks, Jake,' I say. As I watch him go I notice, squeamishly, that he walks more slowly than I remember, and that his balance is slightly out of alignment.

'Come,' Jonathan says, 'let's go.' On the way I go in again briefly to see Jane, while Jonathan waits for me at the door. We embrace quickly because visiting time is over. She gives me, with furtive enjoyment, the last Guinness bottle. Under the eyes of the nurse I stuff it up my jumper. Guinness in the cleavage.

'Stay with us, dear Katherine, won't you?' she says. 'I insist on it.' When I return to Jonathan I give him the bottle. He is amused.

'What kind of a woman are you that keeps the Pope's piss stuffed up your jersey?' he says.

We walk fairly quietly towards the underground station. Jonathan gives me a kindly arm, an arm sleeved in brown Marks and Spencer knitwear worn into a sizeable hole at the elbow.

'Do you like holes in your elbows?' I say. 'Would it be overbearing to offer you a tasteful patch?' He doesn't altogether hear me.

'I've been sitting at a typewriter a lot,' he says. 'I've gone into holes.' It is only at the underground station a few yards further on that he stops suddenly. 'Tasteful, did you say?' he says. 'Tasteful or useful?' I tell him I said tasteful.

'I offered you a tasteful patch. But I could do you a tasteless one if you insist,' I say.

'Kiss me,' Jonathan says. I kiss him by the cigarette kiosk at the entrance to the underground station, feeling the sudden shock of the unfamiliar mouth.

On the platform we stare across at the ads on the other side of

161

the track. Jonathan has his hands in his pockets and is silently whistling.

'Jacob says you got married,' I say. Jonathan raises his eyes momentarily to the seeping barrel vault of the tunnel roof.

'He decided to predispose you in my favour, I see,' he says, with some amusement.

'He did, as it happens,' I say. 'He said that I would like you, and I do.' Jonathan smiles.

'Let's say that we've both done some fairly thorough anthropology on the extended family,' he says. 'And what exactly did Jake tell you?' I tick the items off on my fingers.

'That you taught in a school in Athens, that you got one of the students pregnant, that you married her and subsequently divorced her. You know how Jacob likes to give one the nitty gritty.' Jonathan nods.

'That was some school, Kath. The one I taught in. English, French, German and volleyball, I taught. I even taught some of them to play the flute. Sweated labour, it was. A truly corrupt old boozer ran the joint. A German war criminal, I suspect.' Jonathan always did have a good ear for mimicry. On this occasion he throws himself into the role of Teutonic headmaster with a truly Hitlerite zeal.

'I TEACH ONLY RAINER MARIA RILKE,' he says. 'YOU VIL DO ZE REST.' On the strength of his power to amuse me, I forgive him his transgression.

'The wonder is I ever found the time to get the girl pregnant,' he says. 'My son is very sweet, Kath.'

'I'm sure he is,' I say. A yearning for our babies is a thing we have in common.

'Is. Was,' he says, resignedly. 'I've ceded him to the kinship network. He is being reared by his besotted grandparents, and he enjoys a great excess of Athenian male relations who do instead of me. I was there briefly two months ago. I do know what you mean about wanting to hide them under your coat. My wife, as was, has gone back to school. There she is, giggling over ice-cream cones with her chums. Unbelievable. She's the same age as Annie, but more girlish. Her family extends into the Fulham Road, I may say. She's coming to a language school in Knightsbridge this September. Knightsbridge isn't my beat.'

162

'Were you ever in love with her?' I ask.

'No,' he says. 'I liked her. She liked me. I'd have liked her a lot better if she'd known how to count. I showed her how to calculate her menstrual cycles and she messed it up, of course. February has twenty-eight days, not thirty-one.' I resist the temptation to remark that he also taught biology.

'I like them all,' he says. 'They've always been very decent to me, her family. God, but they don't half eat a lot of sweet stuff, Kath. Have you ever eaten that Greek nougat? Jesus, it has your teeth out in seconds.' It is apparent to me that in a paste of nuts and honey he sees epitomized his desperate claustrophobia.

'I'm one of those incompetent women who got pregnant, Jonathan. I forgot to take a pill,' I say.

'Kath,' he says, 'I'm sorry.'

'Do you find it a relief being home?—seeing the map of the London Underground on the wall?' I say, thinking as much of myself. 'Do you think maybe it never happened to me?' Jonathan nods his recognition.

'Even more so when they say "Inside Only" on the buses,' he says.

'And when the fruit vendors' barrows have those notices that say "Please do not squeeze me until I am yours," ' I say.

'Those especially,' Jonathan says, smiling. 'Victims of cultural shell-shock, aren't we? Hot milk and Elgar for us both at bed-time.'

'Ugh!' I say. Across the track the Union Jack is displayed upon the cheese ad. Someone has risked life and limb to scrawl 'NF' across it. Jonathan takes my hand in his own.

'And what think you, coz, of the Flag?' he says. 'The Flag that in our innocent youth belonged to Carnaby Street, you see, and now belongs to the National Front.' Lots of water under the bridge.

'What's your baby's name?' I say.

'Alexis,' he says. 'I mean to pitch a tent with him one day on the Sussex Downs.'

'Do you still go fishing?' I say.

'When I can. Not all that much.'

I no longer care much now for the routine sufferings of fish. My heart has grown older. I have embraced a dead baby.

163

40

Jonathan returned with me to Jacob's house where we sat for a while on one of the sofas.

'I thought your mother looked well,' I said. 'I was relieved to see her look so well.'

'I think she's perfectly okay,' Jonathan said. 'She's a tough old bag. Jake was paralysed with anxiety last week. He was convinced she was three-quarters dead.'

'Poor Jacob,' I said. 'Dear Jacob. Ought we to cook him something, do you think?'

Jacob evidently didn't cook much with Jane not there. He had one onion, one egg and a few withered potatoes sprouting at the eyes. The cupboards contained a sparse collection of useless and rather way-out tins from the delicatessen. We sliced the potatoes and the onion between us and baked them in Jake's wonderful oven with some milk and black pepper. Jacob came back with his arms full of Hampstead afterthoughts. Pâté and salt beef and rye bread and *apfel strudel*.

'We cooked your spuds,' Jonathan said. 'Your cupboards are full of Polish ear-lobes in tins. Why do you keep nothing edible, Jake?'

Jonathan left us early, saying he would come for me the next day. Jacob found me some puce Habitat sheets and directed me to Sylvia's bedroom. A nice little room with Abba posters and little woolly souvenirs. Hanging on the door of her cupboard was a shimmering cerise disco suit. We were none of us getting any younger.

'I'll leave you one of my Mogadon, shall I?' Jacob said thoughtfully, before we turned in.

'I've brought my own, thanks, Jacob,' I said.

We made for Kentish Town the next evening, Jonathan and I, which was a lot smarter than I remembered. When I lamented this, Jonathan undertook to find me the last greasy spoon in the area—which he did. We ate kebabs stuffed into unleavened Greek bread, and washed them down with beer. Then we ate pastries oozing sugar syrup. At least I did. Jonathan said no thanks, it reminded him too much of his mother-in-law. I told him Roger's story about the Holy Ghost and the blackberries and the wrath of God. Jonathan couldn't remember the episode.

'But I'll tell you why not,' he said. 'Why the Holy Ghost didn't descend. 'Tis my belief that Rogsie *is* the Holy Ghost.' Then I said that I could drink some of that Turkish coffee, that sweet Turkish mud.

'Greek mud,' Jonathan said, 'if you please. Unless you want the waiter to up and black my eye.' I felt very comfortable with him. I was impelled to confide in him.

'It's not altogether true that I've just come back,' I said. 'I've been with my mother for five weeks. In Dorset. I've been in the outpatients' clinic. I've been very sad, Jonathan. I may have seemed rather high yesterday, I know, but I've been a heap. I cry very easily. Ignore it, won't you?' My tears began to ooze a little. 'In the trade it's called "discharging," ' I said, 'all the snot and tears. It's called discharging. That is what the psychs call it.'

'Let's call it crying,' Jonathan said. 'Use the paper napkins. It's what they're for.'

At Jacob's door I remembered my debts to him. I drew three pounds out of my purse and handed it to him.

'This is yours,' I said. 'You paid for my supper.' Jonathan declined to take it.

'Come off it, Kath,' he said. 'No need to be scrupulous over the price of a kebab.'

'Oh, but there is,' I said. 'I'd like us to have proper financial arrangements. I've had some most improper ones in the past.'

'Pay for my next haircut,' he said.

'I'd rather pay for my own dinner,' I said. 'My guess is that your haircuts cost more than three pounds. There's something very becoming has happened to your hair.' Jonathan laughed and pocketed the money.

'Good thinking,' he said, appreciatively.

For nearly two weeks Jonathan escorted me to and from Jacob's house in this way, like a devoted custodian, sensing that I was a poor convalescent creature fit only for chicken broth and hot water bottles. Elgar and hot milk. I went with Jacob, at first, to visit Jane each day. Jonathan came in the evenings and walked with me, sometimes with Jake also, on the Heath. I recalled occasions when we had done this before, because Jacob often went for walks in Sussex with Jonathan and sometimes also with me. It was delightful to do what I had done before in a sense. It filled me with a quiet muted pleasure. I cared for Jane, who had come out of hospital but couldn't lift things and needed to rest.

Rosie came one day. A lovely, tall, dark creature with cropped hair and no breasts, wearing vibrant ethnic leg-warmers against a sudden unseasonal chill and matching mittens strung on a woollen cord around her neck. Looking at her made me wonder whether John Millet, before he died, took her to the hairdresser. Rosie fell into my arms with a childish cry of delight. She had brought with her a young man who was neither black nor proletarian of whom she was manifestly fond. He hung back shyly, holding the flowers which Rosie had brought for Jane. Then they went, hand in hand.

I walked again with Jonathan on the Heath.

'She's very pretty,' I said, 'your sister.'

'She's okay,' he said. 'Would you say she fancies that kid? That little druggie?'

'Druggie?' I said. 'He seemed like a nice middle-class boy to me. Jacob claims that she only likes brick-layers' apprentices.'

'Syringe marks all over his arm, for Godssake,' Jonathan said. 'Sleeves rolled up especially for us to notice. You are as blind as my mother, Kath. Why don't you wear glasses?'

'I'm too vain,' I said.

'Listen,' he said suddenly, rather tensely, 'can we get the hell out of these parts and go to my place? Can I get you on your own somewhere without my family?'

'Sure,' I said.

'Wait for me,' he said. 'I'm going back to tell Jane not to expect us back till late. Okay?'

'You don't think I ought to stay with her till Jake comes in?' I said.

'For Godssake, Katherine,' he said. 'Can you not understand that if I don't unzip my bloody flies and climb into you, I will go bloody mad?'

Jonathan knew a bus that would take us to Kilburn. It took forever to come.

'What's the state of you?' he said. 'I'm not going to hurt you, am I?' He had touched a morbid fear of mine: that those parts of me, so recently a mess of septic swelling and staple-clips, were no longer capable of functioning.

'I don't know. I haven't tried since just after I got pregnant. I've been very celibate. Though I haven't always been so celibate,' I tell him, fired by some curious puritanical need to breast-beat, some hangover from the Methodist Sunday School. 'The year I went to Italy, after your brother dismantled my character, I went through about thirty men in less than a year.' Jonathan, as I ought to have predicted, was nobody's conscience but his own.

'You remind me of Jake's joke about the cakes at the Jewish wedding,' he said without concern. 'Mrs Goldberg five, Mrs Goldman six, but who's counting? Do you know that joke?' I told him no.

In Kilburn High Road, I said to him, 'Do you ever still do that alto singing that your mother made you do?' Jonathan shrugged.

'It could be my party trick, I suppose,' he said, 'if I ever went to parties, which I don't. In short, no. I don't get a call for it, Kath.'

'But I'm calling for it,' I said.

'You mean you want me to sing to you?' he said incredulously.

'Yes,' I said, laughing.

'What, here? In the street?'

'Yes,' I said.

'Are you out of your mind?' he said. 'You want me to sing like

167

a transvestite in the street? This is Kilburn, lady. Do you want six drunken Irishmen to step out of the pub and beat me to death?' Jonathan was so solid, somehow, death seemed remote.

'They'll think it's me,' I said. Jonathan conceded and, after looking furtively over his shoulder, sang a small rustic stanza in Italian which beseeched a barefoot nymph not to disturb the dewfall on the grass. Quite unlike the usual hey nonny no.

'I can't sing any more of it,' he said. 'After that you need more voices.'

'That was lovely,' I said, because it was. Quite beautiful. 'Some soothing rustic trad for us pavement bashers.' It had got of late to unnerve me that I always walked on concrete.

'It's not trad. It's Monteverdi,' he said. Monteverdi and I shook hands across the gap and put down our cudgels.

'I'll tell you something you'll hate, shall I?' I said to him. 'You're cultured, Jonathan. You always were.'

41

In bed, Jonathan loomed over me, pausing like a compassionate executioner.

'Scream at me to get out if I hurt you,' he said. He didn't. What he did to me caused me instead to stir quietly like a moth emerging slowly from a cocoon. Jonathan, who is a flamboyant and copious talker, didn't talk during the act, a thing which pleased me since I preferred the uninterrupted and more primitive pleasure of muscle and gland. Afterwards he carefully picked off the few dark chest hairs which he had shed into the sweat between my breasts.

'You okay?' he said.

'Yes,' I said.

'You've got some intriguing ridges where you've been stitched,' he said. 'It doesn't in the least detract.'

'Have I?' I said.

'You've also still got some lactation going on in your right breast,' he said. 'Do you know that?' I shook my head. He got up to pee. I watched him go, feeling reluctant to leave the warmth of the quilt. When I did, I found that the bathroom was not in fact the bathroom at all, but a small makeshift kitchen. A narrow wedge-shaped afterthought like a slice of brie, with enamelled sink and ancient gas cooker.

'Where is your loo?' I said to him.

'On the landing,' he said. 'You'll have to get dressed. I used an empty milk bottle, but it's a system which favours a gentleman.'

'Some gentleman,' I said as I climbed resignedly into my clothes. 'First it's your mother's wellingtons and then it's milk bottles. What next?' A domino theory of personal hygiene.

'I'll make some tea,' Jonathan said without contrition. He had evidently become a prodigious drinker of tea.

Jonathan's landlady's loo was a delightful period piece with a wooden seat, brass hinges and a porcelain handle saying PULL in elegant blue characters, fixed to the clanky chain. It bore its name in the bowl. It was called The Chine. Over the bath was a notice which said 'Not more than two baths a week, please.' I was tempted to lift it and post it to Michele. I could contemplate, after all, the prospect of writing to him without tears. I would write some day very soon and tell him that I had slept with the English Jew, which went to prove that he never made a meestake and that my life, while somewhat precarious, was no longer in pieces. I would transcribe for his amusement the notice pertaining to the landlady's ablutions, and tell him that I would always love him, which, in a sense, was perfectly true.

Jonathan had made the tea and was waiting for me in bed with it when I returned.

'Take your clothes off and come back to me,' he said. We drank the tea with our knees under the quilt. On his bed Jonathan had an incongruously expensive down quilt poppered into an elegant greenish trellis-patterned cover.

'Jonathan,' I said, 'how was it when your wife gave birth?'

'Two hours,' he said. 'No vaginal stitching. Very good medical care. She was dead lucky, I suppose. And you?'

'Lots of technology,' I said. 'Haemorrhaging. An appalling ache in the back. I won't tell you. Not now. I was too bloody Anglo-Saxon to scream, Jonathan. I lay there apologizing for my own pain. For about ten days I was not so much myself as a compound of Hoffman la Roche. It wasn't half expensive. The doctors got it wrong. My cervix got messed up. My stitches went septic. The works.'

'I'm sorry,' he said. 'I loved your patchwork crotch, if that is any comfort to you.' He anointed my vaginal lobes with a few brief kisses.

'Jonathan,' I said, 'was it ever difficult for you when we were younger? Did I ever make you unhappy? I mean long ago?' Jonathan thought.

'I suppose I persuaded myself that I didn't care,' he said. 'I was okay. It made me more objectionable than I might have been. That's all. I persuaded myself that women were all much the same, once you got their knees apart. I went on a grotesque promiscuous binge. That year Roger came back I made my way with a vengeance through the girls' netball team.'

'When you were seventeen?' I said, finding this hard to believe. 'Do you know what I was doing at seventeen, Jonathan? I was sighing gently over portraits of Lord Byron in school library books.' Jonathan, smiling sweetly, kissed my cheek.

'You see how much less depraved you were than I?' he said. 'You can't get much more depraved, I expect, than to shove your cock endlessly up navy skirts behind the sports pavilion. I probably did for the drainage, clogging it up with used French letters. Dearest Kath. Lovely woman,' he said euphorically. 'This is a very special day for me. "This is the birthday of my life, because my love has come to me." '

'*Is* come,' I said, because he had misquoted. It shocked me. For this, I thought snootily, he got a first at Oxford.

'Is come,' he said, without apology. 'That's even better. It's sexier. My love is come.' He kissed me all over my mouth. 'Why is it you come so beautifully, my love? My love is come—to me, under me, with me, all over me. The birthday of my life is come, because my love is about to come with me for the second time in one evening. Kath, sweet, beautiful, ravaged Kath, will the scars up your esteemed fanny stand it if I turn you over and fuck you from behind?' I nodded shakily, because I could not speak. It was too much of joy.

I woke Jonathan at one o'clock in the morning, saying that I ought to go home.

'Home?' he said, yawning, blinking vaguely.

'If you will put me in a taxi, I'll go to Jake's,' I said. 'I'm sorry to wake you.' I had been watching him sleep, in that curious protective mothering way in which one watches the sleep of a man who has entered upon it after visiting sexual pleasure upon one. Jonathan mumbled into the pillow, blinking against the light.

'They'll know you're with me,' he said. 'Go to sleep.'

'I think it's bad form,' I said, 'not to turn up. I ought to be there

171

in the morning.' Jonathan sat up suddenly and looked at me, shaking off sleep.

'Hello, my love,' he said. 'Are you talking to me?'

'I'll come back tomorrow, of course,' I said. 'After I've had lunch with Jake. Okay? Jon, please wake up. I'm a bit reluctant to step out into the street at this hour on my own. As you said, this is Kilburn, isn't it? I mean, I haven't yet been on the Women's Self-Defence course like your sister.'

'Sure,' he said. The agony of the night air, after the warmth of bodies and the down quilt, was quite terrible for us both.

At lunchtime the next day, having previously spent some minutes trying to tone down, with nettle-rash cream, a compromising abrasion on my upper lip caused by Jonathan's moustache, I met Jacob who was lunching with his publisher. He offered me over the table to the publisher, vouching generously for my abilities. Was I in the corridors of power?

'That's excellent,' said the publisher. 'We'll advertise the job, of course, but it's yours.' Then I took a bus to Jonathan's flat where I found him sitting at his typewriter, wearing, of all things, the aged black pullover which I once made. A quality garment, made to last.

'You can walk this morning,' he said. 'All that bashing at your maimed interior has done you no violence.'

'It's the afternoon,' I said. 'It's half-past three.' Officiously, because intensity is difficult to bear, I quoted him am and pm. Jonathan had a curious quiet heaviness about him.

'I love you,' he said, not without some pain. 'Dare I love you? Tell me that, Kath.'

'I've got a job,' I said shiftily, through fragility and fear. 'Your father's publisher is going to advertise for a copy-editor but fix it for me. Shocking, isn't it?' Jonathan held me.

'Terrible,' he said. 'They're a funny lot, these publishers. They publish all this left-wing stuff because only radicals read, and then they send out the printing work to Hong Kong for the cheap labour. It's a bad world, Kath. Come. Lie in my arms on the darkling plain. Live with me. Don't go away tonight, please. I need you. I need to stuff you full of my spew. Have some tea.'

'I'll stay with Jake for a week or two,' I said, 'if you don't mind.'

Jonathan made us tea, which we drank with our knees again under the quilt.

'This quilt,' I said, 'this quilt is a fine thing, Jonathan. How do impoverished writers in garrets buy things like this?'

'In sooth, somebody stole it for me from Heal's,' he said. 'She had a Christmas job there. I didn't ask her to, mind.'

All the residual adolescent trouble-maker within me stirred at the thought that a man who had received stolen goods was about to make love to me.

'I'm not altogether impoverished, as a matter of fact,' Jonathan said. 'I am a man of property. You are in bed with the clandestine owner of a heap of damp stones in Kilkenny. A house, Kath, but it's still in my grandmother's name because I'm scrounging dole money, you see. It's been used for storing hay, so it's got rather damp. I intend to live in it. Rogsie says he will spend two weeks in it with me in September and we'll make a start on repairing it. He knows about damp-coursed concrete and reinforcing joists. I've got some money too, just a bit, to fix it up. Jane is going to come and set up the garden for me when it's habitable. It's near where she spent her childhood holidays. Will you share it with me?' I tried not to respond.

'Is this a hand-out from your grandfather?' I said.

'Indirectly,' Jonathan said. 'He died last year and left some of the loot to Roger and me. Not Jane, of course, the old bastard, but she doesn't need it anyhow.'

'She's got the aunt's money,' I said, much amused. 'What about your poor sisters? Will you have to keep them in the groom's cottage?'

'My house is the groom's cottage, and worse,' he said. 'The sisters are okay. They've got the other grandmother's house in Golders Green coming to them. Lots of boats coming in. All most embarrassing for Jake. Roger has just moved his family into that house the grandparents had in Oxford. Remember that house? It's a bloody palace. Room for the grand piano at last. It's a hard life in this country today for the industrious middle class.'

'It jolly well is,' I said. 'Ask my stepfather. Your grandfather wasn't middle class. What you've got is the pickings of the declining minor aristocracy. It's money stolen from the Irish peasantry.'

'We'll halve it and say no more,' Jonathan said. 'Let's eat.'

It was wonderfully evident to me that evening that Jonathan could cook. Without engaging in that dreary gourmet show of stone mortars and egg-yolks, he produced an edible meal, frying up vegetables in a pan.

'Would you like to see Rogsie again?' he said. 'Would that lay a ghost for you? A confrontation with your teenage crush?'

42

Meeting Roger again was not a thing I sought out and neither did he. He had my telephone number after all. I met him willy-nilly when he came to collect Jonathan for the ferry crossing to Ireland one weekend. A month before I had moved in with Jonathan, which was working well. It suited me comfortably and Jonathan was overjoyed. I went to work each day for Jacob's publisher and left Jonathan at home to peg out washing and stir the soup in between his bursts of typing. He was very nice to come home to and strove to nourish me each evening with dishes culled from *The Pauper's Cookbook*. He washed the plates—thanks either to his mother's resolute indoctrination or in spite of it—without the familiar conflict between immediate gratification and deferred punishment. My earnings came to more than his dole money, which he ceremonially gave up.

'Sit down, my dearie,' he said to me one evening. 'Nice cup of tea? Your pipe and slippers?' Then he brought me the day's *Guardian*. 'How's you, my love?' he said. 'I have been having such a lovely orgy of dominating male fantasies about you today.' He was wearing a funny little gingham apron which looked like the kind of thing schoolgirls make in their first year at high school in preparation for the next term's cookery class. A thing left behind by his ex-wife. 'All while I was running the iron over your Viyella shirt,' he said.

'Oh, good,' I said.

'I thought you'd be pleased,' he said, sitting down beside me. 'You like your blokes to kick you around, don't you? First there's my brother who assaults your mind and then there's the fascist lunatic who assaults your body and nearly kills you on the road. But they've neither of them got anything on me when it comes to proper male brutality.'

'What's your line then, Jonathan?' I said, wondering if all that murdering of fish he did in his youth was what made him so kind.

'I plan to rape you with my new Bisset mop while you read Jill Tweedie,' he said.

'Having first tied me to the bed with your apron strings,' I said. He kissed me.

'My brother telephoned today,' he said. 'He sends you his love. He's coming down on Sunday to take me to Ireland. Tell you something funny about Rogsie—shall I?—thinking of male domination. If he's late back from his seminars of an evening, his wife doesn't feed him. He slopes off to the Chinese takeaway to sustain himself. There's some good, old-fashioned petticoat government in that house. All that monosodium glutamate is damaging to the brain, you know. He *is* a mathematician, after all. Deterioration of the brain is an occupational hazard.'

'Does that mean I won't see you for a fortnight?' I said. I had never enjoyed anybody's company as much before. We contemplated the prospect of separation bleakly.

'Bloody terrible, isn't it?' he said.

Over the years I had envisaged that, in meeting Roger again, I would make myself invulnerable by the careful magnificence of my appearance. I found this a useful thing to do when I was feeling insecure. In the event, he came to the door before we had got up in the morning and I received him improperly dressed in the giant T-shirt in which I slept, thinking, self-consciously, that I had not yet brushed the night's fur from my teeth. We embraced briefly and awkwardly in the doorway, where he let in a rush of cold air. Roger had not changed at all in appearance. There he was, the same comely schoolboy, shaking lank hair from his eyes, not knowing quite where to look, fidgeting a little with his keys which he had attached to a large plastic key-ring made in the image of a fried egg. Life-size.

'I'm early,' he said. 'Is Jonathan awake yet?'

'Of course I'm awake,' Jonathan said from within, his early morning voice tellingly an octave lower than usual. He climbed out of bed in his Marks and Spencer underpants.

'Coffee,' he said, 'that's what meets the case.'

'I'm early,' Roger said again. His speech, which had never been as pronouncedly Sussex as the others, had lost all trace of region. I have this trait myself. I am so eager to please my reference group that, unwittingly, I assimilate its accent. I develop marbles in my voice when I talk to strangers and always talk posh on the telephone. Jonathan doesn't have this problem. He can catch any accent he chooses but his natural speech is still unreconstituted Sussex grammar school.

'Have some coffee, Roger,' I said. 'I like your fried egg.'

'My wife gave it to me for my birthday,' he said. 'It helps me not to lose my keys. I have a tendency to lose keys.' He looked so young that it seemed to me an affectation on his part that he should not only have a wife and be entrusted with keys, but that he should presume to be absent-minded with it as well.

'Aren't you tempted to gnaw upon it?' I said. 'Would you like some breakfast?' Roger smiled his dimpled smile, tolerating the jape but not amused by it.

'Just coffee,' he said. Jonathan pulled on his jeans over his underpants and followed this with the previous day's sweater.

'What else shall I take, Kath?' he said.

'Ibsen?' I said. 'Woolly socks? Your flute?'

'Kath has made me some socks, Roger,' Jonathan said. 'Two, to be exact. One for each foot. Socks to go fishing in. Not so much socks as an art form, they are. They ought really to hang in the Whitechapel Gallery, these socks. They exhibit an inspired union of form and function.' They were Fair Isle socks with lovely scolloped tops. Roger didn't respond.

'You aren't planning to go fishing, I take it?' he said. 'Because I'm planning to have you hump bags of cement.'

'You don't think I might catch the supper?' Jonathan said. Roger might have made quite a creditable schoolmaster, after all, had he not been seduced by fellowships and the pursuit of the Infinite.

'We'll open tins,' he said firmly.

'If you say so, Gaffer,' Jonathan said. 'And what about my woman? Have you got room in the boot for my woman?' Jonathan embraced me, thoughtfully, giving me the security of that well-defined status, sensing that I might be a little at sea. Roger smiled again, I suspect rather wishing that he had the

177

power of entering into Jonathan's high spirits, but remaining aloof from it.

'Could we make tracks soonish, Jont?' he said.

I sat alone among the coffee cups after they had gone, feeling the after effect of Jonathan's unshaven cheek upon my face, and stared rather morosely at the floor. Roger had been so miserably undemonstrative that it had left me feeling very flat. He had not brought himself to engage in so much display of politeness, even, as to ask what I had been doing with myself all these years, or how it felt to be back.

I felt a bit like a hermit in London without Jonathan. My friends had all left, following men and jobs. John Millet was dead, who might once have stepped in and taken me to *Manon Lescaut*. I got dressed and walked through Kilburn into the Finchley Road and on through Hampstead Village, towards Jacob's house. On the way I bought a pint of milk which I drank for my breakfast, and a Sunday newspaper. The newsagent's young man chatted me up jovially.

'Get off, Ron,' said the newsagent, 'she's got her own young man, haven't you, miss?' I was flattered to be called miss. The day warmed up nicely as I walked. Jacob and Jane were drinking coffee on their roof when I got there. Jacob called to me, over the balustrade, to come up and fetch a cup on my way. They had a large thermal coffee-pot up there and some hot croissants, wrapped in a cloth. The last of the terry-cloth baby's nappies, I suspected.

'And what have you done with Jonathan?' Jane said. It was very nice there, on their airy perch.

'He's gone to Ireland,' I said. I surprised myself by engaging in a compromising and foolish snivel. Nothing more than a fleeting moist eye.

'Give the child a nose-rag, Janie,' Jacob said. Jane sought me out a crumpled tissue from her dressing-gown pocket and gave it to me. I blew my nose hard and laughed.

'I'm afraid that, one way or another, my sons cause you a lot of trouble,' Jane said.

'Jonathan isn't trouble,' I said. Jane raised an eyebrow. She habitually perceived Jonathan as her *enfant terrible* and nothing would shake her.

178

'Jonathan was always trouble,' she said.

'Nonsense,' Jacob said. 'In any case it's not your sons, Janie, it's men. Men cause Katherine a lot of trouble. That's not unusual. Men are well-known trouble-makers. There's only one kind of person causes more trouble than men, and that's women. You were lucky in this respect. You settled down early to a righteous and sober domestic life with me, didn't you, sweetheart?' Jane threw him a wonderful black look.

'If you are going to re-write history,' she said, 'I'll get this on the record for Katherine. The only reason that Jacob and I are so nice to each other these days is that we both of us know we may well be dependent on the other any day now to push us around in a bath chair.'

'I hope you will have one of those stylish wicker ones,' I said, 'like a chaise-longue on wheels.' I wondered, in the face of their example, whether I would be necking with my bloke at sixty, or if one ought not to presume to expect these things. I ate croissants with them and stayed for an hour, looking at an old photograph album. I love people's photographs. Photographs of people, that is. I cannot bear tasteful shots of historic buildings and scenery. I like those to come on postcards or in Kenneth Clark. There was Jane with her Angela Brazil haircut and swimsuit, fooling on the sand with her brother, who, five years on, wanted to make fisticuffs with Jake. There was Roger on Jacob's shoulders on Hampstead Heath in little dungarees. There was a wedding photograph, showing Jane manifestly pregnant on the arm of Jacob's professor outside the registry office, and another of Jacob, with an arm around each of two mothers—his own and Jane's.

'She came to our wedding, you know,' Jane said. 'She slammed the door on the old man for once, and along she came.'

There was a picture of Jonathan leering toothless out of a wigwam in cardboard feathers, and a press clipping of Jonathan as Julius Caesar wearing tinfoil oak leaves jammed over his ungainly frizz and making hamming gestures towards a male junior, who was got up as Calpurnia. Forget not in your speed Antonius to touch Calpurnia. Oh shit, Caterina, shut up, because the babe is dead. Dead, for Christssake.

179

43

Jonathan threw down a clutter of back-pack and wellingtons when he came back, and took me for a moment in his arms before he fell heavily into a chair.

'Make us some tea, Kath,' he said. 'We've been working like war horses. Rogsie doesn't believe in tea breaks. There's a new floor, all the plaster is off the walls, we've got a man to make rafters and a new front door. Roger is going to make us new windows in his garage. He's got all the measurements there in his pocket diary, haven't you, Rogsie? All squashed in between the autumnal equinox and the maths prelims. Sit down, Rogsie. Don't do that bloody nervous hovering.' Roger smiled.

'He's a wreck,' he said to me a little smugly because, appearances to the contrary, he was stronger than Jonathan and better at humping cement. 'I must go,' he said. 'I must look in on Mother and Sally is expecting me. That was good for us, Jont. I enjoyed it. It's a good idea to fix one's mind on a manual task from time to time.'

'Speak for yourself,' Jonathan said and laughed on a yawn. 'That was above and beyond the call of brotherly love, what you did. Thanks, Roger. You were prodigious. See him out, Kath, because my legs don't work.' I walked Roger to his car in total silence. In the back he had a large spirit level and a bag of tools wedged between the door and the child seat. He took the fried egg out of his pocket.

'Goodbye,' he said. 'It's been good for me, Katherine, to see you and my brother so happy. I've had you on my conscience intermittently over the years.' Did Roger imagine himself to be dispensing patronage to his brother? Who giveth this woman to this man? And for whom was it good? For me and for Jonathan, surely. Why should it be good for him?

'There's no need,' I said. 'I haven't been idle, you know. I haven't been hemming sheets these years.' Roger nodded.

'No, I'm sure of it,' he said. 'But I was unkind to you. They were things I felt I had to say, those things I said.'

'I stole your travelling bag,' I said. 'I can't even give it back to you because somebody stole it from me.'

Roger smiled and touched my cheek, briefly, with the fried egg. It was, I think, the most affectionate gesture I ever got from him. Because he made the gesture I took the chance to hit him below the belt.

'Do you really go to church, Roger?' I said. 'Did the Holy Ghost appear to you in the blackberry patch?' Roger laughed, but he wasn't put out.

'It's not a thing you are required to understand, Katherine,' he said. 'It has to do, if you remember, with the peace which passes all understanding.' Another verbal coup.

'You're damned clever, Roger,' I said admiringly, 'no wonder you're a don. You always did talk back in that smart way. Shall I tell you something that came as a great surprise to me? I'm clever too. When I had a spell in the loony bin, a while back, the shrink measured my IQ.'

'I never had any doubt of it,' Roger said. 'Listen. If you should ever need my help, Katherine, you've only to ask, okay? Remember, I'm your friend.' King Cophetua and the Beggarmaid.

'Thanks,' I said. 'Goodbye, Roger.'

'Come and see us,' he said. 'Sally would love to meet you and my daughter is always pleased to see Jonathan. You will come, won't you? Come soon.'

'Yes,' I said. Jonathan was almost asleep when I got back.

'Jon,' I said, 'could one actually fancy a man who prayed to God? I mean, be screwed by a bloke who'd just got off his knees?'

Before he fell asleep Jonathan, sensibly, offered me John Donne.

44

Meeting Roger's wife was an event for which I prepared myself with care. I groomed before the glass, having clothed myself in tight burgundy velvet trousers and a soft matching knitted thing with Fair Isle bands around the yoke and wrists, which showed the contours of my nipples. Thanks to Michele, who went in for expensive bribes, I had some long Italian millionairess boots which came up over my knees. My cheekbones were aglow with artful gleam and I had bundled my crêpe hair under a maroon beret with studied carelessness. I pulled over the lot my hand-quilted chintz jacket splashed with faded pink roses, which I made once out of my aunt's discarded curtains. Then I stared at myself in the glass, gorging on self love.

'Let's not miss the train, shall we?' Jonathan said. 'What a grade A sex object you are. Jesus, I've gone out with some birds in my time, but never with one who wore such high-class fisherman's waders. She was a head girl, you know, Roger's wife,' he added sadistically. I stopped in my tracks.

'You're having me on,' I said. 'You're trying to scare me.' Jonathan laughed.

'Gospel,' he said. 'Head girl of that direct grant girls' school in Cambridge. Now I've made you sweat.' He held my hand on the way to the underground. 'I love you, Kath,' he said. 'It was worth it to me, you see. If I'd got you long ago I wouldn't have you now, would I?' I shook my head. In all probability he wouldn't. They seldom come off, teenage crushes, do they? Perhaps it is possible to come together only after one has been through the fire, battered and maimed, like Jane Eyre and her Rochester.

We walked from the Oxford railway station along the Oxford

canal, passing occasional barges as we went. Even the dossers who hobnobbed under the bridges looked younger. We made our way up into salubrious north Oxford, to what used to be the grandparents' house. Roger's grandmother had moved, with a friend, to a cottage in Wolvercote. Sally was there to meet us, but Roger was still in his Institute. She had brown curly hair and pretty, laughing eyes which fixed one in a most forthright manner, quite unlike Roger, who shifted his eyes about nervously and blinked a lot. She had a skin like the bloom on an apricot, and a slightly disfiguring swollen lip where some-body had accidentally bashed her with a briefcase as she boarded a train the previous day, but it did nothing to shake her self-possession. The crucifix was not visible to me, since she was wearing a high-necked sweater. Unlike me, she had taken no trouble to adorn herself—she didn't need to: she had more self-assurance.

'Hello, Jonathan,' she said warmly. She offered her cheek for a kiss. 'And this is Katherine. I'm so glad to meet you at last.' She shook my hand. 'Come in.'

The house was all changed. It was, as always, palatial in its solidity and proportion, but innocently unadorned. Stripped of the grandparents' rather looming antiques, it also had none of the arty clutter of needlepoint cushion covers and appliqué'd hangings that I went in for. There was new, stone-coloured Wilton carpeting throughout, and the white walls had no pictures. There was one educational wall frieze in the vestibule, because Sally was obviously a conscientious, pedagogical mother. She had magnetic numbers on the door of the fridge and she had painted the letters of the alphabet, in lower case, around the walls of the downstairs loo with marker pens. Her kitchen was large and beautifully appointed. The plum trees, visible through the kitchen window, were heavy with fruit. We drank a pleasant cup of coffee with her. There was no sugges-tion that she would report me for wearing my beret at a rakish angle.

'Roger is bringing home a colleague for lunch,' she said. 'His wife has just had a baby. They may well be a little late. I wonder if you people would care to collect Clare for me? She's with a friend in the next street. That would please her no end. She

183

considers you a great treat, Jonathan.' She had a way of managing one with politeness. When she said, 'I wonder if you would care to?' she meant, 'Do it.' Perhaps that was what Roger liked. Somebody to boss him around. Somebody to tell him to stop chewing grass and go and practise the G Minor. That never occurred to me before.

Jonathan and I walked the tree-lined streets till we found ourselves admitted into the neighbour's kitchen, where Roger's daughter was watching her friends paint on computer printouts. A three-year-old, with her mother's straight glance and none of her father's apprehensiveness. She accosted Jonathan like a brisk committee woman.

'You weren't supposed to get me, Jonerfun,' she said. 'Mummy was supposed to get me.'

'And why haven't you got a stack of paintings to your name, like the other chaps?' Jonathan said, calling her bluff.

'Because I just like to play running around,' she said. 'Is she your wife?'

'She's Katherine,' Jonathan said. 'She's my friend.' He crouched to button up her duffle-coat.

'Are you going to marry her?' the child said. The hostess laughed a little, nervously.

'No,' Jonathan said.

'Why not?' said the child. Jonathan smiled.

'Because I see no reason why I should tolerate the interference of Church and State in my love affairs,' he said, being deliberately incomprehensible to her. 'Or of your good self, you nosey little bugger.' She giggled with delight at the insult. We said goodbye and went out into the street where she ran on ahead of us, scruffling through fallen leaves.

'Would you like one of those, Kath?' he said. 'One of those little people? Would you like it if I got you up the spout?'

'Forget it,' I said, 'I'm all right.'

Roger entered, accompanied, talking shop.

'Sorry I'm late,' he said. 'This is Donald.' His colleague was bald and bearded, but I knew him.

'I know him,' I said. 'We don't need an introduction.' Donald O'Brien looked baffled. I enjoyed his slight embarrassment.

'I'm sorry,' he said, in that gorgeous unreformed accent. 'Remind me.'

'Eleven years ago,' I said. 'South Parks Road. On a wall. In the rain.' Donald snapped his fingers.

'Bullseye,' he said grinning broadly. 'You were waiting for your boyfriend.' He was a relief beside Roger, being, as he was, so composed and affable. I gestured commandingly to Roger, feeling the irony of being a woman who had, for a time, enjoyed the admiration of all the men in the room.

'Roger was the boyfriend?' Donald said in disbelief. He enjoyed the idea no end. 'Wouldn't you know it? I made a pass at your girlfriend, Roger, but I'll tell you this: I couldn't move her. She insisted on waiting for you in the rain. I couldn't lure her away for a drink.' Roger weathered the coincidence, picking a little at his fingernail. We went through to the living room where Donald sat down beside me on the sofa, beaming effusively.

'You had more hair on your head and less on your face,' I said, 'but I'm glad to say that your accent hasn't changed.'

'Really?' he said. 'Because back in Melbourne they tell me I sound like a Pommie.'

'Well, they're quite wrong in Melbourne,' I said, 'because you sound like Barry McKenzie. You wouldn't want to sound like a Brit, would you? You're not going to tell me you actually live here, in this penal colony, are you?' Donald laughed.

'You don't forget much, do you?' he said.

I flirted with him because he invited it. We engaged in a great effusion of warm mutuality. I did it, I think, to show up Roger, who must have perceived it as a reproach to himself, who knew me so much better, but found it much more difficult to engage people.

'Nothing,' I said magnificently. 'I forget nothing. I'm like an archaeologist on past conversations. I will quote you chapter and verse if you like.'

'Only you can't remember to visit the dentist,' Jonathan said. I'd stood up the dentist the previous day. Darling Jonathan, bless him, was wanting it to be known that he was the one who was party to my domestic habits. That he was the one who knew the colour of my toothbrush. There was credit to be got from knowing me. I was playing the enjoyable game of upstaging Roger in his own house.

'What's an archaeologist?' Clare said.

'A man who digs up bones,' Donald said.

'A man, eh?' I said, laughing. 'You big Aussie sexist.'

'Digs up bones?' Clare said incredulously. 'Is he a dog?' It made us all laugh. Donald took her on his knee. It was curious how much pleasure the meeting gave us both when we did but sit on a wall together for twenty minutes such a long time ago. We were both having hard times, I suppose. Roger was making me more miserable than I had realized. Donald was suffering the absence of Melbourne.

'And now you live here?' I said. 'And you've married one of these awful Oxford women you complained about, who has just had a baby?'

'She's from Sydney,' he said. 'She's just had her third baby, as a matter of fact. Another male, I'm afraid.' He had a thing for Clare, quite obviously, and wanted a daughter. Then blow me if the man didn't pull out from his wallet, upon the instant, a picture of the wife and kiddies. On a beach. Aussie beach. Wife in bikini. 38.22.38. Undulating blonde hair. Sons grinning under blonde fringes.

'Wow!' Jonathan said, who was sitting on the other side of me. He was not slow to see merit in a half naked woman with unmistakeable attributes. 'This is a woman who has had two children?' he said.

'She's bloody handsome, Donald,' I said. 'She's quite something for a bald colonial mathematician, isn't she? I'll bet she's dead nice and all. Do you always keep her in your wallet, along with your money and your credit cards?' I was behaving like a shrew with Donald because I knew he had the strength to weather it, and indirectly I was passing a message to Roger. The message was that if he were to try on me now what he pulled over me in my youth, I would have his bloody balls in the mincer and make no mistake. Donald laughed.

'Jesus, baby,' he said.

'Jesus, baby, what?' I said. He laughed again.

'Jesus, baby, I never knew you had the power of tongues. It's good to see you again. I mean, really.'

Roger opened some very nice college wine for us to drink with our lunch. We ate in the kitchen at a slinky black table with shiny chrome legs. There was a wonderful serpentine aluminium tube which ran out through the kitchen wall. It must have been a central heating ventilator or a thing for extracting cooking fumes. It was then that it dawned on me that everything in Roger's house was new. I wondered what had happened to his instinct to feather his nest with other people's junk. My guess was that Sally simply wouldn't have it. Sally's lunch had been efficiently prepared beforehand. Things had been drawn out of the freezer in plastic containers. It gave the gathering a nice homeliness. It gave one the feeling of being present at a Tupperware party, but Clare wouldn't eat her pâté. She was quite a presence for Sally to contend with, because Sally wasn't pliable. She placed a value upon behaviour. She liked sitting up straight at table and eating what was on your plate. Clare defiantly dumped her pâté on my plate and dug her heels in. Sally apologized to me.

'She really is a very naughty little girl,' she said. I was not comfortable with the word 'naughty.' It had to do, in my philosophy, with seaside postcards and the music hall.

'Why don't you stop moralizing and make her chips?' Jonathan said impertinently. To my great surprise, Sally blushed suddenly and looked rather coyly at Jonathan. She was completely undone.

'She's a lovely kid,' Jonathan said. He picked up the wine bottle to fill her glass. 'Why aren't you boozing, sister?' he said. She smiled at him primly. I found it hard to be rational about Sally Goldman. The bloody woman was not only bossy, I thought enviously, but she had feminine wiles of the most blatant kind.

'I'm pregnant,' she said. The place was an obscene seething hive of fecundity. 'Only just, but that's when it's most important to be careful, of course.' Jonathan smiled at her, and did sums in his head.

'He came home after laying my floor and got you pregnant,' he said. 'That's nice. A little brother or sister for Small here. 'Phone me when you're eight months pregnant and I'll take you out to dinner, because he won't will he? That miserable

187

husband of yours.' Sally shook her head, pouting prettily. She was flirting with him. Flirting. With my bloke, the hussy. And I with my wretched contraceptive pills in Jonathan's kitchen. A foil package in a jam jar. Pills which I probably didn't need anyway. But how do you know whether or not to believe some morbid, scandal-mongering Italian nurse? You had only to look at IRA funerals, as Jonathan once said, to see how much Catholics liked death and bad news.

'Will you let me feel your foetal jerks through your flesh?' Jonathan said. 'I fancy pregnant women.' I was almost ready to run the bread knife through his leg. Sally disguised her pleasure in his attentions under a small rebuke.

'Why don't you and Katherine get married and have your own children if you like it all so much,' she said. 'Frankly, being pregnant makes me feel like a cow.'

'It wouldn't be a marriage in the eyes of God,' he said, to have her on. Sally looked at him sceptically.

'A fat lot you care for the eyes of God,' she said.

In the afternoon, when Donald had gone, Jonathan and I took Clare to the Science Museum where his niece challenged Jonathan's powers of rhetoric with regard to the afterlife. She didn't like the dinosaur bones, she said.

'They're dead,' Jonathan said.

'But they can come alive again,' she said. 'Jesus came alive again, didn't he?'

'Search me,' Jonathan said. 'He ain't never been no friend of mine.' Upstairs, while Jonathan grappled with the resurrection, I made a sentimental journey to the limestones and cast an eye over the stencilling on the iron girders.

'You were flirting with Roger's wife,' I said accusingly on the train.

'Self-defence,' Jonathan said. 'You were flirting with that Aussie.'

'Did you like my charming Aussie?' I said.

'He was all right,' Jonathan said without enthusiasm. 'He obviously gets you ten foot in the air.'

'You exaggerate,' I said. 'I'd have him for a weekend, but not for keeps.'

'It's all right,' he said. 'You do the same for him. He was in the air, same as you. If I hadn't been there he'd have asked you upstairs.'

'He hardly needs me,' I said, 'with a wife like that.'

'Miss Down Under for 1975 has been out of the market for a week or two, if you remember,' he said. 'She's just had a baby.' A great thing about Jonathan and me was that we gossiped something chronic. No holds barred. All that malice we wouldn't venture before others. I think he got it from his mother, because Jacob was too good on the whole—he never displayed this flaw.

'There's a lot of breeding in Oxford,' I said. 'The place is like a bloody factory.'

'There's too much leisure,' Jonathan said, 'too much coming home for lunch,' but the joke didn't altogether work for us. 'Flush those bloody pills of yours down the loo, Kath,' he said. 'Go on. Like you did with the Valium. All those million highly-motivated sperm for Gods sake. You don't think one of them might pull it off?' I turned to the window, straightening my shoulders, thinking that Jonathan was Jacob's flower child was he not? That people couldn't just go around having babies in bedsitting rooms when they'd got jobs to do; that no baby would ever again be like my baby; that no baby would ever again gnaw its purple mottled fists with such dexterity and charm. I watched the wet green flatness of the Oxfordshire fields thinking suddenly of the baby's mob caps. English babies didn't wear those little cotton mob caps to keep off the sun like babies in Italy wore; like Janice had bought in the clothing chain-store on the way home from work, the sweet thing. Suddenly I found that the fields had developed watermarks like the undulations in shot taffeta because my vision was blurred with tears.

'My baby had some mob caps,' I said. 'She hadn't grown into them of course. I mean, she couldn't even hold her head up, Jonathan.' I bored my fists into my eye sockets to mop the copious flow.

'I've made you cry,' Jonathan said bleakly. 'Oh God. Christ, my lovely, I've made you cry.' He reached for my hand, but I shook him off with a sudden viciousness.

'If you want a baby so much,' I said, 'why don't you bugger off and fuck some bloody Sunday School teacher with her female parts intact, like your brother does? Perhaps she's got a sister for you.'

The outburst caused us to lapse into a silence which lasted till the ticket barrier.

'You've got the tickets,' Jonathan said. 'Are you going to hand them over then, or not?' The ticket man was waiting. I had them in my handbag.

'Sorry,' I said. I produced them and we passed through the gate. 'Hey, Jon,' I said with some embarrassment, 'I'm sorry. I was shitty to you.'

'I was boring,' Jonathan said curtly.

'But Jon,' I said, 'if you were to bugger off, I'd feel bereft, you know.'

'Who's buggering off?' he said. 'Not me, snotface. I'm sticking here with you. Like a bloody barnacle. Listen love,' he said earnestly, 'if I'd known the woman was pregnant, we wouldn't have gone.'

'I know,' I said. 'You don't have to persuade me that you're nice, Jonathan. It shows.'

'If you want to know why I sounded so pleased about her boring pregnancy,' he said, but I put a hand on his shoulder to stop him.

'Because you're nice,' I said. 'Why shouldn't you be pleased? There's no harm.'

'Because I was so bloody glad that it was Sally who was having Roger's babies,' he said, 'and not you. If you must know. I'm sorry to say this to you, Kath. I know it's what you might have wanted. Sometimes I think it still is. But I have to see it my way, don't I?' It made me weep profusely onto his chest. 'I've made you cry again,' he said. 'What's the matter with me?'

'I'll chuck away the pills if you like,' I said. 'Right away.'

'If *you* like,' Jonathan said. 'Only if you like.'

'Okay, if I like,' I said. 'Of course I like, Jonathan. I mean, how churlish it would be of me not to like to have your baby. Can we just not talk about it please?'

'Sure,' Jonathan said. 'We'll just screw like blazes and not utter a word on the subject. Right?' I laughed.

'I'll tell you this, though,' he said, 'and then I'll shut up. If I make you pregnant, you get me too. You understand? No woman is going to pull that matriarchal shit over me again, Kath. Not you. Not nobody. You'll have to stick with me.'

'I think I could realistically envisage doing that,' I said. 'I find you a very thinkable proposition.'

'Lady,' Jonathan said. 'I find you a rave-up.'

45

The consultant had already seen me twice in his hospital clinic, but he had asked me to bring Jonathan to his private consulting rooms in Seymour Place. He liked to do Mr and Mrs together. He talked blandly and interminably over the top of his expensive glasses, intoning soothingly. He himself, he said, could see no striking and tangible reason why Mrs Browne should be unable to conceive a child. He addressed himself to Jonathan who appeared to have dominion, in his eyes, over my substandard private parts. I stopped listening to him from time to time and began to amuse myself by imagining the situation reversed. Were Jonathan to have consulted him, let us say, over a hernia in the groin, or retreating testicles, would he have been addressing me over Jonathan's head in this way? Does one man ever discuss, over another man's head, the problem of an incompetent penis? Mrs Browne's cervix did display evidence of considerable surgical repair, he said. And there was a significant area of scar tissue in what he called 'the front passage,' but he had known women in such cases go on successfully to bear subsequent children by Caesarian section. Mr Browne would, he hoped, indulge him if he ventured to suggest that it might not *altogether* be advisable to rule out the possibility of emotional factors inhibiting conception in this case. That, taking into account Mrs Browne's highly regrettable previous experience of childbirth, and her experience of death —not once but twice (here he folded his hands like a clergyman and paused briefly to cast an eye over his notes)—for we must not disregard the matter of her father's untimely death, he said, which occurred when Mrs Browne was, ah, was, let me see, was it nine years old? The sentence had no end. It was nothing but qualifying clauses. He clothed his propositions endlessly and skilfully in yards of wool. I had inherited from my mother a habit of treating men of the medical profession with an almost obsequious deference. Clean pillow-cases for a home visit and best knickers for the surgery. One always apologized for calling out one's GP to a fever, making the assumption that what one's doctor both liked and deserved was patients who didn't get sick. It was therefore a marvellous joy for me to watch Jonathan calmly take apart this high priest of female plumbing.

'She didn't come here to have you iron out her head,' he said. 'She came here to have you repair her reproductive equipment. What she wants to know is whether that is a thing which your particular tribe of mechanics can or cannot do. Spare us the "O" level psychology.' The consultant, to my very great surprise, was unshakeable in his excessive politeness. He absolutely accepted Mr Browne's point, he said. *Absolutely*.

'Goldman,' Jonathan said. 'Goldman is my name.' The consultant paused for a moment and looked again at his notes. Mr Goldberg was *absolutely* right, he said, in that he and his colleagues could never, of course, *altogether* be sure that there were not factors beyond what they perceived, which inhibited conception, but he would like to stress, he said, that in this case, given the circumstances, Mrs Goldberg might, subconsciously (and he would like to say *altogether* understandably), be balking at the alarming possibility of experiencing, once again, the agony of pain and death.

'Garbage,' Jonathan said. Since I assumed we were about to be thrown into the street I gathered up my handbag in readiness and sat on the edge of my chair, but the consultant waited for Jonathan to proceed.

'You have made no test of her response to pain and her fear of death,' Jonathan said. 'You haven't locked her up with man-eating rats, for example, or made her walk the plank. You are fobbing her off with a hypothesis in the absence of knowledge. Nobody will blame you for your absence of knowledge, but the cover-up is dishonest. A collection of Italian butchers, who operate under the badge of your profession, have carved her up incompetently and your instinct is to make less of this and more of her psyche, because you are all members of the same closed shop. Blame the patient and save your face.' He turned to me. 'I can't sit here and listen to any more of this, Kath,' he said, 'I'll wait for you outside.' He swept out, leaving me behind. Jonathan was always a master of the exit and entrance. Like Mr Knightley, he appears in doorways, knocking mud from his boots. As a card-carrying female masochist, I find both this, and his terrific cheek, quite essential to my sense of wellbeing.

The consultant determined to be protective towards me, which was embarrassing in the extreme. I could see that if I stayed much longer, I would find myself in the marriage guidance department. He hoped I would forgive him, he said, but might he be permitted to ask whether these outbursts were typical of Mr Browne's behaviour? Poor Mr Browne. He couldn't have been more innocuous.

'Only when he's on acid,' I said, treading in my master's steps, before I left. In the waiting room, Jonathan was sitting among a collection of women and reading *Cosmopolitan*. He was the only man I knew who had always had the confidence to read women's magazines in public. He was reading the *Girl's Crystal Annual* the day I met him. I went up to him and kissed his cheek.

'Bolshie, aren't you?' I said. Jonathan looked up.

'Hello, Mrs Goldberg,' he said. 'What a timorous creature you are. You let a hack like that trample all over your subtle and lovely head. Jesus, I can get psychology like that in the barber's shop for free.' Jonathan, being a short-haired male, had developed the conviction that if people got their hair cut more often they wouldn't need psychiatrists.

'I took a stand,' I said. 'I told him you were on acid.'

'What?' Jonathan said.

'I thought you'd be proud of me,' I said.

Jane loved my account of Jonathan's behaviour. She fed us tea and chocolate brownies that afternoon and laughed with delight.

'Good for you, Jontikins,' she said. 'Now tell me, Katherine, why is it that we need men to say "garbage" for us? Why don't we say it for ourselves? I think perhaps Annie will say it. I have great faith in Annie. And she'll be utterly charming with it, too.

Still, I have to say, it's got you no nearer having a baby, has it? Perhaps you could adopt one? It may well require you to get married, of course, but you couldn't have any serious objections to that, could you? All it takes is a registrar to mumble a few civic proprieties. You may borrow my ring for the occasion if you're short of funds.' Jacob slapped his brow.

'Jesus, Janie,' he said, 'you can't say these things to people. Have you no sense of decency?'

'I merely thought it expedient if they wanted to adopt a baby,' she said.

'There's another thing,' Jacob said. 'Adopted babies are brown. Brown babies are admittedly very nice, but only in Hampstead. These people are proposing to live in the Irish Republic among the bigoted Catholic peasantry. You want Katherine to carry a brown baby on her hip? She'll have all the local women crossing themselves in the market-place as she goes by.' Jane smiled.

'She'll have that happen in any case,' she said. 'You couldn't have failed to notice that Katherine is glossy.'

'But think, Jane, how we'd look in the agency files,' I said.

'What's the matter with you?' she said loyally. Loyalty was one of the many good things about Jane. 'I think you are both perfectly lovely. If I were choosing parents for myself I should have no hesitation at all in choosing you and Jonathan.'

'For heaven's sake, Ma,' Jonathan said. 'Of course we'll get married if it's any use, but Kath is a lapsed Methodist who's done time in the nuthouse. She's had an infant, now dead, got upon her out of wedlock by a married Venetian. And me? Look at me, for Godssake. I'm divorced. My kid is halfway across the world. I live off my girlfriend in a dubious attic.'

'By another reading you are also very respectable, Jont,' she said. 'I admit it still surprises me to say it. You are a pleasant young man with a good degree from Oxford. You have a novel in the press. Your girlfriend is manifestly a woman of good sense, for all she's had a bad time in the past. You own a dear little house. Your father is this dear old white-headed philosopher here. I think all you need do is get married.'

'And not say "garbage" to the social workers,' I said.

'And not say "garbage" to the social workers, of course,' Jane said. 'Come on now, Jonathan. Ask her nicely.' Jonathan laughed.

'Kath,' he said. 'Yellow stockings; hand on heart; scouts' honour. Will you marry me?'

46

After I had married Jonathan, my mother expressed to me the opinion that I 'could have done a lot worse.' We paid her a weekend visit where he did all the right things. He opened doors for her, laced his shoes properly and sat down beside her to watch an evening's weekend rubbish on the box. She had reduced her standards for me so considerably since I entered the husband market at nineteen that she was, most of all, relieved. Her next-door neighbour had told her that Jews were 'very good to their own and especially to their wives,' and she had passed this on to me that I might similarly snatch some comfort from the fact. Because I was not nineteen, I made no attempt to deny that Jonathan was Jewish. But nor did I tell her, as I would have done then, that Jonathan had been baptized into the Greek Orthodox Church. The object, after all, was not to be cheeky, but—having done what I wanted to do—to make her happy if I could. In return she respectfully eliminated bacon from our Sunday breakfast on Jonathan's account. Jonathan was charmed by this and asked me afterwards how he could be sure she hadn't gone in for any ungodly mixing of meat and milk in the washing-up.

'She bungs the lot into the dishwasher,' I said.

'We must tell her then that for my next visit I want two dishwashers,' he said. 'For the truly righteous washing up is an expensive business.' I hung about his neck, as they say, like a new wife.

'Before you touch me,' Jonathan said, 'assure me that you aren't bleeding. I cannot suffer the taint of a menstruating woman.'

'I'm not bleeding,' I said. It was then that it occurred to us both that I was not bleeding when I ought to have been.

'Don't get excited. You'll bleed tomorrow,' he said. I shook my head.

'It's the only consistent and dependable thing about me,' I said.

'Bless the woman,' Jonathan said. 'Perhaps she's pregnant. Wouldn't that be a joke?' We had gone through the ritual of marriage, involving if not the Church then at least the State in our love affairs, and for what? For the sole reason that it would improve our chances with the adoption agency.

'There she is,' he said, '*Spare Rib* under her arm. Claws into my defenceless brother. Fee Fi Fo Fum. Big talk with that poor innocent Aussie maths bloke. And look at her. She can't get pregnant until she's got a husband.'

A nice reliable English husband.

For a wedding present, my mother gave me a very advanced knitting machine. It was just what I wanted. We planned to take it with us to Ireland and to use it to earn our keep, topped up with what Jonathan and I could earn from bits of editing and with his capital, if necessary. We planned to do what Jacob called 'some comfortable middle-class slumming.' To this end I had taken samples of my work around shops in the King's Road —of all places—and to other places too. I had got myself some commissions and Sally, in her truly Christian way, had found time between her children and her teaching to hawk my stuff round the rich tourist towns of the Cotswolds. Sally, who has her head screwed on tighter than I have mine, said right away that the place to sell the stuff was Switzerland. She arranged this via the previous year's Swiss au pair. Thus it was that I came, through her, to acknowledge that head girls have uses beyond the field of detention and running on the stairs.

'Roger can set things up for you in New York,' she said. 'He's going to a conference there next Christmas.' Nothing I could think of would have castrated Roger as effectively as to find himself taking my knitwear round the shops in Manhattan, an agent for his kooky one-time girlfriend.

'Roger can't do that,' I said. 'I won't hear of it.'

'Why not?' she said. 'I shall insist upon it.'

'Hawk jerseys?' I said. 'He would have to *talk* to people. I mean ordinary people—people engaging in commerce. Sally, please, I would die of embarrassment if you asked him. Really. I would never be able to talk to him again.' Sally looked nonplussed.

'I don't understand you sometimes,' she said, 'but if you insist, I won't.'

I wrote to Michele after I got married, although he hadn't replied to my earlier letter. I told him that Jonathan and I were married and that I was pregnant again. He responded to this in style by sending us a most enormous Tuscan cake. A cake which appeared to be suffering the effects of hormone treatment. It came with a card addressed, saucily, to 'Caterina and the English Jew' and which said, gallantly, that he had only once made a mistake.

47

I had sailed through my first pregnancy with the serenity of the ignorant. It had not crossed my mind that the process of birth could be anything but textbook or the baby anything but unimpaired in body and mind. I was different the next time. Morbid thoughts overwhelmed me in the small hours, when Jonathan would wake to find me pacing the floor inventing for myself a hierarchy of congenital disasters to see which one I could look squarely in the eye. Once, even, clutching a hot-water bottle in terror, having just dreamed that I had given birth to a dead cat in a pool of gore like Leone's miscarriage.

'Oh Jesus!' Jonathan said impatiently, suffering slightly from interrupted nights. 'After a nine-week gestation period I hope? Don't be perverted Kath.' Jonathan, who had so loyally defended my sanity before the gynaecological consultant, must have had his doubts. Babies had always just happened in his life. They had always come live, with their faculties intact, bringing with them no more than the minor inconvenience of curdled shit and the smell of chlorine bleach. He therefore had no understanding of my intermittent visions of harbouring monsters and dead cats. As far as he was concerned, all this belonged to a genre of mediocre horror. Years of adolescent exposure to low comics had inured him to it.

I was, in addition, a somewhat decrepit case of pregnancy. Not only was I sexually immobilized from the start but I was required, during the first three months, to spend occasional week-long spells in hospital in a special ward for the observation of problem pregnancies. A macabre spirit of female cameraderie prevailed among the victims of fluctuating blood pressure, obesity and diabetes, which caused the sufferers to

200

gather in huddles of quilted nylon dressing-gown and fur-fabric mules, swapping tales of previous disasters. I reverted, as I do in moments of crisis, to re-reading *Emma*, with cotton wool in my ears. Such sleep as one achieved was interrupted by the bedtime trolley peddling laxatives, or by the junior doctors roaring their showy little sports cars into the hospital car park.

It goes without saying that I gave up my job. We lived very largely off Jacob, who came forth with generous and regular handouts in the form of the rent he got for his house in Sussex. He would press the money on Jonathan, saying that giving it away saved him from the crime of owning two houses and that he was 'so bloody rich' anyway, he had no use for it. He was concerned for my comfort and safety to a ludicrous degree, which caused me on the whole to retire to my couch like Volpone at the sound of his foot upon the stair and to reach for my smelling salts. Once he caught me at the knitting machine.

'What the hell are you doing?' he said, like an old fusspot.

'Fair Isle,' I said saucily. 'Oh come on, Jacob, one of the first things I ever remember hearing you say was that childbirth was natural. Women have been known to squat down in the wilderness and to chew up the umbilical cord.'

'Don't talk nonsense to me,' Jacob said. He brought me books to read. Improving books, and bunches of grapes. I could tell that he was trying not to relish too much the prospect of playing with his grandchild because my condition was slightly dodgy and because we planned, after the fourth month, to go away— to which end my hospital consultant had arranged to hand me on to a colleague in Dublin. Jacob was guilty of nagging Jonathan terrifically on the subject, in an attempt to make him change his mind about going, and blackmailed him shamelessly with the fact of my health. Jonathan, in turn, accused Jacob of relishing the idea of women in delicate conditions, so that he could the more easily manage and manipulate them. After a while Jonathan took to going out when he came, which Jacob found a litttle rejecting, I think. Jane came to see me in the mornings without him, always talked sense and on one occasion had the excellent idea of bringing Sally with her, in order that her very newly-born baby might give me hope. Her only failing was to imply unfairly that Jonathan wasn't doing enough for me.

I felt so much for Jonathan during those months. He was being driven mad by his father's alarmism and by his mother's occasional brisk implications that he was exploiting me; by my repeated midnight anxieties and by his own reluctance to use his typewriter for fear of waking me; not least by sexual frustration. I found him one night standing in his socks at the kitchen sink. He had placed his typewriter on two deal boards across the sink and—since there was no electric power socket in the kitchen—had plugged it in beside the record player with the help of a lengthy extension cord.

'Come to bed with me,' I said with feeling. 'I need you.' So Jonathan spilled his seed onto my navel and cried some terrible male tears onto my naked shoulder. That same night he stepped out of bed onto his glasses, which he had left on the floor.

'Oh shit,' he said, irritably. 'Too much sex makes you short sighted.' He liked to think that only Roger was capable of absent-mindedly destroying his glasses and found it compromising that he had done so too.

48

Jacob had evidently enjoyed the drive from Bedales. He liked black comedy. He had brought his daughter Sylvia home for the weekend together with two of her friends. Sylvia's birthday coincided with the weekend that Jonathan and I departed for Ireland. They entered in a girly babble wearing bizarre clothing: white drill cloth dungarees worn with satinized cummerbunds; red stilettos worn with horizontally striped ankle socks; sleeveless padded jerkins like nautical life jackets; harem pants made up in camouflage battle dress tied at the ankles with hair ribbons. The bravest of them had a green stripe powdered into her hair and outsize mirror lenses. Sylvia, who was fourteen, was still occasionally to be caught sucking her thumb. She had abundant frizzy hair like Jonathan's which she wore long and attractively looped up at the temples with apple-green plastic hair grips. Relentlessly, her friends called Jacob 'Professor Goldman.' They used their considerable girlish wiles to draw him out and were delighted by almost anything he said.

'I'm not Professor Goldman,' Jacob said. 'I'm Jacob.'

'Sorry, Professor Goldman,' said the cheeky one with the green stripe.

'He's nearly retired,' Sylvia said. 'He's nearly not a professor any more. Isn't he old? You're old, Jake. You're the oldest father in my whole class.'

'I'm not in your class,' Jacob said. They giggled. 'I won't hang about to shame you, Sylvie. I'll shuffle quietly into the Home for Retired Gentlefolk.'

'He's nice, your father,' said the other one to Sylvia, whispering audibly. 'His eyebrows are cute. Don't you think his eyebrows are cute?'

'They're funny, aren't they?' Sylvia said.

'Hello Katherine,' Jacob said, acknowledging my presence, escaping to the elderly. 'Harpies, this lot, aren't they? Budding Margaret Thatchers, the lot of them.'

'Harpic?' Sylvia said.

'Tell this child, Katherine, with her expensive education, what harpies are,' he said.

Roger was there to say goodbye to us, with Sally and the two small children. Also Annie, who had come on her motorbike with her boyfriend on the back, and Sam, who had come alone. Rosie was expected, but hadn't come yet.

'Meg, Mog and Owl,' Jacob said, introducing Sylvia and her girlfriends. He catalogued us for Sylvia's friends.

'My son Roger, my son Jonathan, my daughters-in-law Sally and Katherine. Sally's babies, with whose names I will not trouble you. My daughter Annie and her friend Mike, wearing his heart upon his chest, as you see.' Mike had a T-shirt with a large Hammer and Sickle across the front and a badge which read 'Nuclear Family, No Thanks.' Annie, who was the most benign product of a nuclear family, had a badge to match. 'Over there,' Jacob said, 'the handsome one is Sam.' Sam caused a slight temporary swoon since he had turned out almost as handsome as Roger was at nineteen, but he carried it more easily, without any of Roger's shy, febrile intensity. He talked motorcycle engines with Mike, and they went out together to cast an eye over Annie's bike which she had parked alongside the climbing geraniums at the front door.

Jonathan had made some delightful gingerbread men for Sylvia's tea, which was to be later that day. First the girls intended to go swimming at the house of a neighbour who owned a pool. They were still children enough, once the living room was empty of Sam and Mike, publicly to strip off their clothing and pull on their charming little scanty black bikinis. I was in the kitchen with Jane and Sally, but we could see them through the open doorway behaving as though Roger and Jonathan were too old to take into account. Roger had very properly picked up a copy of the *New Statesman* in which to bury his head and for a moment had turned, in any case, to look at his tiny son who was asleep in my rush basket under Jane's palm tree. Jonathan was involuntarily staring at Sylvia's friends. One of them had profoundly attractive dimples showing above her buttocks.

'Look at Roger and Jonathan,' I said, whispering to Jane. 'Roger is reading the *New Statesman* and Jonathan is picking the girls over to see which one of them he wants.' Jonathan, who had sharp ears, heard his name immediately. He got up and came through to the kitchen.

'What are you saying about me?' he said.

'Never mind,' Jane said. 'We forgive you because you made such charming gingerbread men.'

After the girls had gone, Annie thoughtfully made a neat pile of the vibrant teenage tote-bags so that we could sit down and drink some wine and eat some cheese without the clutter. Annie was a large square young woman with more than a hint of facial hair. She contradicted the popular myth that men like pretty women. Men loved her. She was always surrounded by groups of attentive males talking sandstone and bronze.

Jane looked terrifically well and blooming. She also looked more beautiful than ever. Her manner of dress had changed since I first knew her in that she humoured Jacob by putting on things which he bought for her. She was wearing such a thing today: a soft light-blue woollen dress which fell from a high collar and which Sally admired.

'Jake bought it for me as a garment suitable to my age and station in life,' Jane said, putting down the compliment. He had quite evidently bought it to match her eyes. It was at this point that Rosie came in. She had with her a man so profoundly lacking in proletarian accoutrements that one could only stand and stare. He was Michele's stereotype of the chinless Englishman, whose existence I always patriotically denied. He was wearing his old school tie. He called Jacob 'sir.' He almost clicked his heels when Rosie presented him.

'How do you do, sir?' he said. Jacob was in and out of his kitchen carrying things for Jane. He paused in the sitting room to review the need for glasses, which the poor young man misread. He leaped out of his chair. 'Sorry, sir,' he said, 'am I sitting in your chair?'

'Sit down, young man,' Jacob said irritably. 'All the chairs in this house are mine.' I escaped, like a coward, to the kitchen where I helped Jane with the food.

'My daughter!' Jacob hissed semi-hysterically to Jane when he came in. 'She's in the clutches of a county solicitor.'

'Calm yourself, Jacob,' Jane said witheringly. 'He looks to me like a nice young man who sells leather goods in Liberty's. He'll last a week, no more.'

'You told me she liked proles,' I hissed. 'I don't believe you.'

'It's the truth,' Jacob hissed back. 'This is all quite new. What is he? Is he from Sandhurst? For Godssake, Janie, he's intolerable.'

'You're neurotic about your daughter,' Jane said. 'You won't be happy until she shaves her head and enters the convent.'

Everyone drank to Jonathan and me and wished us well, but Jacob, who had crabbed at us ever since we conceived the idea of going to Ireland, could not even in the eleventh hour let it rest.

'Well, Jont,' he said, 'we'll have to make the best of this hare-brained scheme of yours, though I'll never know what's wrong with London. The country is for peasants and milkmaids as you'll find out. And then who is going to buy this miserable, derelict house off you?'

'Now then, Jacob, leave him alone,' Jane said firmly. 'Jonathan likes the country. He always did. Just accept that you differ in this respect.' Annie had her mouth open with indignation on our behalf.

'And who are you to say Jont's house is derelict?' she said. 'He's had a builder in it, hasn't he? You haven't even seen it, you old bore. Roggs has seen it and he's not complaining.'

'When are you going to come and see it then, Jacob?' I said. 'You're not going to wait for the half-price fares, I hope?' Jacob smiled.

'Katherine, my sweet girl,' he said, 'do you have any idea what isolation means?' I thought yes, that I did. It meant telephoning the speaking clock at four in the morning from Hendon. It meant being with the Bernards in a crowded city. It did not mean being alone in the country with Jonathan.

'I'll have Jonathan,' I said, sounding hopelessly starry-eyed.

'And a small child?' Jacob said. 'Motherhood is isolating

206

enough, sweetheart. You will be cut off and tied to your child. All this knitting nonsense of yours will peter out because the child will claim your time. And because there's nobody left employed in this country to buy the things you make.'

'Rubbish,' Rosie said. 'The West End is full of shops selling classy jerseys. So is Hampstead. You don't notice. You only notice bookshops. Of course people buy them. I buy them, don't I? We don't all buy our clothes in Oxfam, you know, like some I could mention.' Jane smiled, undisturbed by the jibe.

'Why is it nonsense to knit jerseys, then, Jake?' Annie said. 'Coming from someone who teaches metaphysics, I must say, it's a bit of a cheek isn't it? I mean which do people need more of? Jerseys or metaphysics?'

'The fact is, darling, people pay me to do it,' Jacob said. 'But these two here—God help them, Annie, between them they've got no practical sense at all. Which one of them is it that has the entrepreneurial spirit?'

'Me,' I said. 'My father was a shopkeeper, Jacob. Jonathan knows about the country and I know about selling things. You think I won't work hard. Admit it. You still think I'm a scatty girl with no application.'

'Flower,' Jacob said, 'I think you're lovely.' I laughed.

'Thanks,' I said. 'A lovely scatty girl with no application.'

'He's a sod, Katherine,' Jane said. 'I hope you are fully aware of that.'

'My dear child,' Jacob said, 'what has hard work got to do with it? Money was never made out of hard work. Nobody ever got rich through labouring. Money is made through the exploitation of the labour of others. What you need, Katherine, is enough knitting machines to supply all the local women who will then do the work for you while you people live off the surplus. That's what you have to do. That is the only rationale for going to Ireland, as any good capitalist can tell you. In a situation of high unemployment you exploit the opportunities for low paid, home-bound female labour. Then you hire an accountant to fiddle your books and you cheat the tax man. That's called initiative. That's what you don't have, Katherine, though your charms are many.'

'Notebooks out, chaps,' Jane said. 'I hope you're all taking

207

this down. What a frightful old pedant you are, Jake. I'm bound to say it makes one proud not to have opened a book with footnotes in twenty years.'

'But Jont,' Jacob said, 'the point is that I don't and can't see why you people set out to starve. Surely it is important not to starve? Surely you remember the words of the great Brecht on the subject? "*Erst komt das Fressen, dan komt die Moral.*" '

'Why are you so greedy for them?' Annie said. 'Perhaps you're a frustrated capitalist, Jake. Katherine doesn't want to get rich. She wants to make beautiful things. That's all there is in life worth doing.' Jacob was touched by her sweetness.

'You're a beautiful thing,' he said. 'Once upon a time I made a beautiful thing.' Annie jabbed him amiably in the ribs, and smiled engagingly.

'Two fingers to you, you silly old man,' she said. 'Just because my nose is nearly as big as yours. Don't think that I care.'

Jane moved closer to me in that attractive, conspiring way she had which was always so flattering in its implication about oneself. She put a hand on mine.

'You're getting an awful lot of advice from Himself,' she said. 'This day and every day. I hardly like to add my own, but it is this. Your scheme to make things will work splendidly because —no matter what Jake says—there are always enough very rich people to buy a few very beautiful things. Rosie is perfectly right. Jacob knows this too. He is simply concerned about losing Jonathan's company.'

'That's not true,' Jacob said. Poor Jacob, lying through his teeth, the old bastard. Jane ignored him.

'Your scheme will work on one condition, Katherine, if I may say so,' she said, 'and that is that you wring—I emphasize *wring*—from that stubborn and truculent son of mine, a very specific and very business-like commitment to share the domestic work and the child-care with you.'

'He will,' I said. 'He does. He couldn't be nicer to me, Jane.'

'We're all nice to you, Katherine,' she said. 'You're having a difficult pregnancy. But I'm talking about the long run. I know all about these clever chaps like yours and mine you see. I know all about their nice impressive commitments to the rights of women and the division of labour, because they're very good at articulating these things and it costs them nothing to say it all as nicely as they do. If you are going to earn a living, Katherine, and keep up seriously with your orders, you will not do it and mind a small, active child at the same time. Jonathan must mind that babe for you, either every morning, or for four whole working days a week. Not as a favour, mind, but as a necessity. Along with the shopping and the cooking and cleaning and laundry. Just as women do it. Make him earn the right to sit at his typewriter. That's his indulgence. All the men in this family are distinguished by the fact that they earn a living from their favourite pastime. That is a luxury in a suffering world. Jonathan doesn't even earn a living by it yet, but that is by the by. He will.'

'Just carry on, Ma,' Jonathan said. 'Don't mind me.'

'Thank you, Jonathan,' Jane said, 'I will.'

'Or you could save your breath,' Jonathan said, 'and have my head right off. On a bloody plate. Go on.' Jane laughed briefly.

'Katherine,' she said, 'this is what you do. You put down a schedule for him, in writing, and make him sign it. Get him drunk first if necessary, or threaten to hide his fishing tackle.' Jonathan was miming her behind her back, making horrible, schoolboy yakkity-yak faces which made me want to laugh. 'Photocopy it and leave a copy with me,' she said, 'because if you don't, I have a good idea how it will be in that little house of yours. Lots of lovely fresh fish on the fire and you sitting down to that knitting machine after sluicing the nappies at midnight.' Jonathan had stopped pulling faces at her and was eyeing her suddenly like a gathering storm cloud.

'Are you trying to be funny?' he said. 'Because you're not succeeding. Sharing the work is what I do now. She tells you so herself, but you're so busy grinding your axe you don't even listen to her. What makes you think I'm like Jake?'

'I wonder,' Jane said provocatively. 'Now whatever could make me think such a thing?'

'I don't need Katherine to find my stinking socks for me,' Jonathan said indignantly. 'I'm not like Jake. I cook. I cook all the time. Now leave me alone.'

'My darling Jontikins,' Jane said, 'we all agree that your gingerbread men are lovely.'

209

'Oh shut up, you old cow,' Jonathan said. 'Don't bloody patronize me.'

'And he goes to the launderette,' I said. I held an impeccable sleeve for effect. 'See this shirt. Jonathan ironed this shirt.'

'Look,' Jane said, 'I don't deny for a moment that he is somewhat better than Jake in that respect. The times have moved to make him so. Don't think I haven't heard him in that funny little kitchen of yours, whistling Boccherini over *The Pauper's Cookbook*. I won't say I wasn't impressed, but quite a lot of men will cook now and again if their wives lay in the garlic and root ginger and whatever else is necessary for the star turn.'

'Oh fuck off, you bitch,' Jonathan said. 'Just get off my back, lady.'

'Babies tie women at home, Katherine,' Jane said. 'There is nothing like having a woman at home to create dependence. Jonathan's last baby was born in such very different circumstances, you see. Hosts of aunts and grannies falling over themselves for the privilege of rinsing the nappies. Now look at the poor man. I've made smoke pour out of his nostrils.'

'When Katherine needs your advice she'll bloody well ask for it,' Jonathan said. 'Okay?'

'Or perhaps she won't,' Jane said. 'Not when she needs it most. So I give it to her notwithstanding.'

'Her experience is infinitely wider than yours,' Jonathan said. 'She's had more men in her life than you've had hot dinners. What makes you think she needs your advice on how to protect herself against me, you evilminded crone? She spent four years living with a fascist lunatic.'

'Six,' I said.

'You surely can't mean that charming man who sent you the cake?' Jane said, but Jonathan ignored her.

'What did you ever do but flutter your eyelashes at an arty queer to make Jake miserable, you patronizing bitch?' he said. Jacob was smoking one of his smelly cigars.

'Calm down, Jont,' he said mildly through the fog. 'She patronizes everybody. We all like to display our greatest talents. That is hers. That and enumerating female grievances. Jane took out a monopoly on hardship for the female sex long before anyone thought to burn a bra in a public place. Jane

210

invented the Women's Movement in my back yard.'

'Over your babies' cot sheets more like,' Jane said. 'Over your rubbish bin, Jacob, scraping chop bones off dinner plates. Over the wash basin, picking out your beard remnants while you sat and wrote your lovely books. Now it's your son who's writing books. Why should the same thing happen to Katherine? Why shouldn't she benefit from my experience?'

'Because she can't,' Jacob said shortly. 'People don't. You're very boring, Janie.'

'Being boring has never inhibited you from carping at them, has it Jake?' Jane said. 'Now it's my turn.'

'You sound like any one of a thousand band-wagoning harridans,' Jacob said. 'Women against the world. Women against the bloody works.' Mike leant over to Annie.

'Does he call himself a radical or something, your father?' he said, *sotto voce*. It made them giggle quietly together. 'He sounds like Genghis Khan.'

'Don't,' Annie said, whispering back.

'Your children have grown up for Christssake,' Jacob said. 'You haven't washed a cot sheet in years. Look at them. They're lovely rational adults. You have a cleaning woman to muck out the kitchen for you. If you find yourself having to pick my beard out of the wash basin from time to time, I'm sorry for you, but what the hell else have you got to do with your time, other than harass your daughters-in-law? You can't want to spend your whole life at that damned piano. That is your indulgence, sweetheart, and it never paid the gas bill.'

Jesus, I thought to myself. Jacob, you swine. You absolute bloody swine. Why is it I have always liked you so much?

'My quarrel is with *Jane*,' Jonathan said. 'With Jane, who has this persistent fantasy about me as some jackbooted hood. Don't side-track her with all this clap-trap about the Women's Movement.'

'It isn't altogether clap-trap to anyone like me, Jont, who's had six children,' Jane said. 'Seven, counting Jake.'

'Oh please, Ma,' Annie said. 'Please stop it.'

'I have no quarrel with the Women's Movement,' Jonathan said, 'just so long as it isn't my sperm goes into the freezer to fertilize lesbian marriages.'

211

Sally, who was offering her lovely breast to her small son, tensed slightly, with disapproval at Jonathan's terminology, though she weathered it well enough. In her hierarchy of human secretions, she obviously found breast milk more acceptable than sperm. But Jane smiled, as Jonathan meant her to. In his kindness, he was exercising for her benefit a flair for comic relief.

'You're very sweet, Jontikins,' she said, 'and very clever. Don't be angry with me. It was injudicious of me to meddle in your affairs and I hope you will forgive me.'

Roger's small daughter was frustrating herself with a gyroscope which she could not manipulate. She was bumping up against Roger's thigh, trying to attract his attention, but he didn't hear her—I don't think he really heard any of us. In a house full of talkers Roger never talked much. He always disliked the unremarkable small change of conversation. It was persistently a difference between us—I love what people say to each other. For this reason I like to stand in queues while Roger, in my experience, avoided shops for fear that he might be called upon to say whether he didn't think that the weather had come on a trifle nippy. He had a nice enough gentle manner with his child, but he did not play with her. Not in that wild and wonderful way in which Jacob played with children; that way which made watching adults cry, 'Stop it, Jacob, she'll break a leg. It'll only end in tears.'

'He's not listening to you, Small,' Jonathan said to her. 'Bring it here. I love those things. I'll make it go like the clappers.' He caused the thing to spin on the string in a most accomplished way and gave her the ends of the string to hold. It made me stir with pleasure to think that Jonathan would make gyroscopes spin for my child. Besides, the idiom turned me on. To go like the clappers.

Sally transferred the baby to the other breast and tucked the first away into a copious front-fastening nursing bra.

'Watching you, Sally, makes my nipples twitch,' Jane said, wishing to make herself agreeable. 'I could wish it was me all over again.' But Sally was needing to unload annoyance. She did not like complainers and Jane had broken the code.

'I don't wish to revive what has just passed,' she said. 'Also I

212

do accept your point, Jane, and I do incidentally wish that Jonathan would try not to become abusive, but really, aren't you going to ridiculous extremes? Roger and I don't sign things. We simply help each other. We both teach. We both fetch Clare from nursery school. It depends on which one of us is free in the lunch hour. Anything else would be selfishness, wouldn't it? We have our rules. I cook at the same time every evening for whoever is there to eat and I don't do it again. Roger sees Clare to bed while I do the dishes. We both work till bedtime and if Clare wakes we take turns to go to her. I can't imagine having to wave bits of paper under his nose.' For Sally, living was a simple art of which she had clearly always had the mastery.

'So who was it had a baby in Eighth Week?' Jonathan said, to take her down. 'That's very bad news for an Oxford man. And poor old Rogsie rushed off his feet with the work.'

'All right, Jonathan,' Sally said a little irritably. 'I had the baby in Eighth Week. That was beyond my control.' During Sally's highly reasonable little speech, smacking somehow of the simplicity of toytown, I happened to catch Jacob's eye. He blew me a perfect and very saucy smoke ring, which I acknowledged furtively as if accepting a note passed secretly during prayers, under the eye of the headmistress.

'Roger is different,' Jane said. 'He was always serious-minded, hard-working and obliging. And you, Sally, you are different too. You are much better than Katherine at putting across to people exactly what suits you.'

'She means you're bossy, sister woman.' Jonathan said.

'I mean nothing of the kind,' Jane said. 'Sally is very clear about her own needs, that's all.'

'Not like you, you poor, timid creature,' Jonathan said. 'You let everyone walk over you I suppose? Jesus, Ma, my memory of you is of a dominating virago. Do this. Do that. Especially with Roggs. Simon says clean out the sink. Simon says play the flute. Simon says if you haven't got any French verbs to sort out, bring in the coal. When you've done that stand on your head and recite your twelve times table in Latin.' Jane laughed.

'But it took me years of practice, Jonathan,' she said. 'I was hoping to save Katherine the trouble. I've offended you, my darling. I'm sorry. It isn't my place to give your wife advice. I do hope you can still see your way to having me come in the spring and do your garden for you and see my grandchild. I shall be very scrupulous and not interfere. You may turn me out if I do.' Jonathan eyed her with some sceptical amusement during this piece of caustic humility.

'That's right,' he said, with a degree of affection. 'Crawl, you old cow. Humility is right up your street.'

Rosie's man could bear no more.

'I say,' he said suddenly, 'I don't like to interfere, old chap, but a chap oughtn't to talk to his mother like that. Not in my book.' The embarrassment following upon this utterance brought a blush to Annie's cheek, and Mike stared awkwardly at his feet. Jacob looked around unabashed, as though some-body had just raised a point in a seminar and he was waiting for a volunteer to take it up. Roger looked at him with the contempt he might once have visited on a man who cleaned his shoes.

'And what book is that?' Jonathan said. 'Biggles? Who are you, anyway?' Rosie lost her cool.

'You can shut up, Jonathan,' she said. 'Understand? Jeremy is going to marry me, as a matter of fact. So that's who he is. My fiancé. We came here to say goodbye to you and that's what we're doing. Saying goodbye and good riddance.' She got up to go. Her young man followed, pausing only to nod politely to Jane and say goodbye.

'Goodbye, Mrs Goldman,' he said. 'Goodbye, sir.' They left behind them silence and astonishment.

'Ought I to catch up with her?' Annie said.

'Leave her,' Jane said. 'It's all nonsense. I assure you, it's non-sense. Rosie is histrionic. Like Jake.'

'Go to hell,' Jacob said. He got up and made himself ready to go after her, wasting no time.

'Now I've remembered something I wanted to ask you people,' Jane said. 'Do you want the bed ends of that very nice old brass bed Jake and I used to have? We threw away the wires and the mattress but perhaps Roger could manufacture a new base for you. Jacob and I can't get on with a double bed any more. It makes us sleep fitfully. We come together from separate bedrooms like royalty.'

'Mother,' Roger said, 'at the risk of appearing ungracious, I

214

have to point out that the University pays me to spend some of my time in the Mathematical Institute. It may be my indulgence but it is also my job.'

'Sorry, Roggs,' Jane said. 'Of course it is. I only suggested it because you are so wonderfully clever.'

Jane, Jonathan and I went into her bedroom to admire the bed ends. She had them stored in her bedroom against the wall.

'We can take them like that and find a carpenter,' I said. 'Everything else is on the roof rack. Why not these?'

'I'll bring them when I come, shall I?' Jane said. 'Then I will have to come.'

'Of course you'll come,' Jonathan said. 'You must know that Katherine will insist on it. You must know she is devoted to you, you warped old battle-axe.'

'As I am to her,' Jane said. 'And I want to tell you that I've had enough complimentary epithets from you to last me quite some time, Jontikins. I'm sorry that my private life impresses you with its limited range, but it wasn't for lack of opportunity. I'm sorry if you found my flirtations with John offensive. It's funny. It was Roger who I thought would be the one to mind. He always had such high standards for me. I always worried terrifically about Roger. Do you think it upset him?' Jonathan shrugged.

'I was talking off the top of my head, Ma,' he said. 'Slinging mud. Don't fret about Rogsie. He's grown up. He's thrown away what Kath calls his Hamlet hat. He's done you proud. You gave him no choice, of course.'

'You are nasty to me, Jonathan,' she said. 'You want me to beat my breast. All right, I will. I'm worried about Rosie. I was never a good mother to her. She was always such an ordinary little girl, Jonathan. I wasn't ready to accept it. I thought then that all children came like you and Roger. I didn't know any better.'

'She's all right,' Jonathan said. 'She won't marry that creep.'

'If I come and stay with you, you won't see it as a threat to your well-being, will you, Jont?' she said. 'I mean, you're not anything like as mad as your father, are you? Not meaning anything by it, of course. He's so much more than I deserve. Don't think I don't know that, Jonathan.'

Jonathan was tired of quarrelling with her, of going through that human spider-dance which expressed no more than her own pain in losing him and her own pain in losing her youth; her love for me and her irrational urge to will happiness upon us.

'Katherine is getting more like you as the days go by,' he said teasingly. 'She keeps cracked antique jugs on the mantelpiece full of string and shirt buttons and library tickets. She's developed a thing for that repulsive Staffordshire Salt Glaze.'

'I never knew you disliked it,' I said. 'I think it's beautiful.' Jonathan laughed.

'You never asked me. I think it's disgusting.'

'It's perfectly lovely,' Jane said with finality. 'Of course it is.'

'It makes me think of aberrant growths on the skin,' Jonathan said. 'It puts me in mind of scurfy excrescences.'

Jane took Jonathan in a motherly embrace. 'But that is not the salt glaze, my dear Jonathan,' she said. 'That is *you*. Everything reminds you of something nasty. I only discovered how much when I read your novel.'

'Oh, you've read it, have you?' Jonathan said. 'Is that why you're getting at me today?'

'I am not getting at you, Jont. I merely tell the truth about you. That you are a terrible nuisance like Jake. I'm not denying that you're worth it. I was naive. Forget it. Katherine will throw away the Staffordshire Salt Glaze and you will both be very happy. But about your novel, Jont. God in heaven, isn't it smutty? How do you come to be so smutty, Jonathan? It isn't half good, though. I found it quite terrifyingly funny at times. There's nothing piffling about your smut. Some really noble smut you've got there. With justice, it ought to make you famous. Don't you think so, Katherine?'

Jonathan's novel was actually more than I could cope with during pregnancy, being a spirited if macabre four hundred page satirical hallucination, rich in shots up the female crotch. I had promised myself to read it properly while I breast fed, if it didn't have the effect of curdling the milk.

'You make me think of Swift,' she said. 'Another Jonathan with a nasty powerful mind. It's most appropriate that you are going to Ireland.' Jonathan was pleased and also a little embarrassed.

'You do me too much honour, lovely lady,' he said. 'Carry on. You give me conviction.'

'I thought Swift was kinky,' I said. 'I mean, sexually arrested.' Jane delivered to me, in a glance, the schoolmarm put-down.

'We'll have less of that, Katherine,' she said. 'You know perfectly well what I mean. It's prose I have in mind. I'll tell you what, chaps,' she said conspiringly, 'though I shouldn't tattle and I won't, but just this once. I made strong efforts to keep my copy from Sally when she came this morning, but I don't think I succeeded. I think she's been and taken a peek, don't you? You aren't in her good books today. Have you noticed?' Jonathan shrugged without interest.

After the birthday tea and the gingerbread men, after the schoolgirls, with their concave virgin navels and wet hair, had retired to listen to taped New Wave, after Roger had gone, taking his family back to Oxford with his sweet children clipped into safety harnesses and carry-cot straps, after Annie and her boyfriend had zoomed off in their ghastly rollerball helmets, and Jacob had taken off with Sam for a walk on the Heath, Jonathan and I, with some difficulty, said goodbye to Jane. We drove off in the car, which Sam had put together for us, with our luggage stuffed into the back and tied to the roof. Jonathan heaved a tired and grateful sigh.

'Well,' he said, 'that's the family off our backs.' Jonathan was not in fact menaced in any way by my fondness for his family. He was fond of his family himself but his tolerance for most things ran out sooner.

'If this car were only less jammed up and you less hopelessly untouchable,' he said, 'I would practise some discreet, therapeutic fucking upon you in the next lay-by.'

'Would you?' I said. 'I love you, Jonathan.' I said this gratefully and realistically, because it was true. I fell in love with Jonathan slowly and judiciously. A thing I had never done before.

'I need it after my mother,' he said. 'By what right does the woman talk about me as if she had letters patent from God on

217

the subject?' Jonathan talked sex using words to deputize for the act which it was not opportune for us to commit.

'There's going to be some incessant and prolonged activity in that little house of ours, Kath,' he said. 'Making up for lost time. I'm going to heave my weight off your ribs every morning and leave you in a tacky pool of my ooze.' Jonathan, I considered, had a more than average involvement with his ooze. He liked to make reference to it. (I give you this for the analyst's case-book, merely.)

'Very nice,' I said politely, over the twitching in my groin.

'Then I'll bring you your breakfast,' he said, 'in bed. Boiled eggies and tea for my lovely sexy, oozy, pregnant Kath. We don't really want that old bed, do we? Let's have a new one six feet wide.'

I was very romantic about the prospect of our lives in that house, though, I hope, not without a degree of protective irony. I hoped to be a caustic romantic. I learnt it from Jane. What though my goat boy peed into milk bottles and lived off my earnings? He assured me that he didn't actually play the flute very well either, though it sounded all right to me. I pictured myself sitting by the fire and knitting the Celtic mists and shadowy pools into my cloth. I pictured Jonathan getting up from his typewriter and going out to split wood like a man in Ingmar Bergman, and the child, with woollen mittens flapping at its cuffs, tottering after him.

'And don't think I didn't see you eyeing up the schoolgirls,' I said challengingly. Jonathan laughed and put his left hand on my thigh.

'Sweet, that little blonde in drillcloth, wasn't she?'

'That's my knitting machine in the back,' I said. 'I own the means of production, so you watch it.'

49

The house was beautiful. Like harlequin's coat it was put together through the love of friends. Annie and her house-mates, for the price of a week in the country and warming bowls of soup, slept on our floor at Christmas and painted all the walls. A very nice local carpenter made us some doors and skirtings and a kitchen workboard. He made some window seats, which I varnished and fitted with cushions. We rush-matted the floors. I made patchwork curtains and took unashamed pleasure in what Jacob—damn him—called 'the womanly art of homemaking.' Annie stencilled patterns around the fireplace, having no Roger over her shoulder to put her down, but only Mike, who helped. Jonathan, as Jane predicted, fished and typed, but also fed us all and praised. There were days when I thought we would freeze to death. For Christmas Jonathan bought me a thermal vest and men's long johns. Sally sent, with Annie, her hand-on carry-cot and count-less Baby Gro suits. Roger sent, in the post to Jonathan, some well disposed reviews clipped from the newspapers. The baby was female, born by Caesarian section, suckled first under a plaster figure of the Virgin Mary and later at home on a mattress on the floor of our bedroom. I tried reading Jonathan's novel as I fed her, but gave it up in favour of *Emma*, which is still my favourite. Jonathan, who did indeed bring me boiled eggs in bed, bathed her in a plastic washing-up bowl at the feet of my convalescent self. She was quite different from my other baby, being nocturnal, irregular and greedy in her feeding habits. We called her Stella, having been put in mind of it by Jane's reference to Swift, which caused Jonathan to return to a favourite poem of his youth. Swift's 'Birthday Poem to Stella,' which goes as follows:

Stella this Day is thirty-four,
(We shan't dispute a Year or more)
However Stella, be not troubled,
Although thy Size and Years are doubled,
Since first I saw Thee at Sixteen
The brightest Virgin on the Green,
So little is thy form declin'd
Made up so largely in thy Mind.

Jane came, buttoned up once more in cashmere to keep out the wind and wearing her hair pulled back in a headmistressy bun. She drove me off to plant nurseries where she chose us the best of disease-resistant apple trees and a carefully staggered collection of shrubs and climbing things, so that our garden should have what she called 'winter interest.' She bought us things to make fires in and things to make compost in, a set of tools and a very space-age mower.

'Have them on me,' she said, when we tried to pay her. She was terrific at getting a spade into the earth when it came to digging up rocks.

'This needs cutting back in the autumn, Jont,' she said. 'Pay attention or you'll have me back again in September.' Jonathan wouldn't ever come shopping with us, saying that he'd had enough of shopping with Jane in his childhood and couldn't stand that class-bound way in which she barked at shop assistants.

'I hate my accent as much as you do,' she said, 'and if I do bark at people it's only because I'm so frightened of them, Jonathan. I'm not a poised and coping person like your Katherine.'

'Me?' I said in disbelief.

'Her?' Jonathan said, with equal disbelief.

'Why do you think I had all my lovely babies?' she said. 'It was a way of ensuring that I never had to go out to work. You know me, Jont. I couldn't have run a flower stall.'

'You always played the piano uncommonly well,' Jonathan said.

'Could I have held down a job in the village hall thumping out the music for the Saturday ballet classes, do you think?' she said.

'Why do you knock yourself so much?' Jonathan said.

'Isn't that what women do?' Jane said.

'Only until they read *Spare Rib*,' Jonathan said; since setting up with me he had taken to reading the odd issue of this publication because I intermittently introduced it into our lives, but he didn't care for it much.

'That's not for nice old ladies like me, is it?' Jane said. 'It's for advanced young women.'

'It's for raped lesbians,' Jonathan said. 'Go and buy me some fucking apple trees, both of you.' We did that, leaving the baby tied to Jonathan's chest in a canvas bag—bought cut-price through the pages of *Spare Rib*—and came back, of course, to find her sucking frantically at the wool of his jersey in the vicinity of his milkless paps.

'I like it here,' Jane said, over her tea, while I fed the baby. 'Jake was wrong about this place, wasn't he? It suits you very well. I could stay here forever. Rosie is determined to marry that young man, you know. I don't like it one bit. That's what I'm going back to—planning a wedding.'

50

The last thing I will tell you about is Rosie's wedding. It was one of those weddings where the bride's and the groom's families stand out like opposing football teams, wearing their colours. All the decent hats were, thank God, on our side. We slid into position, late, beside Jane, having been travelling half the night, and placed the carry-cot at our feet. It was just as the organ swelled.

'She's a mouth breather, that baby,' Jane whispered to me across Jonathan. Rosie was beginning to make her way down the aisle on Jacob's arm in white satin.

'Watch this for a lark,' Jane whispered, rather bitterly.

'Shut up and behave properly,' Jonathan whispered back.

I came upon Rosie in her parents' house after the wedding reception, struggling out of white satin in Sylvia's bedroom.

'The bloody zip has stuck,' she said. 'Help.' We giggled over it together, till we had her standing in her pants.

'You looked stunning,' I said, which was true. Rosie laughed, brightly and on edge.

'Isn't it a hoot?' she said. 'God, I wonder if Jeremy's mother has the slightest idea of how many men I've slept with.'

'What are you going to put on?' I said.

'That,' she said. She pulled a rather wonderful brown silk thing from under a coat on the bed. 'Jake spent a day in Regent Street with me, signing cheques,' she said. She climbed into the dress feet first and looked at herself in the glass. 'I'm glad John Millet isn't around to see me,' she said. 'He told me, once, that I had destiny. Did he give you that stuff, Katherine? I mean the hot bath and the black sheets and all?' I nodded.

'Something like that,' I said. 'I think it had to do with power.'

'Do you think he gave my Ma the treatment too?' she said.

'I think Jake got to her first,' I said. Rosie looked at herself in the glass in the brown silk.

'Some people have all the luck, don't they?' she said. 'The only man I ever cared about killed himself. Slit his wrists with one of those knives you use to cut carpets with. You know? Like carpenters have. You met him, actually. He was with me that day I saw you again, after you came back. When Jane had her operation, remember?'

'I remember,' I said.

'Don't tell my parents,' she said. She seemed determined to be alone. 'What's the point? Tell Jonathan I'm sorry I yelled at him that time. I like Jonathan. He helped me lose my 'cello once when I was a kid. It got me off the hook. I haven't got any brains, you see. Not for any of the stuff my mother cares about. You made a lot of difference to me. I used to go to sleep in that dress that you made me. I used to try and copy your writing. I even stole a drawing of you once from John's house, when I was fifteen. I've still got it somewhere. You look as though you were about to burst into tears.' Rosie laughed. 'I'm a bit drunk,' she said. 'I'm off to the bridal suite, no less.' At the bottom of the stairs Roger had sought out Jonathan. I heard him say, with his transcending snobbery, of Rosie's mother-in-law, 'She's like a grocer's wife who has just won a lottery.'

'Me?' I said, to embarrass him, because aggression is the device I have for surviving the pain of Roger's presence. 'Jon, let's go; get the carry-cot and let's go.' Jacob saw us out.

'You did that very well, Jacob,' I said. 'You looked like the real thing.' Jacob smiled manfully.

'It's the last time I give away a daughter,' he said. 'I'm planning to sell the next one.'

That was the last time I saw Jacob. Shortly afterwards he fell down with a fatal heart attack one Sunday morning in his beautiful kitchen, attempting to mouth words, which Jane couldn't catch. I will say, to honour his dear and glorious memory, that I never think of the dialectic without glottal stops; that I never think of *Women in Love* without heavy breathing in

223

the bracken. I have thought, at times, of Jacob's preface which so impressed me, because since then Jonathan has given me a mention in his own. Jacob's is, of course, a pretty piece of dishonesty, through and through. As always, he has his cake and he eats it. It manages, under the guise of a pretty compliment, to take shots both at his fellow academics and at Jane. What he is really saying is that his colleagues have inferior wives. Poor humdrum creatures who edit and annotate, while his own wife is a goddess, who is above such things. What he is saying, also, is, 'Dammit Janie, why the hell can't you be a proper wife to me?' The greatest dishonesty of all lies in his assertion that he never 'presumed to expect' her continuing presence. Of course he did. He took it for granted, as he took for granted that the milk and the *Guardian* came around breakfast. Jonathan's mention of me, by contrast, says only:

'My thanks to Kath, whose earnings have kept me in socks.'

THE END